Murder in A-Major

Morley Torgov

RendezVous
Crime

Cover design: Vasiliki Lenis

Le Conseil des Arts du Canada depuis 1957 | The Canada Council for the Arts since 1957

We acknowledge the support of the Canada Council for the Arts for our publishing program.

We acknowledge the financial support of the Government of Canada through the Book Publishing Industry Development Program (BPIDP) for our publishing activities.

RendezVous Crime
an imprint of Napoleon & Company
Toronto, Ontario, Canada
www.napoleonandcompany.com

Printed in Canada

12 11 10 09 08   5 4 3 2 1

Library and Archives Canada Cataloguing in Publication

Torgov, Morley, 1927-
        Murder in A major / Morley Torgov.

ISBN 978-1-894917-65-0

        I. Title.
PS8589.O675M87 2008   C813'.54   C2008-900032-3

To Anna Pearl, Sarah Jane and Douglas,
Carrie and Alexander, and to Benjamin,
Sydney Allison, Rebecca, and Marshall

Prologue

Madam Vronsky, my piano teacher, politely but firmly removes my hands from the keyboard. Gently she closes the tattered volume of music and places it on the lid of the instrument. She turns to me and gazes intently into my eyes, a questioning expression on her face. For a full minute she stares at me, looking puzzled, sitting on a slim bentwood chair close by, so close in fact that my nostrils pick up the not unpleasant scent of her garlicky breath. She is Russian, warm-blooded but even-tempered, a woman of endless patience. At last she speaks, asking in a voice buttered with sympathy, "Tell me, Inspector Preiss, why are you doing this?"

"You mean playing Beethoven?"

"I mean playing the piano. Why?" She gives me a sad smile and softly repeats, "Why?"

"Because I love the piano," I tell her. "Because I love music. Because I would love to perform these Beethoven sonatas decently one day in the not-too-distant future. All thirty-two." I am not a religious person, but for some reason I add, "Lord willing."

Madam Vronsky shakes her head. "If the great Franz Liszt cannot properly play Beethoven's sonatas…if the great Clara Schumann finds them daunting—" She does not finish the sentence, nor does she need to. The point is made.

"But I don't aim to be great, Madam Vronsky," I protest mildly. "I want only to achieve some sense of fulfillment, nothing more."

"My dear Inspector," she says, "listen to the advice of an old woman. You will only eat yourself up with frustration and disappointment. Eventually your limitations will transform your love of the piano into bitterness, even hatred. So, love music, attend concerts, play for your own amusement...*private* amusement, I mean...but realistically, 'fulfillment' is out of the question, I'm afraid." As though softening the impact of this advice, she places a consoling hand over mine.

Despite her description of herself as an old woman, Madam Vronsky is really not old enough to be motherly to me. I guess her age to be fifty (which makes her my senior by a mere ten years). A riding accident in St. Petersburg years earlier reduced the span of her left hand, cutting short her career as a concert pianist. Instead she became one of Russia's finest teachers, leaving her native country when the music conservatory here in Düsseldorf offered her the post of dean. That I managed several months ago to engage her as my teacher does not speak to my talent; rather it speaks to my brazenness, and my ability to afford her fees.

"Does this mean you no longer wish to instruct me?" I ask, sounding like a spurned lover.

She gives me another sad smile. "How can I be less than honest with a pupil who happens to be one of Düsseldorf's senior officers of the law? In my heart, I feel as though I am falsely taking your money, Inspector."

Now I place a hand over hers. "Thank you for your honesty, but I truly wish to go on."

She sighs deeply, reaches for the Beethoven volume, opens it to where we left off and places it on the rack before me. "Once again, then," she says quietly. "Remember, Opus 7 is marked *allegro molto e con brio*. But for now, try it half-speed. Watch the left-hand eighth notes, and very little pedal. A crisp attack, that's what I need to hear."

Not more than a dozen bars into the opening movement, we are interrupted by a resolute knock on the door of my apartment.

"Excuse me, Madam Vronsky," I say, rising from the piano and going to the door. I open it to find my next-door neighbours, an elderly pair of bachelors, standing there with critical looks on their faces. They are retired senior civil servants with a reputation for crankiness.

"I do apologize," I begin. "I assume you're here to complain about the noise—"

"Not at all," the crankier of the two replies. "We're here to complain about the *tempo.*"

Such is life in Düsseldorf. Play a passage from a Beethoven sonata and, the next thing you know, two old curmudgeons, virtual strangers really, are at your door presuming to advise you that you've played it badly. In a city like Hamburg, where I began my career as a young police officer twenty years ago, such an incident would never occur. By which I mean that, had I played the Opus 7 badly in that city, anyone within hearing would suffer in silence. Hamburg, I should explain, lies northwest of Düsseldorf, and anyone who knows Germany at all understands that as one travels north and west in this country, the citizenry becomes more and more reticent. In fact, by the time one gets to the extreme northwest, say to a city like Wilhelmshaven, one is struck by the fact that the local populace barely speak to each other at all!

Düsseldorf stands in stark contrast to much of the country. None of your stiff-necked Prussianism here as there is in Berlin, nor the sooty nose-to-the-grindstone industriousness of Stuttgart, nor—thank heaven!—the cold-bloodedness of Frankfurt, where men, cooped up in banks built to resemble Greek temples, spend their entire lives doing nothing but entering numbers in ledgers with quill pens.

Düsseldorf lives. And I live in Düsseldorf. And if I never live long enough to play the first movement of Beethoven's Opus 7 up to speed, I can at least legitimately claim to be living my life *allegro molto e con brio.*

My custom after a lesson with Madam Vronsky—an exercise that leaves me midway between exhilaration and exhaustion—is to seek tranquillity in a generous snifter of cognac. Like my self-appointed music critics next door, I am a bachelor and have no one with whom to share these rare peaceful moments (except when a certain cellist by the name of Helena Becker happens to be visiting, about which I will say more later). And so, in solitude, I sat back in my favourite chair and was sipping cognac and feeling my limbs go slack and my thoughts drift into nothingness when there came another knock on my door, actually a series of sharp raps that conveyed an unmistakable sense of urgency. I had already put in a long day at the Constabulary, followed by a strenuous hour with Madam Vronsky and was tempted to cry out, "Go away, whoever you are!" Groaning, I rose from my chair to respond.

At my door stood a middle-aged woman looking breathless and about to collapse. Her chest was heaving, but she managed to utter "Inspector Preiss?" Without waiting for my response, she thrust a small envelope into my hand, turned about abruptly and began to take her leave.

"Wait," I called out. "Can I offer you some water?" I expected the poor woman to expire before she could make her way down three flights of stairs leading to the exit.

"No no, I must return immediately," she called back, not stopping.

"But who sent you?"

There was no reply. It seemed pointless to follow after her, so I closed my door and tore open the envelope—

Chapter One

It was shortly after nine o'clock on that late-March evening when I received that note, delivered to my rooms by the woman who, it turned out, served as the housekeeper to the family of Robert and Clara Schumann. The note was signed "Clara Schumann". The penmanship was graceful and controlled; the message, however, was urgent, summoning me to come without delay while at the same time apologizing for the imposition. At that hour it was always a challenge to find a carriage in the dark, deserted streets of Düsseldorf, but luck was with me, and I managed to show up at the doorstep of No. 15 Bilkerstrasse just as the clock in the Schumanns' entrance hall was striking a quarter of ten.

I found only Robert Schumann awaiting me. The man wore a bulky woollen robe and leather slippers that had seen better times. I thought his attire odd, bearing in mind that I was a guest in his house for the first time and that we could hardly be considered intimate friends or acquaintances. What's more, his hair was unbrushed, and I gathered that he had neglected to shave his face for a day or two. His handshake was weak, the fingers cold and clammy.

Schumann offered no excuse for his untidy appearance, and being aware of the man's reputation as a musical genius, I took for granted that social niceties were somehow inconsistent with creativity. Artists are artists, and that's all there is to it, I told myself.

We stood—or rather I stood—by the hearth in the Schumann parlour. Schumann chose to pace to and fro, rubbing his fingers together as though attempting to force from the bones the damp chill that penetrated everything this time of the year. I was tempted to stoke what little fire flickered in the hearth, but something about the look on my host's pale face told me that creature comforts were not uppermost on our agenda at this moment.

"Madam Schumann's note," I said, breaking an awkward silence, "indicated she was in the midst of some grave emergency."

"This does not concern my wife," Schumann said flatly. I gathered by the chill in his voice that the couple had just engaged in some disagreement, possibly vehement—a feature of married life with which I, though I am a bachelor, am not unfamiliar. "Somebody is deliberately driving me into a state of insanity, Preiss."

"I'm sorry. I don't understand, Maestro—"

He stopped pacing suddenly, and cocked his head to one side. In a coarse whisper, he called to me: "There, Preiss...there it is, it's returned. My ears...it's piercing my eardrums. Can you not hear it?"

"Hear *what*, Maestro?"

"The A...the damned incessant A."

I don't know what, at that moment, irritated him more—the noise he purported to hear, or the look of complete bewilderment on my face. "The note on the musical scale...the A above middle C...as though coming from some hellish tuning fork...or sometimes from an oboe. No, wait...now it's from a keyboard! Don't tell me you can't hear it, Preiss!"

My hearing, like my eyesight, is acute. Yet I heard nothing. And making a quick survey of the room, I saw nothing that could possibly torment this man to the point of madness. There were two grand pianos back-to-back in the parlour, but the lids of both keyboards were shut so that only a ghost could have sent into the air the sound that was now causing this poor soul to tear his hair.

"Are you quite certain, sir," I carefully ventured, "that someone is deliberately producing the A sound that is so repugnant to your ears? After all, certain noises occur throughout the normal course of a day which are entirely innocent, even though one finds them extremely disagreeable."

Schumann rejected this possibility with a curt "Ridiculous!"

This rebuff struck me as rude, and I decided that, genius or not, the man owed me at least a modicum of courtesy. "I'm only trying to be of some assistance, Dr. Schumann," I said with some firmness. "Perhaps you would prefer to postpone this discussion until—"

The testiness in my voice must have had some effect. "I'm sorry, Inspector," Schumann said, "but you seem to take me for some sort of imbecile. I'm not a stranger to my own surroundings."

From my years on the police force, I knew just about every corner, every road, every back alley, even the sewer system, of Düsseldorf. As well, I knew every principal building from one end of the city to the other. "There is a Lutheran church in the vicinity," I said. "When the organist practises, the sounds of his instrument can often be heard through the open doors and windows of the chapel. Two blocks away, toward the river, there is a foundry. Sometimes one can hear the workmen pounding away on their anvils. At times, Maestro, there's a kind of musicality to their hammering and forging."

This time Schumann shook his head from side to side violently.

"Chimes, Maestro," I said. "Are there any chimes in the house? Say from a clock, or maybe wind chimes outdoors, that might be activated by drafts or the ordinary movements of people about the place?"

Schumann thought for a moment. "The only chimes are

those in the entrance hall clock which you heard as you arrived. I have perfect pitch. The sound they make is E-flat. I tell you, Inspector," Schumann said, "it's a waste of time to seek some mechanical answer, some—as you put it before—*innocent* explanation for what is happening to me."

I said, "Perhaps tomorrow, after a good night's sleep—"

"A good night's sleep! My God, man, I've forgotten what a good night's sleep is like. Look at me, Preiss, do I appear like a man who can simply lay his head on a pillow and go off to dreamland? To find even a moment's peace, a moment's rest, I'm obliged night after night to drink myself into a stupor, and even then the sound...the *sound...*"

Schumann's voice trailed off. He stood before me speechless, exhausted, a human wreck in a rumpled robe and tattered slippers.

I said, "First thing tomorrow morning, I will get right to work on this. Trust me, sir; I will spare no effort to get to the bottom of this matter."

"No, no," Schumann cried, seizing my arm, "tomorrow morning is not good enough, Preiss. I am in agony, don't you see? You must begin now, tonight."

"Maestro," I replied, "I see that you're deeply troubled, and rightly so, but—"

Schumann's grip on my arm tightened. "So you, too, are patronizing me now, is that it? You're like the rest of them...my wife, my doctors, my so-called friends. You're thinking I've gone mad and hoping by tomorrow they'll have carted poor old Schumann off to some asylum and you'll be relieved of this nonsense. Admit it, Preiss; that's what you're thinking."

The man happened to be right. And yet, if Robert Schumann was astute enough to correctly read *my* mind, then how could I possibly regard him as being out of *his* mind?

Chapter Two

Throwing my coat over my shoulders, I moved into the dimly-lit entrance hall and happened to glance up the flight of stairs that led to the second storey of the residence. To my astonishment, there on the landing at the head of the stairway stood Clara Schumann. She was clad in a long pale yellow robe tied at the waist with a simple matching satin sash. Her feet were slippered. "Good evening, Inspector," she called down to me. Her voice conveyed a clear message: though she had written the note summoning me, my presence was not welcome.

She began to come down, lightly touching the banister rail with the tips of the fingers of her right hand while sweeping away an errant strand of hair that had fallen over her brow with her left. She held her head high and took each step with a slow thrust of her right foot. I felt as though I was watching an opening entrance by an actress.

She paused briefly at the bottom step of the staircase, and I was able now to make out her features more clearly. Her complexion had an exquisite paleness, as though illuminated by some soft inner light. Her eyes fixed me with a steadiness and self-confidence that almost caused me to look away. It occurred to me that her choice to remain standing for the moment on the bottom step was far from casual; this way we were pretty much of even height, a position more to her liking.

Then a second surprise. Suddenly her mood changed. Brightening, she said, "Now that we are face to face, sir, I believe we have met before." She gave me a cautious smile.

I returned her smile, feeling as though my face was flushed. "Yes, indeed, madam, we have."

"Of course, now I recall. It was at the symphony fundraiser. You were the gentleman who so generously bid at the auction for one of my autographed programs."

"And succeeded, I'm happy to say," I said, "but I must tell you—though God knows I'm not complaining—that the prize cost me the better part of a month's salary. Police service, I'm sorry to say, does not pay as handsomely as one might wish. At any rate, it was worth every thaler, I assure you."

"You're too kind, Inspector. And you surprise me too."

"How so?"

"For two reasons: first, I didn't know that charm was one of the requisites of police work. Second, I never dreamt for a moment that a crime investigator would be interested in music. Tell me honestly now, how *did* you come to be at the soirée that night?" Her voice took on a teasing inflection. "Let me guess, Inspector. You heard the rumour that Richard Wagner and Eduard Hanslick were due to attend and that one of them was going to murder the other."

Clara Schumann punctuated her little joke with a gentle chuckle which I found totally enchanting. "Madam," I said, "the hostility between Wagner and his arch critic is a fact that has every police force in Germany on high alert at all times. How fortunate you are, you and Maestro Schumann, that Mr. Hanslick's reviews are invariably kind."

I was unprepared for (but amused by) Madam Schumann's next statement. "The truth is, Eduard Hanslick is as pompous as an archbishop saying Mass. Mind you, whenever he delivers last rites to Wagner in the press, my husband and I genuflect and utter a little prayer of thanks."

She lowered her voice, as if she and I were about to

exchange confidences. "Now tell me, Inspector, how did you come to be at the gala?"

I said, "Believe it or not, Madam Schumann, I *am* a music lover, though I admit that my attempts at playing the piano are at best a cut above those of an orangutan. Luckily, I've made the acquaintance of Helena Becker—"

"Ah, yes," Clara Schumann said, her face brightening. The simple mention of Helena Becker's name seemed suddenly to elevate my stature. "She's the cellist with the Düsseldorf String Quartet. And very pretty, too."

"Come to think of it, madam, my very first hearing of Dr. Schumann's Opus 41 Quartets—the three that he dedicated to Felix Mendelssohn—was at a performance by the Düsseldorf, and it was at a reception afterward that Miss Becker and I were introduced to each other."

As I was telling this to his wife, Schumann appeared in the hallway. Raising his eyebrows and looking suddenly interested, he asked, "So, Inspector Preiss, and how did you like them, the quartets, I mean? The critic for the *Berliner Zeitung* called them my finest works for strings. Even compared them to Beethoven's."

I thought the pieces marvellous and told him so without hesitation. In a flash, this turned out to be a mistake. "You hear that, Clara," Schumann said, his arms outstretched as though pleading for justice, "everywhere people go out of their way to flatter me. I am treated by everyone as though I am some fragile hothouse plant who can't be told the truth."

"But I *am* being perfectly honest, Maestro," I said fervently. "Please believe me."

Clara Schumann took the final step down to floor level. She was considerably shorter than her husband, but somehow she seemed taller, and she spoke to him in a firm, almost harsh, tone of voice. "You see, Robert, this is precisely what I've been talking about all these months. There is a side to you that is determined not to accept praise. In the bluest sky, you somehow never fail to discover black clouds."

She turned to me. "Inspector Preiss, what my husband needs is a doctor, not a detective. Despite what he's told you, this is a *medical* case, not a criminal case."

This brought an outburst from the maestro. "How in hell, woman, do you know what I've told Inspector Preiss?"

"If you must know, Robert, even from the top of the stairway I could hear every word."

"In other words, you were eavesdropping on a confidential conversation."

"I'm your *wife*, for God's sake. Wives don't 'eavesdrop' on so-called confidential talk involving their sick husbands."

She turned back to me. "And you believe, sir," she said, "that my husband's condition…this business about the 'A' sound…you really believe there is some deliberate evil being done to Robert?" Though she did not put this question to me with open sarcasm, she left no doubt that she considered the whole affair ridiculous.

"Madam, you ask if I 'believe' this or 'believe' that. I avoid elevating suspicion to the level of belief until there's a foundation of solid facts. But I *have* heard and seen enough this past hour so that I could not for the life of me walk out that door without promising to look into Dr. Schumann's suspicions. And the sooner the better."

"Then it's obvious, Inspector," Madam Schumann said, her manner indignant now, "that nothing I say can convince you not to interfere." She turned her gaze on her husband, giving him a look that bore a mixture of pity and contempt. Without taking her eyes from him, she said, "But I warn you, sir, you will *not* like what you find."

"As a matter of fact, I never do," I said.

I let myself out and noted that the chill in the street was only a touch more penetrating than the chill in the house from which I had just departed.

Chapter Three

B ack in my rooms, I poured myself a healthy portion of schnapps, which I downed in a single draught. The strong liquor burned its way through my system like a fine stream of lava, but instead of calming me as I'd hoped, it left me with a restless feeling. It was now just past one o'clock in the morning, and yet I felt totally awake. I moved across the sitting room to the large bay window, parted the heavy curtains and looked down to the small park directly across from my dwelling. Despite the bleakness outdoors, the ornate wrought-iron gateposts at the park entrance, bracketed by tall gas lamps, their yellow light gallantly flickering, presented a warm and satisfying picture. My rooms could not be called lavish, but they were comfortably furnished and a source of pleasure to me.

What was even more pleasing to me was the thought that I had just been admitted to the private world of one of the most illustrious couples in Germany and indeed the whole of Europe, a world light years removed from my origins.

The town of Zwicken, where I was born in 1820, was located in the heart of poor farming country. To characterize our town as "the heart" was not exactly appropriate, for it was a heart that pumped very little blood. The place was not much more than a collection of humble houses and shops leaning against one another for support in their old age. From backyards one could hear chickens and geese clucking away meaninglessly, like village idiots. Occasionally a sow could be heard grunting as she rolled over on her side, inviting her piglets to feed. Horses and cows left their calling cards on the unpaved roadways, obliging pedestrians to step gingerly when crossing, like children learning to walk.

Not long before I was born, Napoleon Bonaparte's infantry and artillery had shuffled and rattled into our town, confusing Zwicken with another and more important centre nearby, Zwickau. Disgruntled over their mistake, the Frenchmen had taken their unhappiness out on the local townsfolk. While their officers turned a blind eye, the troops proceeded to ransack the shops until every shelf was bare. Worse still, with the kind of brute desperation known only to conquering soldiers far from home, they harassed or raped any young woman who could not run fast enough to escape their hungry pursuit.

On the day of their departure for Zwickau, Napoleon's heroes left behind them a town drained of its energy, its resources, and above all its dignity. The populace licked their wounds and patched their scars as best they could. But Zwicken's reason for existence had pretty much petered out, like the footprints of the last French militiamen.

My father, Wolfgang Preiss, operated a small tailor shop on the main thoroughfare of Zwicken, an occupation which, given the state of affairs in the town, left him with much time on his hands. This permitted him to indulge every day and most nights in the labour that was dearest to his heart—writing novels. Though not well-educated, he had read the works of Goethe, Schiller, and several other distinguished German authors and poets, and dreamed of joining their ranks with his tales one day, when the literary world would finally wake up and recognize his own peculiar genius.

He fashioned himself a writer of what came to be known years after his passing as speculative tales of the fantastic. Being a dreamer, he convinced himself, could have its rewards if only he could transcribe his visions into words. These conceptions, and many more, he incorporated into novels in which the protagonist, an inventor, being a prophet of sorts, existed without honour in his own land only to be acknowledged as a true visionary after he was dead and gone. To my father, this theme constituted life's ultimate tragedy.

Alas, publisher after publisher rejected my father's novels. Somewhere between the tailor shop and his wished-for career as an author, our family's meagre finances steadily leaked away.

For years, my mother suffered anxious days and restless nights waiting for the sky to fall and put an end to our seemingly endless miseries. So ramshackle was our house that it became the subject of a local joke: neighbours, it was said, pleaded with us in winter to keep our doors and windows shut tight to prevent the cold within from escaping into the outdoors.

It was after one particularly bitter January day that the boundaries of my mother's vast patience were at last breached, and she could no longer restrain her fury. "Look at this house!" she cried. "It is a desolate place, windswept by hopelessness and neglect!"

Father pondered this for a moment, then nodded appreciatively. "I like it, Emma...yes indeed, I think it's quite wonderful."

Mother eyed her husband with disbelief. "You *like* this house?"

"No, no," Father replied quickly, "I mean the sentence, the way you expressed yourself just then." He paused, gazing up at the crumbling ceilings. "Ah yes, 'a desolate place...windswept by hopelessness and neglect'..." Excusing himself, he dashed off to his writing table to jot down my mother's words in his small, tattered notebook.

Leaping after him, my mother continued at the top of

her lungs: "Wolfgang, listen to me, this family cannot go on much longer clinging by our fingertips to the unsteady ledge of your ambitions! Do you hear what I am saying?"

"Please, Emma, *please,*" my father begged, "speak more slowly. I cannot write so fast. What came after 'unsteady ledge'?"

So it went: my mother uttering printable sentences that seemed to flow naturally from her tongue; my father keeping up the pretense that *he* was the literate one in the family, while at the same time increasingly unable to distinguish fiction from reality.

As for my little sister Ilse and me, we played games of make-believe in which we imagined ourselves the offspring of German nobility, dispatched to this shabby household by a vengeful wicked witch, whose amorous advances our handsome princely father had once made the mistake of spurning. Soon, very soon, we told ourselves, a carriage drawn by eight white horses would clatter up to our doorstep, and our father—the prince, that is—would sweep us off to our rightful palatial chambers.

During much of my childhood and early youth, then, that was how our days were spent. My father nourished his fantasy that any day now the name "Wolfgang Preiss" would replace "Goethe" on the lips of Europe's literati. My mother nourished her fantasy that any day now she would become a widow and, with her looks still miraculously intact, attract a solid provider as a second husband. My sister and I shared a dream that, restored to noble surroundings, we would be brought up as all well-born children should be—by doting servants.

The one fortunate aspect of my childhood was my scholastic prowess, especially in the sciences. My instructors in chemistry and physics at the Gymnasium discerned that I possessed an extraordinary aptitude for scientific investigation. In my senior year, they encouraged me to apply for the only scholarship available to a youth of my social station. And so it was that, shortly before my eighteenth birthday, I found myself at the tiny railway station in Zwicken, about to leave home for the first time. I was to attend the National Police Academy in Hamburg. At last, liberation!

Overcome with uncontrollable grief, my mother and sister could not bring themselves to accompany me to the depot. (In moments when I feel less than charitable, I cannot resist the feeling that their recipe for uncontrollable grief consisted of one part sorrow and ninety-nine parts envy.)

It was while I stood on the station platform awaiting the train that my father drew me aside, seized me by the shoulders and, gazing deeply into my eyes, intoned, "My boy, this above all—"

He halted in mid-sentence. Whatever thought was on his mind seemed to be momentarily suspended above us like some enormous mudslide.

"Yes, father?" I said.

"This above all," he repeated. Again there was a pause while he glanced about him to make certain there were no eavesdroppers, though we were the only people at the depot. Lowering his voice, he said, "If you remember nothing else, Hermann, remember this: avoid surprises!"

Our relationship up to this point was such that I never questioned or challenged my father's advice or his perceptions about the world around us. This was so at first because of the strict rules of filial respect and obedience that prevailed in the God-fearing households of the day. Later it was so because the man was such a patent fool that there seemed no point in taking issue with him on any subject. Still, as we waited now for my train, the grave expression on his carelessly shaven face suggested that it was possible, just barely possible, that the man knew something I didn't. Giving him the benefit of the doubt, I repeated dutifully, "Avoid surprises."

"Good boy!" My father jerked his head with approval. "You see, Hermann," he explained, "there is no such thing as a *good* surprise. Without exception they're bad, all of them. Death, infidelity, insolvency...a sudden knock on the door and—poof!—you're a corpse, or a cuckold, or some brazen bill collector makes off with your trousers. Then there are riots in the streets. And, of course, diseases. An innocent glass of water tonight, tomorrow morning your body is on fire and covered with purple spots!"

Listening to these last-minute cautions, I was willing to bet the few humble banknotes sewn into the lining of my jacket that the old gent had taken one pinch too many of his beloved snuff and sneezed his brains into his hat. Though I'd never been more than ten kilometres in any direction from Zwicken, even *I* knew this much: of the countless evils to be shunned in a port city like Hamburg, surely innocent glasses of water were far from foremost. It was no secret in Germany that Hamburg's waterfront was an immense open sewer, where human waste and wasted humans mingled so freely in the tides that they were often indistinguishable. The city's sidewalks and shady entrance-ways throbbed with brothel life around the clock, offering with one hand a few minutes of pleasure, and guaranteeing with the other a lifetime of embarrassing skin disorders. Innocent glasses of water indeed!

Nevertheless, I was determined that my last few minutes in Zwicken should be spent agreeably. "Thank you, father," I said, "I will try to remember your words of wisdom. I consider myself blessed to be the son of a true sage."

My father's eyes suddenly gazed even more deeply into my own. "Ah yes, Hermann," he said, "that's the other thing I meant to tell you."

"Other thing?"

"Yes. You are not my son. Your mother was pregnant by another man...possibly a French warrant officer at the time of the invasion, though there was also this commercial traveller from Potsdam...when I agreed to marry her. Since you are not my own flesh and blood, my last will and testament leaves nothing to you. I'm sure you understand that it's only fair that your dear little sister Ilse should be my sole beneficiary, bearing in mind that she is to the best of my knowledge and belief my own flesh and blood. Now then, my boy, do try to be of good cheer at all times. Goodbye and best of luck."

The truth is that the sudden news of my dis-inheritance came as nothing more than a very glancing blow. After all, when there's nothing to gain, there's nothing to lose. But the revelation that my mother's egg had been fertilized by some random sperm from out of town left me profoundly unsettled not only throughout the train ride to Hamburg that night but for the many years that followed. To this day I am nagged by doubts about my origins and the taint of illegitimacy.

That I chose to remain a bachelor, despite the odd flirtation now and then, was directly attributable to that conversation at the railway station in Zwicken. Given my parents' incessant wrangling, was it any wonder that I came to regard the temple of marriage as being no more reliable than a tent in a hurricane.

Bachelorhood had its positive side in my case. It left me free to immerse myself in my work in the field of crime in general, and homicide in particular. Not for me the scheduled life...supper at six, bedtime stories for the children at seven, pipe and slippers at eight, lights out at nine. When most men were sitting down to dine, or to listen to the end-of-the-day chatter of their children, or lie snugly against the flannel of their wives' nightclothes, I found myself bending with boundless curiosity over a bludgeoned corpse, or examining a knife planted like a flagpole in someone's chest, or figuring out the trajectory of a bullet lodged in someone's skull.

There is an irony here, of course. For one who was

warned to avoid surprises, I had made it my occupation
to deal with those very things. The surprises I dealt with,
however, happened to *others*, not to me. This fact made
all the difference. No matter how heinous the crimes I
encountered, I was able to view them dispassionately.
Objectivity is the soul of professional crime investigation, and mine had never faltered.

In short, my work was my life.

Still, there came a point in each day when I was able to
lay down the tools of my trade and say "Enough." It was at
such times that, in effect, I managed to hand the crime
back to society, as one hands back to its mother an infant
that has done something bothersome in its under-
clothing. Once removed, if only for a few hours, from the
jigsaw puzzles of my profession, I was at liberty to immerse
myself in a very different kind of life, a life of good food,
good wine, great music, and the company of a beautiful
woman, namely my cellist friend Helena Becker.

And it was the same Helena who now—to my complete
astonishment—interrupted my thoughts about the
Schumanns and my own career with a discreet knock on
my door.

"Do forgive this intrusion, Hermann," she said as she
swept into my suite of rooms. Her face was flushed, and
there was an air of unbridled excitement about her. Before
I could take her cape, she circled her arms about my waist
and pulled me to her. My first instinct was to laugh with
pleasure. In the several years we had known one another,
I had seldom seen her in such a state of elation.

"Don't tell me, Helena, let me guess," I said, inhaling her
perfume and the natural clean scent of her hair, "you've
been to the opera to see Wagner's *Lohengrin* again. I know
how that opera always thrills you, especially the love scenes."

Like a coquette, she fluttered her eyelashes. "Wrong," she
said, not letting go of me. "Guess again, Hermann."

"You were at an orchestral concert, and they played

Mendelssohn's *Italian Symphony*. That's it. The final movement's enough to make anyone want to do something wild and wicked."

"Wrong again."

I have to admit that at this hour of the night, my enthusiasm for playing a guessing game was growing thin. "I'll guess once more," I said, trying to look stern, "and if I'm incorrect this time, I'm going to throw you out into the cold street. Now, then, I've heard a rumour that that dashing Hungarian Liszt is in Düsseldorf and that Baron Hoffman and his big fat frau were throwing a party to honour the man...to which, incidentally, I was not invited. I take it, Helena, that you were?"

Helena gave me a generous kiss on the cheek. "I love it when you play clever detective. Yes, Franz Liszt was at the Hoffmans', and he played his piano transcription of one of Wagner's overtures. My God, Hermann, the passion...I can scarcely describe it...it is so—so arousing!"

The minutes that followed were dizzying. I found myself occupying the space ordinarily occupied by Helena Becker's cello. I could feel her right arm sliding back and forth across the small of my back, as though she were wielding her bow. With her left hand, she fingered the notes, as it were, up and down my shoulder blades, digging deeply.

But when I closed my eyes, it was not Helena Becker's face I was imagining.

It was the face of Clara Schumann.

Chapter Four

The following morning, eager to be alone with my private thoughts, I made a point of avoiding the ritual daily briefing with Commissioner Schilling, my immediate superior, and climbed the three flights to my office at the Constabulary by an out-of-the-way rear set of stairs. My case load happened to be unusually light. For some reason, the crime rate for the City of Düsseldorf regularly fell this time of year, suggesting that a severe drop in temperature could always be relied upon to freeze evil impulses. This gave me time to ponder the problem of Robert Schumann.

How best to deal with it?

More to the point, should a senior police official even bother to become involved?

In the hope of resolving these questions, I arranged to meet Helena for lunch at her favourite restaurant in Düsseldorf's central market area, Schimmel's Coffee House on Linkstrasse. I selected a table in a quiet corner where we could talk and not be overheard. "Helena," I said, "I need a favour." Leaning closer to her, I said, speaking quietly, "What I'm about to disclose must remain absolutely confidential. It concerns the possible commission of a crime. Strictly speaking, it is police business. But the challenge here is so extraordinary that I must look outside the police community for assistance. You see, Helena, the victim—if one can call him a victim at this stage—is none other than Robert Schumann."

I went on to describe in detail my initial conversation with Schumann as well as with his wife, Clara.

Helena, at this point indifferent to the food that lay before her, listened attentively, paused to think about it for a few moments, then said, "I'm sorry, Hermann, but I *am* having difficulty taking this seriously." I detected a slight twitch at the corners of her mouth, as though she were attempting to suppress a laugh. "Let me tell you something," she said. She made a quick survey of her surroundings to make certain she was not being overheard. "In the musical world, and even beyond—though apparently the news has not yet reached the Düsseldorf Police Department—Robert Schumann has long been considered half mad. I find it astounding that you of all people—a man who knows what lies beneath every single cobblestone in Düsseldorf—don't know all the stories that have circulated for ages about the Maestro. I find it even more astounding that you care enough to give this craziness as much as an hour of your time."

I took a moment to compose a careful reply. "It's because, Helena, for the first time in my career, I am dealing with people...*personalities*...who do not fit into the underworld of shabby criminals and victims I'm accustomed to dealing with. Ninety-nine out of a hundred times, I find myself in a sense rubbing shoulders with thieves, prostitutes, murderers, embezzlers...men and women I am reluctant to touch even when my hands are gloved! And along comes Robert Schumann, my one case in a hundred, so to speak, that doesn't involve some disgusting form of human garbage—"

She interrupted me. "Not to mention Clara Schumann, of course?" She gave me a knowing smile, the kind of smile born of womanly intuition.

I pretended not to comprehend. "Meaning what?"

Helena heaved a sigh and rolled her eyes to the ceiling. As though speaking to herself, she said, "Men

are so terribly boring when they pretend to be stupid."
She looked at me again. "Meaning, Hermann, that men
instantly become enchanted with Clara Schumann even
before her fingers settle on the keyboard. Are you going
to sit there and claim to be the exception?"

"My interest in this case is purely professional," I
insisted. "So, can I count on you to help me?"

"Help you how?"

"First, say yes; then I'll explain."

Looking anxiously over her shoulder, she said: "Oh
dear, my goulash must be ice-cold by now. Ask the waiter
to take it back to the kitchen and heat it up, Hermann."

Knowing Helena, this was her way of saying yes.

Chapter Five

T here was a firmness in my step as I walked to my office at the headquarters of the Düsseldorf Constabulary. I felt fueled by a new and different sense of purpose. And yet, in one of those rare moments of introspection that plague an otherwise single-minded sleuth, I asked myself: Was Helena right? Was there some ulterior motive driving me to pursue this case?

Of course, I was genuinely moved by the plight of Robert Schumann. Who wouldn't be, witnessing the state he was in?

But as for Clara Schumann? Well, yes, I *was* intrigued. More than intrigued. Captivated!

Although my hours of work were long and erratic, what spare time was available to me I chose to spend in recital halls, art galleries and libraries. Among my colleagues in the Constabulary I was looked upon as a bit of an oddity, no doubt because I preferred a solitary hour in a bookshop to the after-hours camaraderie of a beer hall.

These extra-curricular interests of mine put me in touch with a number of eminent people in the cultural life of Düsseldorf. One of the connections I'd made was Georg Adelmann, a journalist of note who wrote extensively about music and musicians for newspapers as well as for academic publications, and who I knew to be writing a monograph on the life and work of Schumann. Though he travelled widely gathering information for his articles and treatises,

Adelmann returned to his apartment in Düsseldorf to write his pieces, and I was aware that he was in the city at this time. Before meeting again with Schumann, I was determined to gain as many details about his background as I could. What better source than Georg Adelmann?

I immediately dispatched this note to Adelmann:

Dear Dr. Adelmann:

I understand you are working on a monograph on the life and works of Robert Schumann.

My close friend, the cellist Helena Becker, is about to make her debut as a solo performer. The work she has chosen is the Maestro's Cello Concerto in A Minor. Helena feels that in order to do justice to so passionate a work, she must acquire the deepest possible understanding not only of the music itself but of the man who created it.

Knowing that you and I are acquaintances, and being herself almost painfully shy about approaching you directly, Miss Becker has prevailed upon me to speak to you on her behalf. I would be enormously in your debt if you and I could chat—perhaps over lunch—so that I may in turn give Miss Becker the benefit of your insights concerning Schumann, the man as well as the composer.

Most respectfully,
Hermann Preiss

Chapter Six

I t was billed in the local press as a gala event, the highlight of the new concert season in Düsseldorf. Robert and Clara Schumann would present an all-Schumann program, he conducting his Fourth Symphony, she performing his Piano Concerto. There would follow a reception sponsored by the Music Society, which meant that the cream of the city's upper class, brimming with Champagne and high-society gossip, would retire afterward to their mansions to speculate deliciously on how long a mis-matched couple like Robert and Clara Schumann could be expected to remain husband and wife. After all, he was nine years her senior, now forty-four but looked sixty-four thanks (as I was soon to learn) to heavy bouts of drinking, and the steady consumption of pills for a variety of aches and pains, most of which were rumoured to be imagined rather than real. She was a very different story. Now in her thirty-fifth year, Clara Schumann exhibited an effortless radiance.

The concert was sold out, and I was unable at the last minute to purchase a ticket. Apart from the desire to hear the music, I was eager to watch the Schumanns "in action", so to speak, before my next encounter with the composer himself. A long line of disgruntled people were being turned away outside the hall, told that there was no longer even standing room. One of the privileges of my office, however, was that I was able to gain entrance simply by presenting my credentials to the manager of the box office. Somehow, an aisle seat only six rows from the stage materialized. I took my seat and settled back, anticipating two thrilling hours of music.

The overture, also composed by Schumann, went well, and he seemed pleased with the enthusiastic applause.

The piano concerto went even better. But I thought the Maestro ought to have done the gallant thing and allowed his wife to take solo bows for a performance whose success was largely attributable to her playing. Instead, the two stood side-by-side to acknowledge a standing ovation that I felt was meant for her alone. When an usher emerged from the wings to present the pianist with an enormous bouquet of carnations, I detected a slight frown on Schumann's face, as though it was *he* who should have received the floral tribute.

During the intermission, I mingled with that segment of the audience who, occupying the orchestra and box seats, were entitled to occupy the luxuriously appointed mezzanine lounge. The comforting aroma of hearty good living perfumed the air, thick and tangible, like the scoop of whipped cream that crowned my slice of Black Forest cake. And there were other things in the air, half-whispered remarks. *"For a man who looks as though he's been to hell and back, he still knows how to deliver a good tune..."* *"Can you imagine that young woman having to go to bed every night with a man who looks old enough to be her father!"*

It was just as the ushers were beginning to announce the conclusion of the intermission that I happened to catch sight of Georg Adelmann hastily downing a demitasse of coffee at the refreshment table.

"What great good luck, Preiss," Adelmann said, giving me a cheerful pat on the shoulder. "This will save us exchanging notes. Are you free for lunch tomorrow, say, twelve noon at my club?"

"Twelve noon sounds splendid," I said, "but what club are you referring to?"

"Why, the Düsseldorf Arts and Letters Club, of course."

"But Dr. Adelmann," I said, "you are doing me a favour, and therefore it is *I* who should be hosting our luncheon." An admission here: I was merely being polite. The truth was that I had never before set foot in the premises of Düsseldorf's exclusive and prestigious culture centre, a place reputed to serve some of the finest food and rarest wines in the country, all consumed by men of distinction and wealth. An opportunity to be a guest there was not lightly to be passed up.

To my dismay, Adelmann said, grinning jovially, "Very well then, I agree to be your guest, since you insist."

I had hardly insisted, but now was faced with taking the famous journalist for what would surely be an expensive meal at one of the city's better cafés, one that would seriously strain my budget. My mother had warned me about this kind of thing. "Hermann," she would say, "the rich get richer by saving, the poor get poorer by spending." She cited my father as the perfect example of that adage.

The remaining half of the concert would be taken up with a performance of Schumann's Fourth Symphony in D Minor. Before the Maestro took the podium, I had a minute or two to study the program notes which, at first glance, were somewhat confusing. It seemed that Schumann's Fourth was really his Second, according to the notes, having been composed as the second of his four symphonies in 1841. The composer, however, had been dissatisfied with the original version and revised it ten years later. As a result, the version we would hear this night was a musical rebirth occurring in 1851 *after* his Third Symphony, which was why it was now given the number "Four".

There was something so haphazard about the creative process, especially in the musical field. So much seemed to depend upon impulse, inspirational moments that suddenly flashed then went dark, like the passage of fireflies in the night. How different from my world. In my profession, one necessarily piled fact upon fact upon fact, like constructing a brick wall. My world was one of logical sequences: two was followed by three which was followed by four. Anything different was unthinkable.

The D Minor opened with the strings of the orchestra sighing with a hint of yearning, suggesting autumn and the fading away of another year in the composer's life. The second movement, coming without a pause, began with a plaintive melody played by the oboe at a melancholy pace. Again without a break, the third movement, a boisterous scherzo, followed and promised to lift the dark mood left by the preceding two movements. For the first several bars, the musicians and conductor were as one, and the man on the podium waving his baton with such decisiveness seemed to be enjoying himself immensely.

But then, suddenly and for no apparent reason, Schumann let his baton drop to his side, where it remained for several bars. The Düsseldorf orchestra carried on bravely, the musicians no doubt expecting their leader to resume conducting as vigorously as before. Instead, when Schumann's arm rose once again, his beat was out of time to the music, and the baton moved back and forth in a desultory fashion. Moments later the Maestro seemed to recover; then his beat faltered again. By now the players were exchanging anxious glances. In the house, people were whispering. Even the most untrained ear could tell that the scherzo was disintegrating into a sorry jumble of sound. Somehow the orchestra, with no help from its conductor, managed to complete the third movement.

Eventually, the scherzo folded directly into a fast and brilliant finale. How the musicians managed this transition on their own was beyond explanation but, as suddenly as Schumann's attention had slackened earlier, it had revived and was sustained for most of the final movement.

Then it happened again. The unexpected fall of the

baton, the lifeless dropping of his right arm. The remaining few minutes of Schumann's Fourth were played out in a state of disarray, the musicians ending their mission like troops caught up in a rout. What should have been an ovation instead became a moment of stunned silence. Without so much as a glance at the audience, Schumann fled the stage, leaving in his wake a smattering of polite applause and a sea of confused faces.

Going against the tide of people making their way to the exits at the rear of the auditorium, I advanced to the stage and made my way to the private lounge backstage reserved for the orchestra's conductor. As I approached, I could hear a commotion and recognized several of the voices, the most prominent being the voices of Robert and Clara.

"I am a ruined man...ruined!" Schumann was wailing.

"Calm yourself, Robert...please, try to calm yourself... everything will be all right...Dr. Hellman is here..." That was the voice of Clara Schumann.

Entering the conductor's rooms, I found Schumann sprawled on a sofa, his jacket removed, shirt collar unbuttoned, bow tie undone, legs and arms limp like those of an unstrung puppet. A bearded man in evening clothes hovered over the distraught composer, urging him to drink a milky liquid that he was offering in a small glass. I took the man to be Dr. Hellman, and the substance in the glass some form of sedative. "Please," the bearded man pleaded, "just take this, Dr. Schumann, and I promise you—"

But Schumann's lips tightened like a vise; he would have none of it.

Close by the physician stood another person who was not at all familiar to me but who appeared to be as concerned as the others and spoke solicitously to Schumann, urging him to heed the doctor's advice and drink the potion. He was young, perhaps about twenty years of age, dressed in street clothes rather than formal eveningwear, and remarkably handsome. His full head of blond hair was brushed back off a high brow so that it almost touched his broad shoulders. His eyes were large and the shade of blue that reminded one of those clear clean lakes in Bavaria's mountain country. Had I spotted him on a sporting field, I would have judged him to be an athlete, given his slim but sturdy build and youthful voice. Though he and I exchanged quick glances, neither of us was inclined under the circumstances to engage in introductions, and I assumed that he was probably either a member of the concert hall staff or possibly a conservatory student who happened to be a family friend of the Schumanns, and left it at that.

Looking beyond his wife, Dr. Hellman, and another whom I recognized as Julius Tausch, the orchestra's assistant conductor, Schumann caught sight of me. "Preiss, thank God you're here!" he said, weakly beckoning me to come nearer and stand at his side. Ignoring everyone else, he addressed me as though I were his sole source of refuge. "You see, Preiss, you see, don't you? The 'A' sound? Even on stage when I am conducting, it pours through me like molten metal. They are killing me, Preiss. You must help me, save me!"

As he spoke these words, I happened to glance at Clara Schumann. She was staring at me coldly, as though defying me to respond to her husband's plea. I confess to a fleeting hesitation on my part. It was not easy to ignore the look of hostility on the woman's face. Nor was I eager to antagonize her. Indeed, I'd hoped that she and I would somehow join forces in rescuing her husband from whatever danger was threatening his life.

To Schumann, I said, "You have my assurance, Maestro, that I will do everything in my power to help you. You have my word, sir." And with that, I turned to leave.

"Inspector...a moment, please—"

It was Clara Schumann. She had followed me down the corridor that led to the exit.

"Yes, Madam Schumann?"

"You see what is happening, don't you?" she said. "Your presence serves only to reinforce and even inflame my poor husband's illusions. If you truly wish to be of assistance to us, remove yourself from this matter entirely. Tonight. This very minute. I implore you."

"And if I find that I cannot?"

Her expression froze. Without another word, she turned and made her way back to the conductor's lounge.

About one thing, at least, there was no mystery now: she and I seemed destined to carry on not as allies but as adversaries.

*   *   *

Not surprisingly, the local music critics were in complete agreement in the next morning's papers.

"Once again," wrote one, "Dr. Schumann's lyric gifts show strong evidence of having faded…at best his music merely displays a sense of organization…"

Another opined that the composer "has so little talent for beautiful orchestral sound and apparently no use for it in any event…"

A third critic was even more vicious. "Absent were brilliant debates between different parts of the orchestra such as one finds in the works of Beethoven and Schubert; rather the music emerges in a grey and viscous mass of sound out of which occasional melodies seep…"

Worst of all, Düsseldorf's critics—while generous as usual in praising Clara Schumann's virtuosity—now unanimously called for Robert Schumann to do the right thing by the Düsseldorf Symphony Orchestra and step down as its principal conductor. The most outspoken critic on this point, Gustav Jansen, pointed out that what had once been one of the country's finest musical ensembles was being reduced under Schumann's leadership to an orchestra of only modest abilities. "I appeal to Dr. Julius Illing, as Chairman of the Music Society of Düsseldorf, to take action," wrote Jansen, "before the situation further deteriorates. Perhaps Maestro Schumann might henceforth occupy the honourary position of Conductor Emeritus..."

I thought: how terrible the life of the creative artist...to be stripped and stretched without pity on the rack of public opinion. Then, thinking this, I realized that I was trapped, hopelessly trapped. Trapped by him. And trapped by her.

Chapter Seven

Georg Adelmann and I sat down to lunch at Emmerich's Restaurant des Artistes at noon on the day after the concert. As I feared, Dr. Adelmann possessed expensive tastes in food and drink. Presented with the wine list, he reverentially recited the contents, stopping abruptly at a particularly costly vintage. "Ah yes," he exulted, "a '29 Burgundy! One of the better years. Splendid! You know, Preiss, a good Burgundy *begs* for roasted goose, doesn't it." Which is what he ordered, explaining that he habitually ate only one meal daily and therefore preferred that it be copious. This disclosure became all the more ominous thanks to a fawning headwaiter who profusely congratulated Adelmann on his admirable choices while cautioning him to save room for a cheese platter and dessert.

"Somehow, I'm not at all startled by this dreadful turn of events in Schumann's career," Adelmann said. As he spoke, minuscule bits of the pickled beets that he'd ordered as an appetizer flew from his busy lips, landing on the white expanse of tablecloth between us, leaving the once pristine space spotted as if from smallpox. I made a mental note to keep a safe distance from the man throughout the meal. "You see," Adelmann went on, "from the very moment of his conception in 1809, indeed even *before* that time, the Schumann family was star-crossed. Strange, but some bloodlines seem to have a natural talent for collecting bad luck. They have a kind of magnetism, like lodestone, but unfortunately what they attract more often than not is misery."

"You mean Schumann was born into poverty?" I said.

"On the contrary," Adelmann said, "his father and his uncle had established a rather profitable book publishing business in Zwickau—"

I dropped my fork. "Did you say Zwickau, Dr. Adelmann?"

"Yes. In Saxony. You're familiar with the town?"

"Of course. As a matter of fact, I was born nearby. A small town called Zwicken."

Adelmann sniffed the air. "Zwicken? Zwicken? Never heard of it. I assume, sir, that you were fortunate enough to spend your childhood in a more *civilized* part of the country. At any rate, Schumann's father was an extremely sickly man, but a man of some considerable literary accomplishment. Wrote a dozen or more books, mostly about mythology. By the time young Schumann was old enough to attend school, the family was enjoying some affluence."

"What about Schumann's mother?"

"She was the daughter of a doctor. When Schumann's father, August, wanted to marry Johanne Schnabel—that was her maiden name—the girl's father gave August a hard time. Insisted the young man get into business first. Put a lot of stress on the poor fellow, which he never quite got over. Life-long stomach pains, sore limbs, headaches, that kind of thing. Not unlike the current situation with Robert and Clara. Strange how history repeats itself, eh, Preiss?"

"How so?" I said.

"No doubt you've heard of the notorious Professor Friedrich Wieck, Clara Schumann's father?"

"Only that he is a piano teacher of some importance. I never heard him referred to as notorious."

"Then let me set you straight, Preiss. A dreadful human being, that's the best one can say for Wieck. Did his utmost to make Schumann's life miserable. Schumann was a pupil of his, but his playing ability was somewhat hampered by a small right hand. So Wieck devised some sort of stretching apparatus to apply to young Schumann's hand. Pure torture, and in the end not worth a damn. Ruined Schumann's chances for a career as a concert pianist. And as though that wasn't enough, Papa Wieck bitterly opposed his daughter's pending marriage to the seemingly luckless Schumann. Even went so far as to force a court battle over the issue. Lost, of course, and ever since then the acrimony between the two men has been thick enough to chop with a butcher's cleaver."

"You started to tell me about Schumann's mother," I said.

"Ah, yes. Again, history repeats itself. She gave birth to five...or was it six?...children in short order. Robert was the youngest. Poor woman spent much of her life, even when times were relatively good, in the shadows of chronic melancholy. Young Robert was the child she felt closest to, especially because at a young age he displayed exceptional musical talent. At the age of seven, he began music lessons with a church organist in Zwickau. No doubt about it, Preiss, the man you and I witnessed going to pieces before our very eyes last night in the concert hall was once upon a time a very gifted child."

"Then when did Schumann's life take a wrong turn?" I said. "Look, Dr. Adelmann, many men and women blessed with innate talents run headlong into adversity, but they manage to overcome, even to triumph. Take Beethoven, for instance. He became a legendary figure despite becoming stone deaf. My God, he wrote the great Choral Ninth when he couldn't hear a single note of the piece."

"Ah yes, Inspector—" Here, Dr. Adelmann jabbed his knife in the air to make a point. "But, there are some— and I am one of them—who will go to their graves maintaining that Beethoven's Ninth—the choral part, that is—was a tragic mistake."

I stared at Adelmann as if he'd just uttered heresy.

"You see, Preiss, the piece is barely singable. It was written at least one whole tone too high. Next time you have an opportunity to hear the piece, listen carefully. If you can prove me wrong, I, Georg Adelmann, will deliver to your doorstep an entire case of Germany's best Moselle. The trouble with Beethoven is that he didn't know when it was time to quit."

"And it is your opinion that the same can be said of Robert Schumann?"

"Yes, absolutely. The man's a mess."

"And you attribute this principally to his childhood, then?"

Adelmann suddenly laid down his knife and fork. "If you will forgive my saying so, Inspector, I don't quite see how your inquisitiveness about Robert Schumann's childhood is germane to the purpose of this conversation. As I understood it, you wanted to know more about the man as a full-fledged *composer* so that your friend Miss Becker might— as you put it—better understand the Cello Concerto."

There was a hint of suspicion in his eyes, something I was not accustomed to. (As a detective, it was I who gave people suspicious looks, not the other way around.) "Please pardon the insatiable curiosity of a policeman, Dr. Adelmann," I said. "Interrogation is in my blood. My life is punctuated by question marks."

Still eyeing me with some skepticism, Adelmann said, "I don't know why it is, Inspector, but I have this strange feeling that your mission—how can I put it delicately?— has less to do with your friend's interest in Schumann's concerto and more to do with..." Here my guest hesitated for a moment. Lowering his voice, he said, "More to do with these tales about the Schumanns themselves."

Hoping my expression looked innocent, I said, "Tales? What tales?"

Adelmann sat back in his chair, as though shrinking away from the subject he had just raised. "I have no wish to engage in gossipmongering," he said in a sanctimonious tone.

Nonsense! I thought. Journalists thrive on gossip. Scandals are the condiments that add spice to a journalist's trade, but for the time being I would have to let him pretend he was above spreading such stories. "You are perfectly right, sir," I said, "and I respect your insistence on being discreet in such matters. Nothing would be more unjust than covering a distinguished couple like Robert and Clara Schumann with a blanket of scandal."

I had used the word "scandal" deliberately, waiting to see if Adelmann would rush to deny that there was anything scandalous in the air concerning the Schumanns. That he did not do so sent me an important message. At some point, and soon, I would have to subject myself to a second expensive meal with Georg Adelmann in order to delve into what he called "these tales about the Schumanns themselves".

But for now I would have to be content to learn more about the composer's past rather than his present.

"Schumann's childhood and early youth were blessed on one hand because of his talents," Adelmann said, "but on the other hand were over-burdened with his parents' ambitions for him and their expectations of him. This 'on-one-hand-and-on-the-other-hand' pattern applied to everything in Schumann's growing and developing years. He had a close relationship with his father and his three older brothers, which fed the masculine side of his life; but he was also closely attached to his mother and to her more feminine interests. At times, he was a very sociable and outgoing child; at other times, he was anxious and withdrawn. When he was fifteen, his older sister Emilie committed suicide by drowning. Soon after, his father died suddenly. Schumann was devastated by both losses. So much happiness at times, so much tragedy at other times. Schumann's cheerfulness as a child vanished almost overnight. He became taciturn, daydreamed a great deal and, by his own admission, was unsure of himself in social settings."

Dr. Adelmann paused. Somehow he had managed to consume his plate of food while talking (the tablecloth bearing increasing evidence of this feat) and nodded now with approval as I refilled his wine glass for the third time. For a moment he turned his attention to the whereabouts of our waiter, which I took as a signal that he was ready for one of the desserts that stood tantalizingly on display on a nearby trolley. To my dismay, he selected not one but two— a large bowl of trifle and a generous slice of apple strudel.

Watching Georg Adelmann pitch with gusto into his desserts (he paused only long enough now and then for a noisy sip of his coffee), I was beginning to think that the price I was paying far exceeded the value of the information he was yielding. Wasn't it the same for everyone? I asked myself: friends and relatives come and go, prosper and fail, live and die. I began to fear that the Schumann monograph would prove about as fascinating as a railway schedule and only half as useful.

But just as I was about to consign this luncheon to the wastebasket, Dr. Adelmann redeemed himself.

Studying a large forkful of strudel, he said in a casual way, "You are aware, are you not, Preiss, that some years ago—when he turned twenty-one, to be precise— Schumann conceived the idea that he had produced twin companions, companions of the mind, so to speak? He called one 'Florestan', the other 'Eusebius'. Florestan represented Schumann's outgoing masculine side, the social being, the man of action."

"You mean Florestan, the hero in Beethoven's opera *Fidelio?*"

"Exactly. Eusebius, on the other hand, was named after the Christian saint, of course, and represented martyrdom, suffering, submission. The two 'spoke' to Schumann, or so he revealed to intimates. They provided a kind of balance to his life and his artistic endeavors, gave him a sense of direction, he claimed. Still claims, in fact."

Then, almost as an afterthought, Adelmann said, "And as if that were not enough, the poor fellow was much too preoccupied with sex. Obsessed is more like it."

I wasn't certain I wanted my guest to go on with this particular topic, not at Emmerich's Restaurant des Artistes. God knows I wasn't prudish about the subject of sex. As a police investigator, I had come across just about every kind of sexual activity known to the human species. Still, there were limits to what one discussed openly. "If I may be frank, Dr. Adelmann," I said, speaking as politely as I could, "I would prefer to hear about Schumann's sexual problems in a more private venue."

"Come, come, Preiss!" said Adelmann. "I take it, sir, that you are a man of the world and not some naïve country bumpkin. Word has it that between over-indulgence in sexual intercourse with a variety of young women, and presumably an excessive amount of pleasuring himself, Schumann's most private part—his penis, to be specific—is in dreadful condition. You know, Preiss, one cannot be cavalier about where one deploys one's 'soldier'. The trenches are perilous, and grievous wounds are too often suffered for the sake of instant gratification."

Pompous ass! Besides, given his obvious dedication to his stomach, my guess was that *his* "soldier" seldom if ever saw active service in "the trenches".

"Several highly respected physicians," Adelmann continued, "have speculated—privately to me, you understand—that he probably contracted a form of venereal disease as a young man. How has this affected his marriage? Well now, there's a choice topic for speculation, eh?" Adelmann gave me a wise wink.

As we rose to leave the restaurant, he suddenly tugged at my arm. "I suppose you've heard about Schumann's house guest? Very interesting young man. Composer and pianist. Hails from Hamburg. Been on a concert tour. Apparently stopped over in Düsseldorf. I understand they are very taken with this fellow. You know: kindred spirits, lovers of the romantic movement in music. Like the proverbial peas in a pod, so I'm told. I was introduced to him recently. Quite handsome, even dashing. Tall, blond, eyes like sapphires."

The description immediately brought to mind the stranger in the conductor's lounge the previous evening. "I believe I may have seen the young man you describe last night, after the concert. Do you recall his name?"

"Of course," Adelmann said. "Johannes Brahms. I can tell you, his is a name to remember!"

Chapter Eight

E arly the following morning—a Tuesday—I arrived at my office wanting nothing more than to close my door, sit back in my chair with my feet propped up on my desk, and catch a half hour's sleep without disturbance. I had spent the previous night and early morning hours in a cell-like bedroom, the walls and ceilings of which looked as though they had been painted crimson by some shamefully inept decorator. The "painter" clearly was the same man who had left similar souvenirs of his artistry in two other bedrooms in this lower-class section of Düsseldorf in recent weeks. The victims, all young prostitutes, had their throats cut after suffering multiple stab wounds. As the investigator in charge, I was under orders from the Commissioner of Police to spare no effort in the search for the killer.

But somehow the eagerness and the energy that, up to now, had flowed so unflaggingly in me, seemed to have leaked through my pores, as though through a sieve. Making my way from that bedroom to the Constabulary, I experienced a weariness far beyond anything physical. *Face it, Preiss,* I lectured myself, *this is what you do to earn your living—and not too bad a living it is—so put your heart and soul into it!*

The lecture was falling on deaf ears. Over the course of my stroll back to police headquarters—I passed up a carriage ride, wanting some time to myself—I pondered the reasons for this sudden and uncharacteristic lethargy.

In my heart of hearts, as my career went on, there was this feeling, weak at first but steadily gaining in strength, that there was a tiresomeness about crime that inevitably made the *investigation* of crime tiresome.

What's more, I had grown sick of the locations of crime. The typical sites were tawdry—cheap, sparsely-furnished rooms in flophouses; bordellos with mattresses stained and reeking of every kind of human spillage imaginable; taverns whose ales tasted like recycled dishwater and whose food was repulsive even to the rodents who explored it; alleyways and back streets where footsteps in the dark meant that rape or murder were no more than an arm's length behind. Only in theatrical dramas did these offenses take place in castle corridors and frilly boudoirs, the playrooms of the rich and noteworthy. In real life, evil's preferred domain was the gutter.

Arriving back at my office from this latest investigation, I was in a despondent mood. It quickly brightened, however, when I caught sight of an envelope delivered to my desk just before my return. The handwriting, the imprint on the seal (a treble clef), and the floral scent of the paper, told me this was from Helena Becker.

I broke open the seal and extracted the note. And read:

Dear Hermann—

Robert and Clara Schumann have extended a warm invitation to the Düsseldorf Quartet to participate in a musical evening at their home this coming Saturday at eight o'clock. The guest of honour will be Franz Liszt, who is once again visiting Düsseldorf en route to Weimar. I gather that a number of luminaries in the musical world will be present. Our Quartet will perform Dr. Schumann's Quintet for Piano and Strings with Clara Schumann at the keyboard. The invitation mentions that each of us may bring a guest.

I can think of no one who might benefit more than you from attending this event. Therefore I shall refrain from

*further tempting you to accompany me except to add that
our hosts will offer a light supper prior to the musicale.
(And if you play your cards right, I may offer you further
refreshments later in the evening, Hermann.)*

   Helena

Chapter Nine

The Robert Schumann now planting himself before me, beaming and ebullient, pumping my hand vigorously as he and his wife welcomed me on my arrival at the Saturday evening musicale, was not the Robert Schumann who, only a few nights earlier, had been in a state of collapse after the concert, overcome by panic. Even more extraordinary was Clara Schumann's greeting. Glowing with amiability, she said, "Ah, Helena, my dear, what a charming idea, bringing along Düsseldorf's finest policeman for protection." Turning to me, smiling slyly, she said, "And you, Inspector, are you here to guard Fräulein Becker's priceless cello or Fräulein Becker herself?"

"As anyone can see," I said, "Fräulein Becker is far more priceless than her cello." I knew this was the response that was called for. But my gaze, which should have fallen then on Helena, instead remained on Clara Schumann. For a moment or two, I wondered if hypnosis, a phenomenon I had long regarded with disbelief, was not a sham after all. Attired in a simple emerald gown, her neck encircled by a single strand of pearls, the woman was proof that elegance did not depend on adornments.

Madam Schumann said to her husband, "Robert, dear, why don't you take Fräulein Becker's wrap and help her store her cello against the piano. Meanwhile, I'll escort our famished-looking Inspector to the buffet."

Schumann seemed perfectly happy to obey, and happier still when, as Helena shed her wrap and loosened her silk shawl about her shoulders, he caught sight of her high, firm bosom.

Taking my arm, Clara steered me toward the warmly lit dining room. On her face was a broad smile, but now it struck me as fixed, and I sensed beneath her show of hospitality a cold layer of suspicion. I was not wrong. "So, Inspector," she said, speaking in a low voice only I would be able to hear, "why are you really here tonight? Have you come to spy on us?"

The best way to disarm her, I decided, was to treat the matter of my presence facetiously. "If you must know," I said, trying to sound secretive and speaking just above a whisper, "the real reason for my attendance is standing over there," I nodded in the direction of the far corner of the dining room table. There, hovering over a platter of roasted meats and poultry, was Georg Adelmann, fork poised in his right hand like a spear. Balanced on the palm of his left hand was a large plate already laden with a mountain of cheeses, potatoes, salads and slices of bread.

My hostess gave me a puzzled look. "Georg Adelmann? Are you saying *he* of all people is under surveillance?"

I put my finger to my lips. In a hushed tone, I said, "Please, I beg you to say nothing of this to anyone, Madam Schumann. What I have just told you is in strict confidence."

"The only crime Georg Adelmann commits, if indeed one can call it a crime, is the crime of over-eating," Clara said.

I had begun this business about Georg Adelmann as a diversion, hastily contrived, I admit, but for what I perceived as a good cause. On Clara Schumann's face there was an expression now of such intense curiosity that I had no choice but to carry on.

"Notice, madam," I said, "the exceedingly generous cut of Adelmann's coat. Even for a man of his enormous girth the coat is clearly two sizes too large. My father was a tailor, and I have more than a passing interest in clothing. Trust me, there is a reason for this…a sinister reason."

"Which is?"

"I am willing to wager my badge of office that his coat contains deep inner pockets capable of containing certain items he is in the habit of—to put it politely—appropriating for his own use and enjoyment—small but precious trinkets, household ornaments, perhaps the odd valuable piece of jewellery or tableware."

I suppose it was somewhat shabby of me to cast a shadow over the eminent journalist, one of the Schumanns' stellar guests, but what I had divulged was not spur-of-the-moment fiction. The fact was that, at my luncheon meeting with him at Emmerich's, I had watched with a mixture of astonishment and fascination as Adelmann, with the clumsiness of an amateur petty thief, had folded his linen napkin over a small silver salver and, thinking his actions were unseen, slipped his prize into some secret depository well down inside his suit coat. Physicians who dabbled in this new branch of Medicine known as Psychology had a word for people like Adelmann—kleptomaniacs. My word for this kind of activity was much more to the point: robbery. At any rate, it was one of those incidents a detective tucks away in the back of his mind, like something put away for a rainy day, something that might come in handy in the future. The "rainy day" was here and now.

"Please, don't let this distract you," I said to Clara. "You have my assurance that I will keep an eye on our friend over there throughout the evening." Then, feeling an urge to change the subject, I said, "I'm thrilled at the prospect of rubbing shoulders with the great Franz Liszt. Do you think he'll favour us with a selection or two at the piano?"

"The 'great' Franz Liszt is here officially as a guest, not as a performer. But mark my words, Inspector: he has never needed a second invitation to light up the sky with one of his fireworks displays. Even though he's *not* on tonight's program, don't be surprised if *he* is the one who plays the encores."

She was smiling when she told me this, but I could taste the acid in her voice. I said, "I could easily detect your dislike of the man, even if I weren't a detective."

"You must understand something," she said. "Liszt and his friend Wagner have gone out of their way to discredit everything my husband stands for. They refer to themselves rather grandly as 'The Weimar School' and regard themselves as superior avant-gardists. In one of his recent magazine pieces, Wagner used an English expression—'stick-in-the-mud'—to describe what he calls sarcastically 'The Leipzig School'."

"Then why all this elaborate fuss in honour of an artist you hold in such contempt?"

"The Italians have a saying," she replied. "'If you want an audience, start a fight.' Here, in Germany, we say 'If you want an audience, drop the name Franz Liszt.' She reduced her voice to a whisper. "The truth is, half the people you see here this evening are only here out of curiosity to see Liszt in the flesh, to be able to say tomorrow to their friends that they were in the same room as he."

"Please pardon a frank question," I said, "but aren't you being—"

"Hypocritical?" She gave me a shrewd smile. "Of course." Her smile vanished. "We don't live in a spiritual world, Inspector; we live in the *real* world. At least, *I* do. I'm not always certain about Robert."

By this time the rooms were filling with invited guests. I recognized several persons prominent in Düsseldorf's high society. There were, to be sure, Baron and Baroness Hoffman, as close to royalty as one got in this region, a pair who, unlike their hostess, bedecked themselves with medals and ribbons (in his case) and necklaces, brooches, bracelets and earrings (in her) so that together, as they entered the foyer and moved into the dining room, they formed a gigantic human chandelier. Following after them at a slow, respectful pace was an assembly of lesser celebrities—civic officials (who knew little about music and cared less but relished an opportunity to appear cultured); Dr. Julius Illing, chairman of the local music society; a handful of writers and journalists in threadbare evening clothes, all of whom, despite their influence, looked as though they could stand a good meal and some decent wine.

In the dining room, the Schumanns' guests fell upon the food and drink as though fortifying themselves for a stark desert crossing rather than a gentle evening of chamber music. Inwardly, I congratulated Georg Adelmann on his foresight in arriving early and getting to the buffet before the others.

But where was the guest of honour himself? It was well past the time when Franz Liszt ought to have made his appearance. To be fashionably late for an event of this sort was customary among socialites, and indeed a grand entrance was never truly grand if made precisely on schedule. But a half-hour had gone by, and still no Liszt. Out of the corner of my eye, I noticed the Schumanns glancing at a mantel clock in the dining room and looking a bit anxious. If Liszt was to enjoy the benefits of the buffet, he would have to arrive very soon or be content with scraps.

Georg Adelmann, at last, had filled his stomach and attached himself to Helena Becker in a quiet corner of the drawing room, feasting now on the sight of Helena's figure. The peculiarities of the cello obliged Helena to wear a full skirt performing. Though such a garment ordinarily would reveal nothing about the natural contours of the player, in Helena's case there was something tantalizing about this costume, which did not fail to register on Adelmann. *Splendid!* I thought. I wanted the old glutton to become enchanted with my cellist friend, so enchanted that he might divulge to her information about the Schumanns that he would hesitate to divulge to a police official like me. Catching sight of me across the drawing room, Helena nodded and gave me a sweet smile. I smiled back with what I hoped was a signal of encouragement.

A full hour had now passed, and still no sign of the guest of honour. The Schumanns kept eyeing the mantel clock. Some of the men began checking the time on their pocket-watches. People were beginning to murmur discreetly, some guessing that Liszt had forgotten, although it seemed preposterous, others taking it for granted that the famed virtuoso traditionally eschewed banquets in order to maintain the lithe figure that he presented on stage. "No doubt he will show up," Adelmann said, "offer profuse apologies, charm everyone with his pretense of humbleness, and outshine even the jewels on Baroness Hoffman's encrusted bodice."

At nine o'clock, after exchanging worried glances, Robert and Clara Schumann summoned everyone to take their seats in the drawing room. Looking exasperated, Schumann said, "Ladies and gentlemen, the players are ready, and we are going to proceed with our program despite the absence of our guest of honour, who has probably experienced a delay in his travel arrangements. He should grace us with his presence before long. Before we present Beethoven's D-major Trio, and my own Piano Quintet, we have a very special and pleasant surprise for you. You are going to hear for the first time a young composer, who in my opinion is already a soaring eagle in the musical heaven and who will play for you two of his recent pieces for piano. Because our young genius is inclined to shyness, I will tell you that he calls the first a rhapsody, and the second an intermezzo—"

Schumann turned slightly and, looking over his shoulder, called, "Clara, if you will—"

Behind Schumann, a door opened and Clara Schumann emerged from an anteroom leading by the hand the same tall, handsome fellow I'd seen that night at the concert hall. For someone so athletic in appearance, he seemed to be taking hesitant, small steps, like a schoolboy being trotted out before a roomful of grownups to recite a poem. Letting go his hand, Clara motioned for the youthful composer to seat himself at one of the two grand pianos, her gesture gracious and, I thought, a bit too theatrical.

Nor did I fail to take note of another gesture. "Distinguished guests," Clara said, "please welcome from Hamburg...Johannes Brahms." Then, as she passed behind Brahms on her way to her seat, her hand brushed across the back of his neck. The touch was so slight, so subtle, that I doubt anyone in the room noticed, anyone, that is, except me. Ascribe it to the particular angle at which I was seated, or ascribe it to the fact that a detective's vision tends to be binocular, even off duty. But there was no denying: that brush of Clara Schumann's hand against the back of Johannes Brahms's neck was not accidental.

Though I am no music critic, I felt almost from the opening bars of the *Rhapsody* that we were in the presence of an enormously gifted musician, a man with powerful melodic ideas and the technique to give voice to those ideas. The *Intermezzo,* softer, more poetic, sounded to my ears like a long sigh. It was not so much an expression of passion as it was a deep sigh of yearning, of longing for someone who was just beyond reach.

The final lingering note of the *Intermezzo* was followed by enthusiastic applause and a few shouts of "Bravo!" Schumann strode to the piano and lifted Brahms by the shoulders, turned him about to face the small audience, then stepped back, leaving the young man, looking awkward and sheepish, to bask alone in the admiration and approval of everyone in the drawing room.

My attention wandered for a moment to the back of the room. There, standing by herself, as though isolated from the rest, was Clara Schumann. She did not join in the applause. I saw no outer demonstration of enthusiasm on her part for the performance we had just witnessed, but on her face there was a look that seemed to me to go far beyond admiration and approval. It was a look that seemed to match the mood of Brahms's second selection, that same sense of yearning and of longing for someone who was just out of reach.

By now the clock in the drawing room showed the hour as nine thirty, and our host found himself forced to offer lame excuses for the absence of the guest of honour. To rescue her husband in what was so obviously an embarrassing situation, Clara Schumann spoke out. In a cool, confident voice, she said, "You're all well acquainted with the Liszt legend, I'm sure. First he enters a room in *spirit*. His *body* follows much later."

The room exploded in laughter. Schumann beamed appreciatively at his wife. And Johannes Brahms, who had been ushered to a chair in the front row, gazed up at Clara Schumann with an expression I can only liken to pure undisguised adoration.

With characteristic poise, Madam Schumann took charge. "While the heavens are opening and Maestro Liszt is preparing to descend, we will proceed in the meantime with the Beethoven."

As the musicians took their places to perform the Beethoven Trio, I watched Clara Schumann return to her place at the back of the room. But even there, in a relatively dark corner, she continued to be the centre of my interest. And despite the purity and beauty of the Trio, and Helena Becker's intense contribution to the performance, my attention kept shifting constantly from Clara in the rearmost row of seats to Robert and Johannes in the front row, and back to Clara.

Why, I asked myself, had she chosen to distance herself from her husband and his bashful but appealing protégé? Was it diffidence on her part? Hardly. Clara Schumann was a woman accustomed to occupying the centre of the stage. Despite mothering six children, she was not a subscriber to the popular view of German womanhood, a view that regarded females as domestic creatures whose public activities should be limited to attending church on Sundays.

Was she jealous of her husband's reputation as a composer? While all Europe acknowledged her virtuosity as a pianist, her own accomplishments at writing music had been eclipsed by her husband's, judging by critical accounts I had read. That she was serious in her efforts no one doubted, but being serious was one thing, being inspired quite another. A piano concerto she'd composed was acknowledged by critics as competent, a compliment akin to declaring that, as a chef, the woman knew how to cook a pot roast.

Putting aside for the moment what I took to be her infatuation with this fellow Brahms, was it possible that she saw in him both a formidable competitor with Robert in the area of composition, and a formidable competitor with her as a performing artist? Behind her ostensible pride in promoting the young man from Hamburg, was there a fear that he might turn out to be *too* successful before long? In the financially uncertain musical world, every commission to compose received by Brahms would be a commission Robert Schumann failed to receive; every engagement to perform as a pianist would be an engagement Clara failed to obtain. With six children to feed and clothe, every thaler counted these days.

There was another possibility: I recalled her question earlier in the evening: *Have you come to spy on us?* My impromptu answer at the time might have served to persuade a gullible person, but Clara Schumann did not strike me as one who was easily gulled. By choosing to sit as far from Brahms as she could, was she hoping to dispel any suggestion that Johannes Brahms's proximity was vital to her own wellbeing? Ever since the night of Robert Schumann's breakdown at the concert hall, the notion had been rooting itself in my brain that there were blanks in the Schumanns' marriage. Were these blanks now being filled one way or another by a young and vigorous Brahms? Call it a policeman's instinct for the suspicious; call it cynicism; whatever the reasons, I was sure the relationship between Clara Schumann and Johannes Brahms contained all the ingredients of a secret and passionate love affair, one that was bound to evolve, if indeed it had not already done so.

Applause and cries of "Encore!" were still in the air following the Beethoven piece when suddenly and rather noisily, the wide doors leading from the foyer were thrown open.

All eyes turned to the back of the drawing room.

There at last, poised like a statue, magnificent in silk top hat and long black cape, stood Franz Liszt.

Chapter Ten

Careful not to disturb a single strand of his long, perfectly combed hair, Liszt doffed his silk top hat and handed it to a waiting servant, then waited calmly as the servant slipped the wool serge cape from around his shoulders. His manner was that of a prince accustomed to being attended in this way.

"A thousand pardons for this rude intrusion," Franz Liszt called out. "I was unavoidably detained. Alas, when it comes to timing, Germany's railways are not as gifted as Germany's musicians." With a helpless shrug, he added simply, "The evening train from Weimar—" Everyone in the room seemed to understand. There were sympathetic nods and the odd wise chuckle here and there.

Schumann made his way toward his newly-arrived guest, a broad smile on his face. Extending a hand, he said (a little too loudly, I thought), "My dear Franz, Clara and I are honoured to have you under our humble roof!" The two men embraced, heartily slapping one another's backs. Detaching himself, Liszt said, "I am chilled to my very bones, Schumann. A hot cup of tea or better still coffee—"

"But of course," Schumann said, then called across the room, "Clara, my darling, would you fetch our dear Franz a cup of coffee, a slice of cake. The poor man looks starved."

"I would be happy to, Robert dear," Clara replied, giving her effusive husband a look that could have turned him into a pillar of salt had he glanced back at her.

As Schumann led Liszt to a front row seat that had

been set aside, I had an opportunity for the first time to study the man at close range and in a setting other than a concert hall stage.

Everything about him—his outgoing charm and extreme handsomeness, his easy sophistication, the smoothness of his voice, his impeccably tailored evening-wear—everything bespoke a man of the world, a man of grace and civility.

At Liszt's insistence, the program resumed without another moment's delay. With Clara Schumann performing the piano part, Robert's Quintet would occupy the second half. In his brief introduction before the players commenced, Schumann, standing close to his wife at the keyboard, one hand laid tenderly on her shoulder, repeated what was already well-known, that he'd written the piece for Clara and dedicated it to her some ten years earlier as a kind of small concerto for the piano, one capable of being performed without all the fuss and bother of a large orchestra and concert hall.

"If the Quintet overflows with love," said Schumann, his voice growing hoarse, "I make no apology." At this, I expected Clara to make some equal and loving response, no matter how slight, to reciprocate. Instead, she sat at the piano with head bowed, hands folded in her lap, her expression frozen in what looked like profound embarrassment. She seemed to desire nothing more at the moment than that her husband should shut up.

A quick look across the front of the room to where Brahms was seated revealed an expression on his face that was remarkably similar to Clara's.

I was struck, too, by another odd fact: having introduced Johannes Brahms with such fanfare this evening, surely Schumann would have gone out of his way to introduce the promising young man to the titan who had just taken his seat nearby. Why did he fail to do so? Was it oversight? Was it deliberate? And granted that Brahms appeared a rather shy fellow, wouldn't he nevertheless have taken the trouble to introduce himself to Liszt? One could dine out for months afterward on such an event. *Yes, I swear before God, Liszt said he'd heard of me and insisted I look him up next time I visit Weimar...*

I had heard the Schumann Quintet played on several occasions in the past, but never with such energy and passion and sparkle as the performance at the Schumann house on this February night.

Once again my attention was drawn throughout, as if by a magnet, to Clara Schumann at the keyboard. Whether displaying her nimble technical skills in solo passages or blending with the other players in more sombre sections of the quintet, it was she who set the tone and the pace. It was she who gave the entire performance its soul.

And it was her name, shouted with admiration, that filled the room the moment the final chord sounded. *"Clara!...Clara!...Bravo Clara!...Magnificent Clara!..."*

People shot to their feet applauding, calling for an encore, in an ovation that focused on the slight figure in the emerald green gown. Behind her in the shadows stood her husband, his eyes watery, joining in the applause, looking somehow as if he'd had little to do with all of this.

In the front row stood Johannes Brahms, a soft smile on his smooth face. I have some acquaintance with that kind of smile and knew where it had its origin. If Brahms was not hopelessly in love, then my powers of perception were hopelessly failing.

I cast my eyes to another part of the front row, where Franz Liszt too had risen to his feet. But his applause? "Polite" would be a fitting word to describe it. In fact, after a moment or two Liszt ceased clapping, looked about as though he were dumfounded by the outpouring of enthusiasm that surrounded him, then resumed applauding in a mechanical fashion, the corners of his lips upturned in a patronizing smile, as though what he had just heard was music to be tolerated rather than enjoyed.

When finally it became evident that the players were too exhausted to favour the audience with an encore, Robert Schumann stepped to the centre again. Looking directly at Liszt, he said, "And now, dear friends, do we dare hope that our guest of honour, Maestro Franz Liszt, will make the evening perfect...or perhaps I should say *more* perfect...by playing for us?" Schumann gestured toward the two pianos. "These keyboards have never before felt the magical fingers of Maestro Liszt, and—" Here Schumann began to chuckle at the witticism he was about to deliver. "And it may be said, ladies and gentlemen, that a grand piano is not truly grand until it has been touched by the master himself, Franz Liszt."

Liszt half rose from his seat to acknowledge the applause that greeted Schumann's announcement, then promptly sat down in what his host must have taken as a sign of modesty. This apparent reluctance on Liszt's part was not what I had expected. From all accounts, and bearing in mind what Clara Schumann had said about him earlier in the evening, I assumed that Liszt would not require a second invitation. Yet here he was, seemingly glued to his chair and shaking his head from side to side in a very determined refusal.

Schumann, opening his arms expansively, said, "You are too modest, my dear Liszt. The piano awaits you. Please!"

"Thank you, my dear Schumann," Liszt called from his seat, "but I could not possibly play now. I mean, my music would be totally inappropriate after what we have just listened to...after music that is so...so very *Leipzig.*"

The expression "so very *Leipzig*", heard clearly from one end of the room to the other, had an immediate and strange effect; it seemed to drain all the oxygen out of the place, leaving everyone momentarily speechless and immobile. Something in the way Liszt had uttered it smacked of condescension.

What followed after a split-second of stunned silence was dreadful. In a sudden, violent rage Schumann lunged at Liszt, seized him by the shoulders and lifted him from his chair with a force that was nothing short of an assault. "How dare you speak of our work in such a demeaning way?" Schumann shouted.

As a mere onlooker, I found Schumann's actions frightening. Liszt must have found them terrifying.

Without another word, Schumann released his hapless guest of honour, swung swiftly about on his heels and stalked out of the drawing room, slamming the heavy doors behind him.

Considering the gross indignity he had just suffered, Liszt managed to regain his composure, outwardly at least, with incredible aplomb. Calmly, carefully, he straightened the lapels of his tailcoat and pulled the collar down snugly back into place. His oversized black bowtie, which had been knocked askew, was restored to its proper location and given just the right pinch at the ends to tighten the knot. With firm downward strokes, Liszt brushed the creases from his slim-fitted trousers. Once again he was every inch Franz Liszt: the perfect pianist, the perfect man-about-town.

But now he was also Franz Liszt, the *im*perfect guest, the man who—perhaps innocently (although I wondered about this)—had managed to transform what had begun as a brilliant evening into a smouldering ruin. Everyone in the room glared at poor Liszt as though he had just dumped a cartload of refuse in their midst. To his credit, he realized he had made a grievous mistake. He lost no time in offering an apology to his hostess. "I do beg your pardon, most sincerely, Clara. The fault is all mine. Blame it on a slip of the tongue."

This excuse only added fuel to the fire. Clara shot back, "I would prefer that you confine your slips of the tongue to Weimar. They are not welcome in this house."

Her anger left Liszt no choice. "I won't burden you further with my company, madam," he said. Given that he had just been invited in no uncertain terms to leave the premises, his tone was respectful, even gracious. "May I say only this, madam: you and your husband are the only people in the world from whom I would accept so calmly the insult just handed me."

All of us watched in deathly silence as Liszt turned and began to make his way out of the drawing-room. But as Liszt passed in front of Johannes Brahms, he paused. "Young man," he said, "I regret that I arrived too late to hear your performance. Perhaps on another occasion. By the way, that piano—" Liszt pointed to the instrument Clara Schumann had played on. "That piano is in need of a good tuning. I have perfect pitch, and the 'A' is at least a full quarter-tone too high." Shaking his head, Liszt added, "What a pity."

Chapter Eleven

I have done with him forever!" "Him" was—of course—
Franz Liszt. The person making this vow for all to
hear was—of course—Clara Schumann.

I had no difficulty understanding her anger. For a
man with a reputation for social grace, Liszt had acted
with incredible insensitivity, almost boorishness.

What *was* difficult to understand, at least for me, was
Clara's apparent indifference to the whereabouts at that
moment of her husband. For all we knew, he might have
been in the attic attempting to hang himself from a rafter.
Or he might have been in the cellar drinking himself into
a stupor—something he was known to do all too
frequently whenever things went badly for him. Or he
might have stormed out into the night, coatless and
hatless, roaring aimlessly into the uncaring February wind.

Stationing herself in the foyer, her head high, her
composure restored despite everything, she bade a polite
"Goodnight, thank you so much for coming" to her guests
as they bundled into their heavy outerwear and,
muttering awkward expressions of sympathy, filed out.

Only four persons remained now: Clara Schumann,
Brahms, Helena Becker and I.

I was committed of course to escorting Helena back
to her apartment, but a sense of unfinished business
hung in the air, and though I had the distinct feeling
that my hostess and her protégé were eager to see the
last of Helena and me, I made no move to assist Helena

to pack her cello in its case, nor did I don my overcoat, which the Schumanns' housekeeper had handed me. Instead, I turned to Brahms. "Tell me, sir," I said, "was there any truth to what Liszt said to you on his way out?" "You mean about wanting to hear me play my own music?" Brahms gave me an ironic smile. "Hardly. Our music is worlds apart, his and mine. Liszt's is the music of a swindler, a showcase of empty confections…bonbons that are hollow inside. I am proud to be called a 'Leipziger'. As far as I'm concerned, it's the ultimate compliment." As Brahms said this, he and Clara exchanged looks of unguarded fondness.

Pretending to be merely curious, I said, "My question had to do with Liszt's observation that the piano was out of tune. Did you agree with him?"

"Nonsense!" Brahms said.

"But he seemed very sure of himself."

"They are always very sure of themselves, Liszt and Wagner," Brahms said. "Both of these 'Weimar' types regard themselves as God's gifts to the human race."

I was anxious not to press the matter too urgently; still, the question of the piano being out of tune nagged at me.

Brahms continued to be dismissive about it. "I know something about piano tuning," he said. "You see, when you play in brothels, as I was obliged to do to earn a living back in Hamburg in my younger days, you play on instruments that are a step away from the garbage heap. So I went to work always equipped with my own tuning fork and set of tools. And later, when I began my concert career, I still continued to carry all this equipment, because one never knew what kind of instrument one would encounter on tour in the backwaters. Trust me, sir; I know when a piano is in tune and when it isn't."

"So, if the middle A was a bit off…say on the low side or the high side…your ear would have detected the flaw?"

"All of us would have noticed it immediately," Clara Schumann interjected. "Besides, in anticipation of tonight's musicale, Robert and I naturally had both pianos tuned this afternoon."

"Tuned by whom?" I asked.

"Our regular tuner and technician, of course."

"And he is?"

"Wilhelm Hupfer. He has maintained our instruments for many years. Willi is almost a member of the Schumann family by now. Nobody—absolutely nobody—understands the intricacies of a piano as Willi does. On several of our major tours, Willi has accompanied us; that is how much Robert and I depend on him."

I asked, "What time this afternoon did Hupfer complete his work?"

Clara thought for a moment. "I would say about mid-afternoon...three o'clock, maybe three thirty."

"Oh no, Clara," Brahms said quickly, "it was much later. It was just after five when he packed up his tools and left. You remember, don't you? Hupfer wanted you to try out both pianos, but you said there was no time because you had to attend to matters with the cook, then dress for the evening."

"Ah yes, Johannes, you are quite right. I'd forgotten." Then, as if to make light of this discussion, Clara said, smiling at me, "When I'm not at the keyboard, my sense of time is often less than ideal."

"I'm curious, Madam Schumann," I said. "What would motivate a man of Liszt's stature—a man who professes to have perfect pitch, a claim, incidentally, nobody seems to challenge—what would motivate him to remark that the piano you played on was tuned too high?"

"You must not take whatever Franz Liszt does or says too seriously," Brahms said. He seemed in a rush to answer. "Are you aware, Inspector," he said, "that in America there is a famous circus operated by a man by the name of Barnum, P.T. Barnum, as he's widely known. And this man Barnum, they say, has offered Liszt a half million dollars in American money to tour with the circus? Imagine, our hero Franz Liszt playing in a circus tent! Elephants dancing to Liszt's tunes, clowns doing somersaults, and the biggest clown of all, the musical acrobat himself, banging away at the keyboard! Only God in heaven knows whether or not Franz Liszt possesses perfect pitch, but *I* know that those pianos are perfectly in tune."

"No, Brahms, I'm afraid Liszt was right, and you are wrong—"

The four of us turned to discover Robert Schumann coming down the stairs from the second storey of the house, taking the flight of steps slowly, one step at a time, gripping the bannister firmly as though he were afraid he might topple. "I hate to contradict you, Johannes," Schumann said, pausing several steps from the bottom, "but the moment Clara struck middle A and the players began to tune, I realized that something was decidedly off. In fact, throughout most of the second half of the program, that middle A kept pounding away at my brain. It was as though a carpenter were hammering it into my skull."

From where he was standing, Schumann called to his wife. "Clara, did you not try out the pianos this afternoon while Hupfer was still on the job? You know he always insists you do so before he packs up and leaves."

Clara Schumann glared up at her husband. Then, turning her back to him, she spoke as though she no longer cared about family confidences, privacy, discretion or pride. "I am fed up, Robert...fed up and tired. I cannot be all things to all people any longer. I cannot be everywhere at once. No, I did *not* try out the damned pianos when Willi was here. And where were *you*, may I ask? Brooding as usual in some neighborhood tavern? You didn't show up until after six. I had guests to prepare for, children to feed, a thousand-and-one last-minute details to attend to. There was simply no time...*no time!*"

It was the kind of outburst that could have only one effect on any guest witnessing it—embarrassment. After a painful moment of silence, I cleared my throat a bit noisily and said, "It *is* growing rather late, Madam Schumann. I'm sure you must be exhausted. If you will excuse Fräulein Becker and me—"

Without looking at us, her back still to her husband, Clara said, "I hope you are satisfied once and for all, Inspector Preiss, that my husband is a sick man. And to make matters worse, he is not content to stumble alone into madness, but insists upon taking me with him."

How could I possibly respond to this statement? I decided that no response was the best response.

*   *   *

Once Helena and I were settled in our carriage, I said, "I still fail to see what is so inflammatory about one composer calling another composer's music 'Leipzig'. The policeman in me looks upon all these artistic differences as petty, even silly. I picture Schumann and Liszt engaged in a duel at dawn tomorrow, facing each other at twenty paces, armed with loaded powder-puffs."

"Don't fool yourself," Helena said. "These people are geniuses. Their convictions run very, very deep. So do their prejudices and their rivalries. What you witnessed tonight is far from over and done with."

After a few minutes of silence, she suddenly said, "He was right, you know, Hermann."

"Who was right?"

"Schumann. He was absolutely right."

"You mean about the—"

"It was off, yes, the middle A. The second she sounded the note for us to tune our instruments, I said to myself that it was on the high side."

"I don't understand, Helena. You are professionals. Why didn't you say something right then and there?"

"Because it would have meant that Hupfer would

have to be summoned, and we would have had to wait while he re-tuned. It could have taken forever, don't you understand? Anyway, I didn't want to cause a fuss."

"Did any other player notice?"

"I looked at the others, and yes, we all noticed it was sharp. But as you said, Hermann, we are professionals. So we simply carried on. Maybe Hupfer was not up to his usual standard this afternoon. Maybe these days the old man's got too much wax in his ears."

"Or maybe—" I looked away, hesitant to complete my thought.

Helena said, "Or maybe what?"

I shook my head. "Nothing. An idea just flew through my brain. Really, Helena, it's too far-fetched."

"Tell me anyway, Hermann."

"Follow me for a moment, then. Before Brahms made such a point of correcting her, Madam Schumann said Hupfer finished his work by about three or three thirty, right?"

"Go on."

"If she was accurate about the time—and something tells me she *was*—that would have left enough time for someone to tamper with the pianos. Someone who had the right tools and knew what he was doing. Especially someone who had a reason." I paused. "Sometimes my imagination runs off with itself." Then I added, speaking to myself, "But sometimes it doesn't."

We spent the rest of the carriage ride in silence, the two of us seated close together. My thoughts, however, lingered back at No. 15 Bilkerstrasse.

When we arrived at her lodgings, I said, helping her down from the carriage, "Would you like me to come up...for a while?"

"Not tonight, Hermann."

It was just as well. In truth my offer was half-hearted, for what was going through my mind at that moment over and over again was the name "Hupfer".

Chapter Twelve

T he old gentleman who overhauls my gold pocketwatch is permanently hunched from years of bending over his cramped worktable. His eyes are frozen into a permanent squint from peering into the miniature innards of timepieces. His hands have become small lobster claws after a lifetime spent handling the delicate tools of his trade. The fellow, now in his sixties, who services our firearms, has about him the reek of gun oil and the acrid smell of spent gunpowder. His fingers, no matter how thoroughly they are scrubbed, bear the stains of his trade that will go with him some day to the grave. His workshop is a dungeon, and he seems more like a prisoner in it than a free tradesman. Much the same can be said of all the other technicians and tradespeople and artisans upon whom we rely from day to day. There is a uniformity about such men, an air of pride mixed with fatigue. They have reached the peak of their respective vocations but have somehow become beaten down by daily repetition and the limitations that separate craft from art. When they die, their tools die with them, and that is the end of their story.

Or so I was convinced until the morning I met for the first time Wilhelm Hupfer—"Willi" to the Schumanns. His workshop was as spotless and orderly as a medical clinic. Though he was shorter than I, he stood ramrod-straight, which made him seem taller. His white cotton coat—the kind worn by physicians and research scientists—was starched and immaculate. He was clean-shaven and clear-eyed. His hands, resting comfortably on the lid of a giant Bösendorfer he'd been repairing, were like those of a surgeon. When I mentioned this to him, he smiled a bit. "Ah yes, Inspector," he said, "skilled like a surgeon to be sure...but much, much more sensitive. Let me show you what I mean."

Lifting the heavy mahogany lid of the Bösendorfer grand and propping it up, he pointed to the inner workings that resembled a harp laid flat. With the knuckle of his right index finger, he rapped first the gold-lacquered cast-iron frame that formed the foundation for the wooden pin blocks and wire strings, then the thick solid spruce planking, braced by horizontal struts that formed the inner rim of the casing. "Looks strong, doesn't it, Inspector. Strong enough to withstand an earthquake, eh?" I agreed. "And strong it certainly is," Hupfer continued, looking down lovingly at the instrument as it lay bare beneath him. "The great Liszt plays one of these. Been playing one since he was a young man. Used to break the strings on other makes. They said he could tear open the guts of a grand piano the way a lion tears open a gazelle. Not so with a Bösendorfer, however."

"I don't understand," I said. "If a piano like this is so sturdy, why does it require the delicacy of a surgeon to maintain it in proper working order?"

Hupfer gave me the smile of an expert who loves any opportunity to enlighten the ignorant. "That is my favourite question, Inspector," he said. "Look here, if you will—" He motioned to me to bend closer to the piano's busy interior. "I'm going to press a key...say middle C...like so—"

I watched as the felt-tipped hammer struck the double steel and copper strings that gave off the sound of middle C, then fell back into place in the row of hammers.

"Looks simple, doesn't it? You bang the key, it bangs the strings, it comes back. God's in his heaven, and all's well in the world, right?"

By this time, even a dullard would discern that what this man was talking about was anything but simple. "You're the doctor," I said. "Please go on."

"The motions of the action must be adjusted to within a tolerance of a millimetre...*or less.* For instance, the backcheck—that's the part that catches the hammer on the rebound after it has struck the string—the backcheck must be regulated so that the hammer is caught precisely twelve millimetres from the string; otherwise the instrument will not be capable of proper repetition."

I looked on fascinated as Hupfer reached across to his workbench and selected a fine needle. Holding the needle like a scalpel, he gently but firmly prodded the felt tip of one of the hammers, loosening its dense fibres. "This is how we 'voice' the piano, one hammer at a time, to achieve the warm, mellow tone, the right volume, the evenness of scale that the piano virtuoso demands. This instrument was built in 1839, Inspector, about ten years or so after the Bösendorfer firm was established. As a matter of fact, it was purchased by a member of the Hapsburg family at the Vienna Industrial Exhibition that year, after it was awarded first prize and a gold medal. Alas, the Hapburgs paid more attention to the royal stables than to their pianos, and so I have had to perform major 'surgery' here. But when I am done..." Hupfer paused to give the keyboard an affectionate pat. "When I am done it will be like new. No, *better* than new! Shall I tell you something, my friend? You could transport this piano to the far ends of the earth, and the minute a simple scale is played on it, any expert will recognize one thing immediately."

"And that is?" I asked.

"That I, Wilhelm Hupfer, voiced the instrument. I know one standard and one standard only, sir... perfection."

"You do indeed possess all the abilities of a skilled surgeon," I said, shaking my head admiringly.

"All except one: the ability to become as rich as a skilled surgeon. An expert like me never receives the public recognition and the rewards he deserves. Who does? The performer. His impresario. His manager. Even the flunkies who lay out his wardrobe, shave him, and empty his chamber pots."

I attempted to lighten the moment. Smiling sympathetically, I said, "Your rewards will come in heaven, I'm sure."

Hupfer was not amused. His face took on a hard expression. "Oh no, Inspector," he said, "they will come much sooner, and here on earth. I have been a patient fool long enough."

"Do you work on other makes?" I said.

"Of course," Hupfer replied, his tone implying that my question was foolish. "A surgeon does not confine himself to one kind of patient only. No, Inspector, I am qualified to operate on just about any piano known to mankind. Naturally, I do not meddle with cheap mass-produced instruments that are beginning to come onto the market. One does not engage the services of a French chef to cook a meal of sausages and sauerkraut."

Hupfer removed the prop and carefully lowered the lid of the Bösendorfer. "Tell me, Inspector, are you thinking of acquiring a fine piano for your own use? Is that why you wanted to see me this morning?"

"No," I said. "As a pianist, I'm afraid I fall into the category of 'sausages and sauerkraut'. I'm guilty of having bought one of those cheap mass-produced pianos as befits my talent. I would never dream of requesting an expert of your renown to so much as *smell* what passes for a piano these days in my living quarters."

I hoped my humble admission would strike Hupfer as appealing. After all, what delights a proud man more than when another debases himself before him? I wanted this fellow to feel thoroughly superior. More to the point, I wanted to catch him completely off his guard when I posed my next question.

I said, trying to sound idly curious, "How do you account, sir, for the fact that Madam Schumann's piano was out of tune last evening?"

Hupfer's eyes snapped open with shock. "I beg your pardon. I do not understand the question."

"You worked on the Schumanns' pianos yesterday, did you not?"

"Yes. Mostly on the one she was going to play, not the other one. The Maestro gave Madam Schumann a brand new piano a few months ago for her birthday…from the Klems factory in Düsseldorf. Hardly a masterpiece as instruments go, but for a price of a couple of hundred thalers, nothing to sniff at either. The case is embellished with a floral pattern. I wish to God they had spent more time embellishing the *action*. But, as I said, it's a decent enough instrument for home use. Each and every piano has its own problems, Inspector, but because the Klems was almost new, all it required was a thorough tuning." Hupfer's eyes narrowed. Almost sneering, he said, "And who, may I ask, ventured the opinion that it was out of tune?"

"Franz Liszt."

"You want me to believe that Franz Liszt said her piano was out of tune?"

"Yes."

"Surely this is some kind of joke."

"No, I heard him very distinctly."

"He said this to her, to Madam Schumann?"

"No, to young Brahms, during a brief exchange as Liszt was departing. After he left, I had a conversation with the Schumanns and Brahms regarding this very subject."

Hupfer's expression brightened instantly. He let his shoulders go slack, at the same time heaving a sigh of relief. "Good. I'm sure *they* agreed that the Klems was in perfect tune. I mean Brahms and the Schumanns."

I pretended to be preoccupied with a minute scratch on the Bösendorfer's outer keyboard flank. "That's not quite how it happened," I said, bending close to examine the blemish, as though I was keenly interested in it. I sensed that Hupfer was growing tense again.

"What do you mean, 'that's not quite how it happened'?"

"Well..." I took my time, my nose almost touching the polished mahogany now. "Madam Schumann and their friend Brahms were absolutely certain that the piano was perfectly tuned and that Liszt was wrong."

"Yes, yes, of course. I'm not at all surprised."

"But—"

"But what?"

I straightened myself. "But Maestro Schumann disagreed with his wife and Brahms. In fact, he agreed with Liszt. Emphatically so. He said the moment middle A was sounded in order for the quartet to tune their instruments, he sensed that it was off. And a friend of mine who plays in the quartet verified this. Pretty strong evidence, wouldn't you agree?"

"I would agree and I would *not* agree, to be frank, Inspector."

"Meaning?"

"Meaning that a grand piano is a complex piece of machinery. There are close to twelve thousand parts, from the tiniest screws to the largest slice of spruce planking, that make up an instrument of that sort. Sometimes what goes on in the bowels of a piano is as mysterious as what goes on in the human body."

I began for the first time to detect a tone of defensiveness in Hupfer's voice. It seemed that only a moment ago he was boasting about his standard of perfection; now he was asking me to make allowances. Although I was no expert when it came to pianos, I knew that many of these instruments—even the finest of them—occasionally developed cracks in their soundboards. I felt that I had now found a crack in Willi Hupfer's personal soundboard.

"How long would you typically spend tuning a piano like Madam Schumann's?" I said.

"As I told you before, her Klems is relatively new, so I spent no more than an hour, maybe a bit longer, because the action was slightly heavy in the bass. On an older piano, tuning can run to about two hours, depending of course on its condition. Too much humidity or too much dryness can cause the hammer arms to bend out of shape. Also there may be a problem with moths. Moths can eat into the felt on the hammers, which then fail to strike the strings with the proper angle and force. One must have regard for all these variables, Inspector."

"And did you?" I asked.

"Did I what? Have regard for all the variables? Are you questioning my thoroughness, sir?"

"Not for a moment, Herr Hupfer, I assure you."

"Then why these questions?"

Should I reveal the purpose behind my visit? After all, if there was a purely technical explanation for Schumann's persistent complaint about hearing the A sound, who better than Hupfer to assist me to get to the bottom of it? On the other hand, if there was—as Schumann was convinced— some form of skullduggery at work here, what if Hupfer was involved in the plot? The self-confidence he had displayed during the initial part of my visit was beginning to fade with each of my questions. His hands fidgeted nervously with a small brass screwdriver, and his right eyelid suddenly developed a noticeable twitch.

"Herr Hupfer," I said, "what I am about to discuss with you must be treated in strictest confidence. I understand that your ties to the Schumanns are extremely close, and I trust therefore that I may rely completely upon your discretion."

"Naturally," Hupfer replied, then smiled shrewdly. "Funny

thing, Inspector. Something told me you didn't come to my shop merely to learn how to tune a piano."

"No, Herr Hupfer, I came for the opposite reason. I need to know how to *un*tune a piano. To be more precise, I need to know whether a piano can be tampered with in such a way that a particular string will resonate without actually being struck. In other words, will some unrelated or indirect action cause a string to emit a sympathetic sound, so to speak, in a consistent pattern?"

Hupfer took a moment to reflect. "Well, we do encounter a very annoying situation from time to time with pianos...a buzz."

"A buzz?"

"Yes. Striking a key will sometimes set off a rattle...a buzz is more like it...that may come from any of the instrument's moving parts or vibrating surfaces. Tracking down the source can prove exasperating even to a first-rate craftsman like me."

"And do you always succeed?"

"Of course!" Hupfer chuckled softly. "You see, Inspector, pianos *talk* to Wilhelm Hupfer. That's right, I said talk. I give them voice, and in their way they speak to me. I have only to touch one or two keys...I choose them at random, and immediately the instrument comes alive and confides in me. 'Willi, I am suffering from a warped soundboard'... 'My damper springs are loose'... 'I've lost the brilliance in my treble'. Each and every piano that is fortunate enough to enter my little domain becomes my mistress, and we quickly become intimate. At least that's what Frau Hupfer, my long-suffering wife, tells people."

"That's very reassuring," I said. "But have you any insights as to how a persistent sound can be produced despite the fact that the relative key has not been depressed?"

Hupfer shook his head. "With all due respect, my friend," he said, "I was already completing my apprentice-ship while you were still in swaddling clothes. In all my many years of experience, I have never encountered the situation you describe, and I doubt very much if it can occur. It would be highly improbable."

"But it is *possible?*"

"Possible?" Hupfer shrugged. "Well, I suppose anything is possible when you bear in mind the thousands of components that make up one of these grand pianos. But I must tell you that if tampering was a criminal offense in Germany, more than half of the piano tuners in this country would be behind bars. The vast majority of men who dare to call themselves piano technicians belong in railway yards oiling steam engines."

"Are you saying, then," I asked, "that if it were possible to corrupt the workings of a piano so that, no matter what was being played, one note protruded and kept protruding and protruding, the tamperer would have to possess a high degree of skill and be highly knowledgeable in the field of sound?"

"Certainly such a person would be no run-of-the-mill piano tuner. Indeed he would have to be fifty per cent genius...and fifty per cent devil. I doubt such a person exists, Inspector."

"Humour me for a moment, Herr Hupfer," I said. "Let us suppose that your half-devil half-genius *does* exist. Could he manipulate the mechanical apparatus to achieve the result I've described?"

"Humour *me* for a moment, Inspector," Hupfer said. "What has all this got to do with the Schumanns? You are asking me about matters which are pure conjecture...no, more than conjecture...bizarre, even grotesque. I cannot bring myself to think anyone would want to commit such a foul act, especially where the Schumanns would be the victims. Granted, it's common knowledge that the Maestro's moods can be extremely difficult to deal with at times. Up one day, down the next; more often than not these days as unpredictable as the weather. And poor Madam Schumann has not had an easy time of it for as long as I've known the couple. It is a miracle the way she carries on. Surely the two of them are regarded by everyone as objects of sympathy. Nobody would deliberately set out to cause them harm and embarrassment. Nobody in his right mind would dare commit such an act even as a prank."

"I think you are missing my point," I said. "Forgive me for being blunt, Herr Hupfer, but I am not seeking your advice as to who the tamperer might be and what his motive might be. I must ask you to focus on one question and one question only: can a piano be tuned or untuned in such a way that, regardless of what is being played at any given moment, one note will stand out?"

Giving him what I hoped was a friendly smile, I said, "I do apologize, sir. You see, Herr Hupfer, I'm unaccustomed to being in the awkward position I'm in. I mean, sir, in all frankness, I'm not certain whether I've embarked on a genuine criminal investigation, or whether I'm foolishly chasing the wind."

"Then you must forgive *me* for being blunt, Inspector Preiss," Hupfer said, looking me straight in the face. "In my opinion, sir, you are chasing the wind."

Chapter Thirteen

The house of Dr. Paul Möbius at No. 12 Dietrichstrasse had the advantage of a corner location, which meant that, unlike the block-long row of which it was part, it offered a side entrance for the use of the doctor's patients. Were it not for the discreet brass plaque above the doorbell engraved "Paul Möbius, Doctor Of Medicine, Please Ring", this could have been the residence of any of the well-to-do families who inhabited Dietrichstrasse. The exterior of the four-storey structure was a hodgepodge of wood, brick, stucco and stone, the kind of mongrel architecture that certifies not that the occupants have taste but that they have money.

I did as the small sign at the entrance bade. Three minutes went by. I rang again. The door opened, and a middle-aged woman, out of breath and flustered, holding a mop, greeted me.

"I'm Inspector Preiss," I said. "I have an appointment with Dr. Möbius."

The woman dropped her mop. "Oh my God," she said, speaking in a hoarse whisper, a look of alarm in her eyes, "the doctor is not yet back from his morning rounds at the hospital." One look at her told me she was Möbius's housekeeper, harassed, overworked, probably underpaid, a person for whom the world came to an end at least once every hour of her working day.

"I don't understand," I said, more than a bit annoyed. "I was to meet with the doctor *before*, not after, he made his hospital rounds. Has there been some mistake?"

"Oh my God," the housekeeper repeated. "This is terrible. I'm so sorry, sir." The woman seemed about to fall on her knees and beg forgiveness for some error or oversight of which she was entirely innocent. "Please," she said, "sometimes the doctor changes his schedule without telling anyone. You know how it is with important men, sir. It is not for me to question his comings and goings. The Lord willing, he will return soon, that is all I can tell you."

"I should like to come in, then. I assume one is permitted to wait in his office?"

She looked uncertain. "Your name again?"

"Inspector Hermann Preiss. Of the Düsseldorf Police."

"My God, the police! Yes, yes, we mustn't keep a police officer waiting at the door like this. Please forgive me."

I entered, stepping carefully over the mop, and followed her along a dark corridor which led to a room at the rear of the ground floor. In a hushed tone, as though she had guided me to a holy site, she said, "This is Dr. Möbius's office. You may wait here." Then she retreated, walking slowly backwards, bowing her head humbly, the choreography of a person born into lifelong domestic servitude.

If it is true that a man's office is a reliable reflection of his personality, then what was I to make of the eminent physician whom I was about to meet for the first time?

Consider the furnishings: seating for two, no more. I suppose this made sense in a room where intimate thoughts were disclosed. But observe the seating arrangement: an oversized wing chair, severe, authoritative, its bottom cushion permanently disfigured by an occupant with an abnormally large rump; next to it, a writing table, its position and condition indicating the doctor was left-handed and very careless about cigar ashes and spilled drinks. The other chair, which I took as I awaited his arrival, must have been salvaged from a rummage sale. Too low, too narrow, very uncomfortable. Not the kind of chair you would lean back in, taking your time, rambling on about whatever was troubling your mind. The message this chair conveyed was: come to the point, time's up. Next patient.

An additional point here about Dr. Möbius that had nothing to do with the state of his office: for a man who was very caring when it came to his own precious time, he seemed to care very little about other people's. He was now more than a half hour late for our appointment. It was he who had insisted on our meeting sharp at nine in the morning. Now, glancing for the tenth time at my watch, I began to fume. In fact, I rose from my skimpy chair and was gathering up my coat, hat and gloves, intending to leave, when suddenly his private office door was thrust open, and in strode the doctor.

Without a word of explanation or apology, he motioned me to sit, pointing imperiously to the miserable piece of furniture from which I had just freed myself. He, of course, settled himself down in the wing chair, extracted a fat cigar from a leather pouch in his breast pocket, and, rolling it slowly between his O-shaped lips, began to light it, sucking and blowing and momentarily obliterating his face behind a cloud of smoke and flame. From behind that cloud, his first words managed to find their way into my ears.

"In the profession of Medicine, Inspector, punctuality is next to Godliness. I would therefore be very much obliged if we may come directly to the point. Ethically I am bound, sir, not to disclose any confidences regarding my patient, Dr. Schumann. Doctor-patient confidentiality is the most sacred cornerstone of the practice of Medicine. We must therefore restrict ourselves to generalities, by which I mean certain theoretical questions, the answers to which I have applied myself throughout my career with, if I may say so—no small diligence and success."

I had the distinct feeling that this was going to be a

one-sided discussion, based upon the doctor's opening statement and tribute to himself. "Have I made myself clear, Inspector?" Möbius said, his thick eyebrows knitting together and forming a single dark streak above his spectacles. My inclination at this point was to tell him to go to the devil and that I was not accustomed to being lectured to in this fashion.

After acknowledging the ground rules, I began my interrogation. "Dr. Möbius, you have opined in your lectures and writings that creative activities, such as those engaged in for example by Dr. Schumann, necessarily lead to a serious state of degeneration."

"Most definitely," Möbius replied. "Not a doubt in the world about it." He leaned back in his chair and patted a heavy gold chain that extended across the vast expanse of his abdomen like a suspension bridge. "Years of research have produced evidence that is beyond dispute, sir." Möbius sniffed audibly, his way of both punctuating a sentence and expressing self-confidence.

"Examples are legion," he went on. "Take Mozart. Died at thirty-five. Schubert? Dead at thirty-one. Mendelssohn barely made it to thirty-eight. By the age of only thirty-three, poor Beethoven had become stone deaf. Moreover, he suffered from fits of rage. Degeneration, that's the reason. Everything breaks down...the body, the mind. Inner forces push and pull these so-called creative people apart, don't you see? Creativity and disease are blood brothers among people in the arts. Painters, composers, writers...they flirt with illnesses of every description. Had I the authority, I would confiscate every easel and palette in Europe...every musical instrument, writing stand, pen, ink pot...and I would retain these instruments of disaster under lock and key until Medicine has found a way to cure men and women of their addictions. Believe me, sir, creativity is a form of incurable addiction, plain and simple!"

"But what about Haydn and Handel?" I said. "They

lived to ripe old ages. Bach, too, lived a full life, not only musically, but domestically and spiritually."

Möbius's hand waved dismissively. "Rare and unimportant exceptions."

"I take it, then, that you place little stock in Dr. Schumann's complaint concerning the 'A sound'."

Möbius gave me a cold look. "I have already made it clear, have I not, that I am not at liberty to discuss a patient's condition?"

Straining to remain civil, I said, "Very well, then, let us continue to speak in theoretical terms. Can one legitimately claim to be hearing a particular musical sound even when that sound is not in fact being produced anywhere within earshot?"

"People who engage in the auditory arts," said Möbius, "are inclined to suffer from auditory hallucinations. They hear music when no one else can possibly do so. There are studies, incidentally, that indicate people in the *visual* arts suffer a similar fate, except that they are constantly confronted by forms and colours not visible to others. It's a maddening process, to be sure, and one would do well to avoid such so-called creative activities because of the often frightening consequences and the terrible price they exact."

"Surely you're not suggesting that people turn their backs on music, painting, even literature, and devote themselves solely to running banks and shops and factories!"

Möbius poked his thick cigar into the air, indifferent to the length of ash that tumbled to the carpet. "Stability, my dear Inspector...stability of character, that's what society rests upon. Engineers, doctors, scientists, *they* are the meat and potatoes of the nation. All the rest is mere desserts, items on the public's menu that are frivolous and therefore entirely dispensable."

"Is it possible, Doctor, that what you call auditory

hallucinations can be stimulated by some outside means? Could someone other than the creative artist himself trigger a hallucination?"

Behind the small oval-shaped spectacles set in delicate silver frames, Möbius's eyes seemed to fade into blank patches of grey. "I have no idea what you're referring to, Inspector, not the slightest," he said with a shrug.

"Very well then. Let me re-state the question. Maestro Schumann maintains that someone is, or some persons are, deliberately attempting to drive him insane by producing, perhaps by some direct mechanical means, the sound of middle A on the musical scale, which sound occurs regardless of what piece of music is being played at any given moment. Indeed, even if *no* music is being played, that middle A sound may suddenly find its way into Schumann's ears. Is this possible?"

Again a blank stare from the doctor. "Is *what* possible?"

I put my question to him again. "Is it possible that the 'auditory hallucination' in this case is being created or produced from some source outside his own mind, and is therefore not, strictly speaking, an auditory hallucination?"

Dr. Möbius was silent for a few moments. He seemed more interested in examining his cigar, which had gone cold. Without looking up at me, he said, "I deal in matters of science, Inspector, not idle speculations."

"Is this your way of informing me, sir, that there is no legitimacy to Robert Schumann's suspicions?"

Still looking away, Möbius said, "You may draw any conclusion you wish, Inspector. I can say nothing more on the subject." From his vest pocket he withdrew a heavy gold watch. "And now, sir, if you will excuse me—"

I rose, collected my outerwear, and made my exit without another word.

On my way out the side door of the house, I began to throw over my shoulders my greatcoat and muffler, and failed to notice a man mounting the steps as I was descending. We collided midway. I swung round. "I do beg your pardon," I said.

Ignoring my apology, the man dashed up the remaining steps, and I was able only to catch a quick look at him. In the split second of this encounter, I recognized him.

The man being let into Dr. Möbius's house was Wilhelm Hupfer.

Chapter Fourteen

I returned to my office at the constabulary headquarters on foot rather than by carriage. I wanted time to gather my thoughts after what was, at best, an hour of pure frustration spent—*wasted* is perhaps a better word—in the company of Germany's reputed leader in the new field of Psychiatry, Dr. Paul Möbius. A feeling of defeat weighed heavily on my shoulders, and my mood was not at all lightened by a typical February sky that pressed down from the clouds, a vast ominous quilt of grey stretching from one end of the city to the other. Nor was my mood improved when, approaching my desk, I spotted a note carefully propped up, so it could not possibly be missed. The gold seal representing the Düsseldorf Police District at the top of the note meant only one thing: a summons to appear before the Commissioner.

"Close the door, Preiss," was the Commissioner's curt greeting as I entered his office. Behind his handsome desk, my superior was pretending to peruse the detectives' assignment ledger. His thick eyebrows hung over his spectacles like nightshades, always a sign that a storm was brewing. "Schumann... Schumann...I see no reference to a Schumann matter here. There's no official complaint on file. No criminal report of any sort. I have no record of having appointed you to investigate anything pertaining to this fellow."

"Indeed, sir, you did not."

"Then by what authority are you engaged in this wild goose chase?"

I nodded in the direction of a nearby chair. "It's a bit complicated, sir. May I sit?"

"No, Preiss, you may *not* sit. I ask you again, who authorized this waste of police resources and taxpayers' money?"

My mind began to race. How had this scowling bundle of facial hair learned that I had become involved in the Schumann affair? I thought my movements in and out of the affair had been discreet these past few days. I'd forgotten that any reasonably trained detective on our staff could have snooped in my daily calendar and put two and two together. God knows, there were enough junior inspectors who were jealous of my rank in the police force and considered me stand-offish.

His jowls shaking with indignation and impatience, the Commissioner repeated his question. "Well, Preiss, for the third time, who authorized you?"

I was forced to think quickly. Then, keeping my voice low, as though disclosing a sacred confidence, I said, "I take it, sir, that Baron and Baroness von Hoffman have confided in you about this Schumann matter?"

The simple mention of these two local aristocrats suddenly drew the Commissioner to attention, even though he was seated. "Confided in me? About what, precisely?"

I replied, "About their extreme distress concerning threats upon the life of their dear friend Dr. Schumann. Surely, they must have brought it to your attention, sir. Perhaps, in your own desire to be circumspect...after all, this is a potentially embarrassing situation for many distinguished people who are suspects. Perhaps the matter was not recorded and a formal file opened—"

"Are you suggesting that my office has been lax in this regard?" A crack in his voice told me he was now backing down.

"Sir, I assure you that I meant no criticism of the Commissioner's personal staff. It would most certainly not be my place to—"

"Indeed, it most certainly would not," he broke in. "Rank and discipline still have their place, you know."

"Absolutely, Commissioner." I paused, as though letting his little sermon sink in, then said, "But I feel compelled to mention that I did happen to have a brief chat with the Baron and Baroness just the other night...at the Schumanns', as a matter of fact." I knew of course that Baron von Hoffman was chairman of the regional board that determined retirement benefits awarded to dutiful (and obsolete) senior civil servants. Facing his own retirement, the Commissioner was keenly aware that the Baron held the key to the old policeman's future. With the mere stroke of a baronial pen, that future could be a grove, or a grave.

"You're saying the Baron and Baroness have a personal interest in the outcome of this investigation, Preiss?" The Commissioner's voice had now lost its edge.

"With all due respect, sir," I replied, again keeping my voice low, "I must emphasize that I have been urged by them...I mean the Baron and his wife, of course...to attempt to keep my investigation as secret as possible. There are, as I said, a number of suspects, people in high places."

"Say no more, Preiss. I am not pleased, I must tell you, that you have undertaken this investigation entirely on your own. However, I'm prepared to make allowances."

"I do thank you, sir. You are most understanding."

"Mind, Preiss—" The Commissioner rose from his chair and stood to his full height. "This is not to be deemed an open ticket, you understand. I am prepared to go along with all of this...but not forever."

"Meaning, sir?"

"Meaning that you must conclude this business one way or another. If you manage to resolve it, well, I suppose it'll be a feather in your cap of sorts. If you *don't,* I will expect you to make up for much lost time. You have a fortnight, and not one hour more. That's all, Inspector. You may go."

Chapter Fifteen

I was hungry for any new piece of information that might be of help to me, and, faced now with the Commissioner's ultimatum, I lost no time arranging that evening to meet Helena Becker for a late supper at Café Amadeus on Prinz Mannheimstrasse in Düsseldorf's commercial district, where at that hour there was little likelihood of our being recognized and interrupted. With its thick carpets, heavily-draped windows and generously upholstered booths and banquettes, it was ideal for intimate conversation. In the booth Helena and I occupied, the glow from a glass-encased candle at the centre of the table had painted her skin a soft shade of gold. "You look more ravishing than ever, Helena," I said.

She did not return the compliment. "You look worn-out, Hermann." She was studying my face, to which the candlelight was apparently not at all kind.

"I've not been sleeping well for several nights, now," I admitted.

"Ah yes, the Schumann case—"

"Case? I'm still not sure it's a *case*, Helena. Everywhere I turn, it seems, there are blank spaces. No smoking pistols, bloody daggers, poison-pen letters. There's nothing but a possible lunatic who insists he hears a particular musical note in strange places and at strange times. And yet I cannot for the life of me let go!"

"Perhaps I can relieve your frustration a little," she said. Taking her time, she glanced to either side of her, then behind her and over my shoulder. At last, satisfied she could speak without being overheard, she leaned closer. "Well, Hermann," she said, "I've a piece of news for you...an important piece from a very reliable source. It will cost you, though. I'm thinking of the veal schnitzel and a very good Riesling to go with it."

"Done! What news?"

"Johannes Brahms has slept with Clara Schumann."

"And how do you know this, Helena?"

"Because *I* slept with Franz Liszt."

"You...*you*...slept with—" I could not bring myself to complete the sentence.

Without the slightest hesitation, without so much as a tinge of embarrassment, Helena nodded. "But I don't understand why you're so shocked, Hermann. I thought a policeman learns to expect the unexpected."

"The unexpected is one thing; the preposterous is quite another."

Helena's complexion suddenly reddened. Instantly, I realized I'd blundered.

"You mean," she said, "it's preposterous that Franz Liszt would want to sleep with *me.*"

"No, of course not!" I protested. "What I meant was, it's preposterous that *you* would want to sleep with Liszt. Not since Nero has any man had such a reputation as a debaucher of women!"

"Do I detect a note of jealousy in your voice, Hermann? Maybe I'd better clarify something...just to ease your pain. We didn't exactly *sleep* together."

I couldn't resist a sarcastic response to this. "So by a strange coincidence, Helena Becker and Franz Liszt are simply a woman and man who suffer from insomnia and happen to find themselves in the same bedroom."

"Not quite," Helena said. "What we did was, we shared a bed...in his suite at his hotel. You see, he'd noticed me that night at the Schumanns' and gotten my name and address from Georg Adelmann. A beautifully-penned note and a magnificent bouquet of flowers followed next day. And that evening we had a late repast in his hotel suite. And then—"

Her account ended abruptly, punctuated by a shrug as if to say *"Well, what would you expect to happen next?"*

"And then the two of you went off to bed," I said, trying my damndest to be insouciant about all this. "Do go on, Helena."

She pretended to be remorseful. "You've mentioned how much you loathe surprises, Hermann dear, and I *am* truly sorry to be so blunt about all this. What is it the British say... 'Truth will out'?"

"I hope for your sake, Helena, Liszt's capability was up to the task at hand. He's no spring chicken, you know."

"Liszt's 'capability' is probably every bit as impressive as your own. The fact is, however, that it did not need to be tested. In other words, there *was* no task at hand."

"Oh really? Well now, let me guess the reason," I said. "Liszt was scheduled to play a strenuous recital program the following day and had to conserve his strength. Funny thing, Helena; I thought that excuse applied only to operatic tenors."

Helena said, "We lay in bed, yes. But Franz—"

"Ah, so it's 'Franz', is it? How charming. The great man permits you to address him by his first name!"

In a matter-of-fact tone, Helena said, "When a man's head is resting on your lap, you can hardly be expected to address him as 'Maestro' or 'Doctor'. Now let me continue, and *please,* do not interrupt. Franz and I lay together, and he spoke about the hollowness that fame has left in his soul. Do you know what he plans to do, Hermann? He plans to retire for a period of time to a monastery. He refers to it as making a pilgrimage. He is desperate for spiritual renewal."

I wanted to avoid the temptation to be snide, but

somewhere near the tip of my tongue there was a trap door, and the words unstoppably came tumbling out. "For a period of time? What are we talking about, twenty-four hours? Be serious, Helena. It's common knowledge that Liszt has been in and out of law courts defending himself against charges of breach of promise to marry, libel and slander, failure to pay bills. I could go on and on. His career before the bar is almost as illustrious as his career on the concert stage. And you're telling me this man is desperate for spiritual renewal?"

"He says he yearns for a new life, and I believe him, Hermann. He is keenly aware that in certain musical circles he merits very little respect, especially in regard to his compositions. Let me tell you what happened to him last year in Weimar. Liszt generously opened his mansion there for Sunday matinées…chamber music, student recitals, introductions of new music, all very stimulating, as you can imagine. Well, on one of those Sunday afternoons, one of Liszt's guests was Johannes Brahms—"

"Sorry to interrupt," I said, "but I was under the impression that Liszt and Brahms met for the very first time just the other evening at the Schumanns'."

"It did seem as though they'd never before met, but it is more likely that both men preferred to forget their earlier encounter with one another. You see, what occurred at the Weimar matinée a year ago was this: young Brahms shows up with a recently completed first draft of his Scherzo. But when Liszt invites Brahms to play it for the small group of friends present, Brahms is too shy or too nervous. So Liszt sits down and sight-reads the piece from beginning to end. A flawless performance, for which Brahms warmly thanks him. The audience too is enthusiastic. Then it's Liszt's turn to play one of his own pieces. And during one of the more dramatic moments, Franz happens to glance over at Brahms. Do you know what Johannes Brahms was doing, Hermann? He was slouched in his chair…*dozing!*"

"So what? How does this qualify Liszt to speak with authority about Brahms's sexual relationship with Clara Schumann?"

"The piano tuner."

"Pardon me?"

"The piano tuner," Helena said. "Wilhelm Hupfer. You remember, his name came up when—"

"Yes, yes," I said impatiently, "Of course I remember. What's *he* got to do with anything? The man's a mechanic. He works with hammers and wrenches."

"Yes, Hermann," Helena said, "but because he's the best there is in these parts, he was hired to tune Liszt's practice piano in his suite at the hotel. Naturally the two men—Liszt and Hupfer—got around to the subject of the Schumanns and their protégé. Well, it appears that our master technician not only has keen ears as befits a man in his trade, but keen eyesight as well. Hupfer was working at the Schumanns' the afternoon of the musicale. And Maestro Schumann was absent at the time. She...I mean his wife...said he'd been out, presumably trying to drink his anxieties away at some tavern or other while she—poor downtrodden woman— was left to attend to...how did she put it?...'a thousand-and-one last minute details'."

"I think those were her exact words, yes."

"Well, Hermann, she miscounted. There were a thousand-and-*two* last minute details."

I raised a hand to stop Helena. "Don't tell me. Brahms was, shall we say, on her list of things to do. What did Hupfer say to Liszt, and what did Liszt pass on to you?"

"There are *two* grand pianos in the Schumann drawing room, remember?"

"Yes." Then I recalled what Hupfer had told me when I visited him at his shop. "Apparently one was fairly new...the Klems, made here in Düsseldorf, not a great instrument but, being new, it didn't require a lot of work. The older piano required much more attention, of course. Hupfer spent two hours working on the older instrument getting it into proper shape."

"But in fact, Clara performed on the Klems instrument," Helena continued. "And before her, when they introduced Brahms, which piano did he play?"

I took a moment to recollect. "He played on the same, the Klems."

"Correct," said Helena. "So a question arises here."

"Yes? What question?"

She picked up a butter knife—one I had been fidgeting with earlier—and began brandishing it as though it was a pointer and she was giving instruction. "Hupfer arrives at the Schumanns' and is prepared to commence his work after being admitted to the house by one of the servants. Madam Schumann is nowhere to be seen at this point, and the servant explains that the Maestro has gone off somewhere and is not expected to return until later in the afternoon. Fine. So Hupfer moves off into the drawing-room. And there, of course, sit the two grand pianos—"

"Yes, yes, Helena, for God's sake get to the point—"

"And just as Hupfer is removing his jacket and about to roll up his sleeves to get down to work, he hears a furtive whispering that comes from the stairs in the hallway just outside the drawing-room, the voices of a man and a woman. Next thing, guess what?"

"*What?*"

"In rushes Brahms. Coatless. No neckwear. Shirtfront partly unbuttoned. And that head of hair...those long blond—"

"Never mind. I gather his hair was unkempt, and he looked dishevelled. What then?"

"'Pardon the intrusion,' Brahms says to Willi Hupfer, 'but it seems I've forgotten something.' And Brahms seizes a small leather bag that's sitting atop the Klems. And in his haste to retrieve it, he spills the contents of the bag on the floor, then begins to scoop them up, muttering things like, 'How stupid of me, how clumsy!' Then, after Hupfer notices that the bag contains tools very much like his own, Brahms feels called upon to explain."

"Helena," I pleaded, "please put down the butter knife." She was waving it uncomfortably close to my face now. "Just tell me what Brahms said."

Not heeding my request, but grasping the knife as though it was a javelin about to be hurled, Helena went on. "Brahms snaps the bag shut and says to Hupfer, 'I'm very particular, you understand, about the piano I'm to perform on being adjusted exactly to my taste, so I prefer to make the adjustments myself beforehand. I therefore took time to regulate the Klems, because I'll be using it this evening.' And then he says to Hupfer, 'Please don't let me interrupt you; I will return later for some last-minute regulating on the Klems.' Why is this so significant? Because, according to Liszt, there isn't another pianist in Europe these days who does his own tuning and regulating. That job is always left to trained technicians, experts like Hupfer. One reason is that most pianos are located in public concert halls, and their proprietors do not take kindly to keyboard prima donnas marching in and messing about with the house instruments. And even when a performance is scheduled to take place in a private salon, the same unwritten rule applies. Technical work is for technicians. Period!"

Helena sat back, put down the butter knife with a resolute smack on the tabletop, and said, "Well now, Inspector Preiss, have I earned the schnitzel and Riesling?"

I was too lost in thought to respond. What were piling up, one on top of another, were questions, not answers.

Sounding annoyed, Helena said, "Really, Hermann, you are the essence of ingratitude. I fill your cup to overflowing, and what do I receive in return? An empty stare. And, by the way, an empty plate."

I took an anxious look at the café clock just in time to hear its chimes announce eight o'clock, which meant that behind the swinging doors at the rear of the place, the chef would be shedding his white cap and apron for the night.

Our waiter, without uttering a word, began subtracting our cutlery, glassware, basket of rolls and tray of condiments, leaving our table naked.

We stood on the sidewalk outside the café now, Helena and I, exiled by a disgruntled waiter.

She said, "Hermann, it so happens I haven't had a shred to eat since breakfast early this morning. Is the fact that I'm starving to death of even the remotest interest to you?"

I'm afraid my answer was entirely out of context.

"Hupfer tells these things to Franz Liszt," I said. My eyes wandered along the street, its stores and offices dark now, its pavement deserted. "Hupfer tells these things to Franz Liszt," I repeated, once again lost in my own thoughts. "But for some reason he chooses not to tell *me*—"

"Hermann, in case you haven't noticed, I'm still here—"

"And then…and then there's his visit to Dr. Möbius—"

"All right," Helena said, sounding like a martyr, "we'll overlook the fact that I'm famished. What exactly have Dr. Möbius and Hupfer got to do with anything?"

My eyes drifted back to Helena. "Helena, dearest, I don't know the answer to your question, but here's what I want you to do."

Chapter Sixteen

I hailed a cab and delivered Helena to the front door of her residence, where the two of us parted with dutiful pecks on the cheeks. The past hour or so had exhausted me, not to mention leaving my appetite for food unsatisfied. I wanted nothing so much as to retire within the four walls of my sitting room, throw on a comfortable robe, and sit before a fire, my mind set free by a liberating snifter of brandy.

Letting myself into the tiny foyer of my apartment block, I was confronted by the concierge, an elderly army veteran with a face scarred by war wounds and hands tortured by a merciless case of arthritis. "There's a man—" With a misshapen index finger, he pointed over his shoulder in the direction of a small anteroom off the foyer. "Been waiting ever so long." His voice suddenly faded to a whisper. "Over an hour! Seems terribly upset about something. I was tempted to offer him tea, but something about him frightened me half to death."

"Thank you, Henckel," I said and stepped across the foyer and into the anteroom.

"Preiss! Thank God! I was beginning to think you'd never arrive."

"Good evening, sir." I tried to sound cordial despite the fact that—like all surprises—this one, on this night of all nights, and at this hour, was especially unwelcome. "To what do I owe the honour?"

"Forgive me for imposing like this, Inspector," Robert

Schumann said. "I must speak with you privately...a matter of extreme urgency."

Schumann trailed behind me up the three flights of stairs to my rooms, taking each step as though he were climbing a mountain. Arriving at the landing outside my door, he was out of breath and gasping for air.

"Brandy, Dr. Schumann?"

He raised a hand to decline. "I wish to be entirely clear-headed."

"Do you mind if I indulge?" Without waiting for Schumann's reply, I poured myself a healthy portion and quickly downed half of it, thinking, *I owe at least this to myself, since obviously I'm to have no peace tonight.*

A closer examination of my guest's appearance explained Henckel's fear of remaining in his presence a moment longer than was necessary. His eyes were bloodshot and watery. His complexion was blotchy, the skin of his cheeks and chin raw in places from being poorly shaved. Beads of sweat surrounding his purplish lips had given his mouth an uncertain formation, like the opening of some unexplored cave. His clothing smelled strongly of cigar smoke and his breath strongly of liquor, though he seemed perfectly sober. I motioned for him to be seated.

"Thank you, I prefer to stand," Schumann said. "Please allow me to come directly to the point of this intrusion. One of my most valuable possessions is missing and presumably stolen, a first draft of Beethoven's Piano Sonata Opus Two Number Two, the one he dedicated to Joseph Haydn. It was left to me by my dear friend Felix Mendelssohn in his last will and testament. Needless to say, it is a priceless document."

"When did you notice it was missing?" I asked.

"The morning after the musicale at our house," Schumann said. "I had gone to the cabinet in my study where it was kept. I wanted to re-examine Beethoven's handling of the opening theme. One visits and re-visits the music of Bach and Beethoven, just as one attends church from time to time...to find God. And it was gone. The manuscript was gone!"

I wanted to know if the manuscript was on display or locked away. This question brought a pained look to Schumann's face. "Stupid vain fool that I am! I was so proud that Felix—God rest his soul—had seen fit to bequeath it to me that I kept it on display in a glass cabinet for all the world to see. And now—" Schumann's voice broke.

"You're quite certain it wasn't simply mislaid, Maestro?"

"Would one simply mislay a treasure chest filled with diamonds? No, Inspector, it was stolen."

"If you are so positive, then you must have a suspect in mind."

I waited for Schumann to go on, but suddenly he seemed hesitant. As gently as I could, I said, "I cannot help you, Maestro, if you withhold information. Whom do you suspect?"

There was a strained moment of silence. Then Schumann blurted out, "Adelmann...Georg Adelmann... it *has* to be him. Can you imagine? A man I trusted...a man to whom I opened my house and my heart...who is supposed to be my friend, my biographer!"

"What makes you so sure it was Adelmann?"

"Because he is a thief. Clara told me he's a thief, 'a petty thief' she said, but apparently he has graduated from petty pilfering to grand theft. I asked my wife how she knew about Adelmann. She said you yourself warned her about him the very night of the musicale." Suddenly seizing my arm, he said, "You must confront him, Inspector, I beg you. He cannot be allowed to get away with this."

Uncomfortable as I was under the grip of my anguished visitor, I replied in a calm, quiet tone, "Maestro, please try to understand. It is not always the most prudent course to *confront*, to use your word. To accuse someone of so grave a crime on the basis of suspicion alone—"

Schumann cut me off. Angrily, he said, "In other words, Preiss, like everyone else around me, you're already convinced that I'm out of my mind. Well, never mind, then. I'll go to the Commissioner of Police himself, if I must."

Quickly I said, "I would not rush to involve the Commissioner if I were you, Dr. Schumann."

"And why the devil not?"

"Because, sir, frankly, the Commissioner is not keen about people in the arts in general, nor does he have much patience for your case in particular. In fact, I have only a few days now to get to the bottom of your original complaint; otherwise, I face some unpleasant disciplinary measures for having neglected more pressing duties. My career could be in jeopardy, do you see?"

Every part of Schumann seemed to sag. "Then I am to end up like the statue in the fairy tale…with my jewels plucked out and taken away, one by one, only not by an innocent sparrow but by a pack of crows and vultures…conspirators, robbers. I give to the world glorious music. And what does the world give me in return? Spite. Envy. Treachery."

"But Maestro," I said, "you have much to be thankful for. Beautiful children. A beautiful and talented wife. The admiration of countless lovers of your music, the respect of a host of your peers—"

"*I hate my life, Preiss! I hate it!*" he shouted, taking me aback. His voice trembling, he went on. "I can no longer bear the sight of myself. Death hangs over every bar of music I compose now, like a storm cloud."

Without waiting to be asked, Schumann moved unsteadily to the nearest chair and collapsed into it, sobbing bitterly, his hands covering his eyes in a gesture of shame.

"Very well, Dr. Schumann," I said, "I will go to Adelmann as early as possible tomorrow. And I promise to report back to you with all due speed."

It was a promise I would very soon come to regret.

Chapter Seventeen

L ike Dr. Möbius (whose premises I had visited a few days earlier), Georg Adelmann obviously felt a compulsion to surround himself with tokens of his eminence: framed honourary degrees, row upon row of them, hung with exquisite care on the walls of his study, evidence not only of the high esteem in which others held him, but the high esteem in which he held himself. Where Adelmann's quarters differed from those of Möbius was in the luxury of the appointments. Though the two residences stood in the same affluent neighbourhood of Düsseldorf, the one occupied by the journalist offered evidence in abundance of a man in love with fashionable furnishings, fine art and Persian carpets that would have done a sultan proud.

Of particular interest to me were the contents of an enormous mahogany breakfront which presided over the sitting room like a high altar in a church. Behind glass doors, its half-dozen shelves were crammed with silver and gold tableware—trays, candlesticks, gravy boats, tea and coffee sets, and ornate serving pieces.

In a voice coated in smugness, Adelmann said "The cabinet is English, of course, from about 1760. But the pieces displayed are examples of our finest German craftsmen from Hanau and Pforzheim. We're finally beginning to outdo the French. I see, Inspector, that you are an admirer of good things."

Without taking my gaze from the cabinet, I said, "You

are too modest, sir. These are not merely 'good things'; they are the mark of a man of superb taste, a brilliant acquisitor, if I may say so."

Adelmann chuckled. "A brilliant acquisitor? Well now, there's a description that's rarely heard. I am deeply flattered."

"I intended my remark to be a genuine compliment, not flattery, I assure you."

"You have a remarkable way with words," Adelmann said. "It's a pity that you chose the constabulary, Preiss. Your kind of articulateness would have been better suited to a more uplifting profession, surely."

Had I carried a dagger at that moment, I would gladly have used it to cut Adelmann's throat. Stifling my resentment, I said, "Man lives in hopes of a better afterlife. Perhaps in mine, I will pursue words rather than criminals." Then, without pause, I said, "That silver salver...the small one, there on the fourth shelf...what a lovely little piece! Wherever did you manage to find one like that? I've been looking for something similar for ages without luck." I recognized the salver, of course, as the one Adelmann had filched that day we lunched at Emmerich's Restaurant.

In an offhand manner, Adelmann replied, "Oh, that salver? Yes, a gift. From some editor or other. A fellow in Heidelberg, as I recall now. I am deluged by grateful editors and publishers and academics with all sorts of fine housewares and art objects. They know my tastes, of course."

It occurred to me that there was a distinct uniformity to these items. They struck me as having been not so much bestowed by a variety of grateful colleagues as accumulated by a single compulsive individual. "What a pity, Dr. Adelmann," I said, "that such a splendid collection is not available for public view. There must be many who would welcome an opportunity to view these pieces."

Adelmann said, a touch of coolness in his voice, "I don't think it would be wise. Prying eyes, idle hands...you of all people must understand. In fact, Inspector, the less said about my collection, the better, I think you'll agree."

Motioning me to take a comfortable armchair, Adelmann offered me a glass of schnapps. "Thank you, no," I said. "It's a bit early in the day for me. Besides, I *am* on duty, Dr. Adelmann."

"Your message indicated there was a matter of some urgency you wanted to discuss."

"Some urgency, yes. And some delicacy. I'm not quite sure how to put it, you see."

"You do not strike me as a man who is short of words, Preiss. How can I help you? It's not about your cellist friend again, is it? A most charming young woman. And such musical talent to boot!" Adelmann leaned forward in his adjoining armchair and gave me an amiable poke on the shoulder. "Makes a man feel inner stirrings, eh?"

"I'm here in connection with the Schumanns, actually... I mean, Robert Schumann specifically."

Looking disappointed, Adelmann drew back into his chair. With a deep sigh, he said, "Will no one rid us of the Schumanns!" A dark look crossed his face, and he seemed about to withdraw from the conversation.

I came to the point immediately. "It seems there is an extremely valuable manuscript missing from the Schumann household...a first draft of a Beethoven sonata that Felix Mendelssohn left in his will as a gift to his friend Schumann—"

Before I could complete my sentence, a startled look appeared on Adelmann's face; then, suddenly, he burst into loud laughter. Bolting from his chair, he went to a chest of drawers, and from the uppermost drawer withdrew a black leather portfolio tied carefully with a broad band of gold ribbon. Holding it aloft, Adelmann said, "You mean *this?*" Adelmann came toward me, waving the portfolio in the air. "Missing, you say? Look for yourself, my dear Inspector. Here it is, the Beethoven manuscript...no apparition, but the real thing." He laughed again. "You call this *missing?*"

"I was only repeating what Maestro Schumann told me, sir; I was not making a judgment," I said.

In an instant, Adelmann's mood turned dark again. "The man truly *is* out of his mind. Missing, my foot! Schumann *gave* me this manuscript. In fact, he pressed me to accept it."

"He pressed you?"

"Absolutely."

"Why did he insist you have it?"

"As a token of his undying gratitude. Those were his very words, Preiss."

"Gratitude for what, may I ask?"

"For not revealing something in his past about which he is deeply ashamed...something I uncovered during my research into his life."

"You mean the business about his sexual activity as a youth...the penis infection? You briefly mentioned these things the day we lunched at Emmerich's."

Setting down the portfolio on a drum table between our armchairs, Adelmann said, "Oh no, Preiss. I'm talking about something far more serious than the peccadilloes of an oversexed youth."

I affected a blank expression. "I'm afraid I don't quite follow—"

"What Schumann was urging me to do was to compromise my professional integrity. You see, I came across several friends of his, *male* friends, but men of some standing in society...educated, not from the lower classes, I assure you...with whom some years ago our friend Schumann engaged in more than a little sexual experimentation."

"Can you speak plainly, Dr. Adelmann?" I said. "Are you referring to homosexual activity?"

"*Activities*...plural," Adelmann replied. "One of these male friends told me Schumann had the appetite of a glutton when it came to such carrying-on. 'Hell-bent' was the way he put it. When I touched on this matter with

Schumann," he continued, "the man's blood rushed to his face, his brow became damp with sweat, his lips trembled, his speech became thick, he stammered. I tell you, Preiss, it was a terrible sight to behold. Seeing him in this state moved me, and I agreed—reluctantly—to avoid any mention of this matter in my monograph."

"Whereupon Schumann prevailed upon you to accept the Beethoven manuscript...as a token of his undying gratitude."

"Precisely," Adelmann said. On his face there was a look of complete satisfaction, as though he had neatly tidied up a minor piece of unfinished business. In a pointed tone, he added, "The affair is best forgotten, really. I assume we need speak no more of this matter."

I nodded in agreement. "Indeed, sir," I said, "you and I need speak no more of it."

But *Schumann* and I would most certainly speak of this. And not tomorrow, but this very day. One of these two—Schumann or Adelmann—was making a fool of me.

I had arranged to have a cab call for me and was about to take my leave when, as my host held the door open, I turned suddenly and said, "By the way, Dr. Adelmann, would you consider returning the Beethoven manuscript to Schumann in exchange for some other form of compensation?"

"Oh no, it is out of the question, Preiss!" Adelmann replied.

"Why is it out of the question?"

"You may ask, sir," he said, smiling at me in a condescending way, "but the reason I cannot return the manuscript is very private and could not possibly be of interest to you."

"I see," I said, not seeing at all. My sense of smell was at work, however, and something very foul was in the wind that fanned my face as I climbed into the cab and ordered the driver to take me at once to 15 Bilkerstrasse.

Chapter Eighteen

T he person greeting me after I was admitted to the
Schumann residence was a stranger to me. Yet,
ordering the housekeeper to go about her duties while he
conducted me into the study, he impressed me at once as
someone accustomed to being in charge no matter where.
His manner was formal, the voice crisp. Deep-set pale grey
eyes seemed to look through me, focused instead on some
person I imagined standing behind me. His mouth, a
simple mean slit, was unsoftened by thin lips formed into
a cautious smile. "Permit me to introduce myself," he said.
"I am Professor Friedrich Wieck. I am already familiar with
your name, Inspector Preiss, thanks to my daughter Clara.
I'm afraid she and her husband are away at the moment."

"Away?"

"Yes. Early this morning, shortly before my arrival
here, it was apparently decided that they urgently need to
spend several days at a spa some distance down the Rhine,
at Bad Grünwald. My daughter left a note. Her husband,
it seems, requires massages and water treatments, or
whatever they do in places of that sort." The professor's
explanation made it plain that he had little use for "places
of that sort". Nor did I fail to note that whenever he
mentioned his son-in-law, he could only bring himself to
refer to Schumann as his daughter's husband. I had no
difficulty believing the stories I'd recently heard about his
influence on the young Clara. It was said that the girl rose
when she was told, went to bed when she was told,

performed when she was told, even dressed and combed her hair under Wieck's strict and incessant supervision.

"Is there something I can help you with, Inspector?" Wieck said. It was clear he could scarcely wait to be rid of me.

To the evident displeasure of the professor, I unbuttoned my coat, laid my hat on a nearby chair, and said, "It's very kind of you to ask, Professor. And yes, as a matter of fact, you may be able to help me." I let my eyes drop to another nearby chair, hinting that I would prefer to sit. My host—if one could call him that—chose to ignore this signal.

"You will have to pardon me, Inspector, but the fact is, I do not have more than a few minutes to spare," Wieck said.

"I beg *your* pardon, then," I said forcing myself to sound forgiving. "I did not realize, of course, that you might have another appointment. I'm sorry if I've detained you. Perhaps later in the day?"

The features of Wieck's face tightened. "Later in the day, I shall be on a train returning to Leipzig, sir."

"But I don't understand, Professor," I said. "You mentioned that you arrived here only this morning. Must you leave so soon?"

"Let me ask you something, Inspector. Do you have children?"

"No, sir. I have never been married."

"Then thank your lucky stars," Wieck said. "There is no ingratitude on this earth as hurtful as filial ingratitude. So long as that raving lunatic continues to manipulate my daughter and draw her farther and farther from me, there is no place for me in this house. I must say, Preiss, you strike me as a reasonably intelligent man. How can you possibly allow yourself to be caught up in this hysterical nonsense my daughter's husband is foisting on the public?"

I began to protest. "Your daughter's husband is a man of great accomplishment—"

With a contemptuous smile, Wieck cut in. "A generation

hence, if not sooner, his name will not be remembered, Preiss. You are a policeman and not expected to understand these things, but take my word for it, neither he nor his music will matter by the time the present decade gives way to the next. What *will* be remembered is this caprice he's indulging in."

I said, "This 'caprice' as you call it, Professor Wieck...I gather that you hold little credence in Dr. Schumann's complaint about the A sound that persists. He insists that it is the product of some kind of conspiracy."

Wieck gave a cynical laugh. "Little credence, you say? *No* credence is more to the point. None. Absolutely zero!"

"But Professor, I myself have been witness to several of his recent episodes. Not even the greatest actor in Europe could feign such anguish."

"Listen to me, Preiss," Wieck said. "He comes to me as a twenty-year-old pupil. From a good family, a family with money, educated people, rather handsome himself I'll admit, and gifted with musical talent. Oh, but on the debit side...a lack of manliness, a constant escaping into childish fantasies, impetuous. I have taught a number of Europe's finest pianists...disciplined young men, and even women, who have valued my ideas and methods. Robert Schumann was never one of them, and never *could* be if he lived to be a hundred...which, God forbid, he may yet do."

"With all due respect, Professor Wieck," I said, "Madam Schumann's career does not appear to have suffered by reason of her marriage to Dr. Schumann. If anything, she is held in the highest esteem by both critics and public."

"Only when she plays truly great music, Inspector. Perhaps you've heard of Mozart, Haydn, Beethoven, Schubert? Those names may not mean much to a police inspector—"

"Oh, I assure you, Professor, I've had some passing acquaintance with them. More than passing, in fact."

Wieck gave me a skeptical look. "Really?" he said. "Well, whether you are familiar with their music or not, take my word for it: when Clara plays *their* music, she plays in the heavens, so to speak. Trouble is, that madman insists that she play *his* music. Have you heard that so-called piano concerto of his?" Without waiting for my reply, Wieck went on. "Thirty minutes of romantic drivel. He says he wrote it for Clara. Some gift!"

One question troubled me now. "You'll have to excuse the inquisitiveness of a simple policeman," I said. "Why, under all these unhappy circumstances, did you choose to come to Düsseldorf?"

"In past years," he said, "I have made it a point to visit, not often mind you, but from time to time, only to see poor Clara, and my grandchildren. But in Clara's letter delivered to me a few days ago, there was a sense of urgency...something to do with the state of the two pianos here. She is concerned that they may be deteriorating due to unfavourable atmospheric conditions...the proximity of this house to the river, humidity, insufficient heat this time of year...matters of that sort, you know. When Clara was a girl, we hoped, she and I, that one day she would inhabit a proper manor house." Wieck's eyes made a quick survey of our surroundings. "Well, Inspector, as you can see... Be that as it may, I will stay only long enough to examine the instruments, then I will be off. I assume, Preiss, that you came here to see Schumann. I'm sorry this proved to be a waste of your time. Good day, sir."

As I began to button my overcoat, there was a knock on the study door.

"Ah," said Wieck, checking the hour on his pocket watch, "right on time. Good." Looking up from his watch, he called "Enter."

The door opened, and in walked Wilhelm Hupfer.

At the sight of Hupfer, Wieck's manner instantly changed from formal to genial. "Ah, Hupfer my good man, wonderful to see you! And thank you for being so punctual." Glancing in my direction, he added: "I was just saying goodbye to this gentleman. Perhaps I should introduce him."

"That won't be necessary, Professor," I said. "Herr Hupfer and I have met."

In a spirit of levity that struck me as forced, Wieck shook a finger at Hupfer. "So, Hupfer, it seems you are already known to the police, eh. What have you been up to? Better come clean, you old scoundrel."

Hupfer looked over at me, a weak smile on his face. "A little jest now and then never harms anyone, does it?" he said. "Professor Wieck is famous for his sense of humour, Inspector."

I was willing to wager that of all the things for which the professor was famous, a sense of humour was not on the list. Nevertheless, I said, "Gentlemen, a police inspector is out of place in the midst of such witty company. If you will excuse me, I'll leave you to whatever business brings you together." As I said this and reached for my hat, I caught a look of immense relief on Hupfer's face. Wieck too looked relieved at the prospect of my departure.

Opening the door, I turned suddenly and addressed Hupfer. "By the way, Hupfer, not that I want to dampen the atmosphere, but do you have some expert remedy for the problems the Schumanns are having with their pianos?"

"Problems? What problems are you referring to, Inspector?"

"Humidity, for one," I replied. "No doubt a result of the proximity to the river, isn't that so?"

Without taking his eyes from Wieck, Hupfer groped for an answer. "Humidity, you say? Why, uh, I wasn't aware…I mean, it's always a possibility in our climate…but then there's plenty of heat in the house…at least, it seems so to me. On the other hand—" Hupfer gave up with a shrug.

Without losing a beat, Wieck called to me as I stood waiting to exit, "Good day, Inspector. We must not keep you. I do hope we meet again, soon."

"I'm sure you do," I said under my breath as I left.

Chapter Nineteen

I returned to my office at the constabulary feeling uneasy. There was something about the conduct of those two, Wieck and Hupfer, that reminded me of an ill-matched twosome caught stealing a pie from a baker's shelf, one much too composed, the other shaking in his boots.

Then, too, there was the constant worry that time was running out for me.

I opened my office door expecting to find on my desk yet another of Commissioner Schilling's unwelcome memoranda. Instead, there stood Schilling himself, looking pink-faced and pleased. Next to him, seated demurely, was Helena Becker.

"Ah, Preiss, there you are, you clever devil," said Schilling, chortling like a walrus. "I've heard rumours about this beautiful young woman of yours. I must compliment you on your taste, Preiss! Well now, I've done my duty; therefore I'll leave you two." Bending clumsily, the Commissioner kissed Helena's outstretched hand. "A great pleasure," he whispered and left the room.

I looked down at Helena. I could tell she'd been making a valiant attempt not to burst out laughing. "What did he mean, Helena, 'I've done my duty'…what duty? I don't like the sound of it."

She rose and kissed me lightly on the cheek. "You've nothing to fret about, Inspector. He simply showed me to your office. He'd spotted me in the main floor lobby, heard me ask the receptionist if you were in, and insisted on accompanying me. Very gallant. I'm glad you showed up when you did, though. I had the feeling I was about to be inhaled. Does he always breathe so heavily?"

"My interest in the Commissioner's breathing is limited to the day he *stops* breathing," I snapped.

"My my, we *are* in a testy mood, aren't we."

"And with very good reason," I said. "I feel like a child playing a blindfold game. Every time I take a step in the Schumann affair, I seem to bump into a wall."

"Well, Hermann, before you give up, I have some news that may brighten your day. You are now looking at the newest patient of Dr. Paul Möbius."

With a touch of pride in her smile, Helena Becker removed a small piece of paper from her clutch purse, unfolded it, and dangled it before my eyes. "A prescription," she said, "for some kind of sleeping potion."

"The handwriting is indecipherable," I said, blinking at what appeared to be a series of animal scratches. "Maybe it's some Wagnerian brew that transforms women into dragons. Or maybe it's an aphrodisiac. Have you considered that?"

Helena said, "When have I ever needed an aphrodisiac? No, I succeeded in persuading Möbius that I suffer severe headaches and can't sleep because of persistent musical sounds ringing in my ears."

"And he really believed you?"

Helena paused to give me one of her coquettish looks. "Well," she said slowly, "he did need a little convincing."

"A little convincing?"

"I insisted that my pains were confined to the region of my head and neck, but *he* insisted that I undergo a complete physical examination. Blubbered something about toxins that form in the lower extremities and that, despite the forces of gravity, work their way *up* into the chest and beyond, eventually affecting auditory faculties. Said this occurred especially in women of my occupation. You know something, Hermann, he almost had me believing him."

"You mean, Helena, that you—"

"Oh yes, Hermann. Naked as a newborn babe. In the militia they call it service beyond the call of duty, don't they?"

"The phrase is *'above* and beyond'."

"Well, in my case it was *below* and beyond. Listen to this: Möbius—after he's done probing here and there and signalling that I can put my clothes back on—then says there are a number of…and here he coughs and clears his throat…a number of rather intimate questions he must ask, and will I consent to answer, all for the sake of scientific diagnosis of course."

"Good God, Helena, surely—"

She pressed her fingers to my lips, sealing them. "So I pretend to be prim and bashful, and I ask what he means by 'intimate'. And he comes right out and says that he thinks my condition, you know, the sleeplessness and auditory hallucinations, are the result of sexual repression—"

"Sexual *what?*" I said and broke into laughter.

Feigning indignation, Helena said, "Hermann, you dare to laugh in the face of a woman who has sacrificed her honour on the altar of your manhood. For shame!"

"Sacrificed your honour on the altar of my manhood? Helena, where in hell did you ever unearth that collection of words?"

"Well, by the time I'd answered a couple of dozen 'intimate' questions, and he'd made careful notes, he put down his pen, gravely looked at me, and that is precisely what he said to me. 'Young woman, you have sacrificed your honour et cetera et cetera.'"

"You told him about us, then? You know, of course, that if Möbius thinks there's even the thinnest thread of a connection between you and me, your visit to him may turn out to have been entirely useless."

"Trust me, Hermann," said Helena. "I was perfect. But there's more, much more. Dr. Möbius then proceeds to deliver a lengthy lecture on the degenerative nature of the life of a creative or performing artist. Words like 'unstable' and 'intemperate' and 'frivolous' and 'licentious' come tumbling out of his mouth, along with clouds of foul-smelling cigar smoke, and I'm beginning to think I'm in the presence of some Druid high priest rather than a doctor who treats mental patients."

I sat back for a moment, digesting Helena's account. At last, I said, "That's all very intriguing, Helena, but frankly—"

"Wait," Helena chided, "let me finish! I went so far as to express contrition over the turn my life has taken. I realized by now that I had raised the curtain on a few of Dr. Möbius's riper fantasies. I could see by the look in his eyes that he saw in me the living example of every lascivious thought that ever entered his head. So I figured his guard might be down."

"His guard? You mean the business about patient-doctor confidentiality?"

"Exactly," Helena said. "And so, in a very casual manner I said, 'I assume, Dr. Möbius, that my symptoms are very much like those of Maestro Schumann. After all, we are both musicians, both steeped in the arts, both frequent performers in public. Rumours have been widely circulated concerning Dr. Schumann's condition, and mine would seem to be the very same, would it not?' Without giving my question a second thought, Möbius replied, 'Oh no, not at all, my dear young woman. Schumann's case has nothing in common with yours, nothing whatsoever. Have no fear of that.'"

"Did you ask him to explain the difference?"

"Of course, Hermann. And he said in that flat know-it-all way of his that there is an entirely different phenomenon underlying Robert Schumann's case. 'You must accept my expert judgment in the matter,' Möbius said. And with that he slammed his notebook closed, wrote out the prescription and handed it to me with an unmistakable air of finality."

"Did you attempt to question what he meant by 'an entirely different phenomenon'?"

Helena shifted a bit closer to me. "Give me your hand, Hermann."

Puzzled, I said, "What's that got to do with—"

"Just give me your hand," she insisted. Obediently, I placed my right hand in hers. "There, you see what I mean?"

I began to understand. Her hand was warm, soft and smooth almost beyond belief, and somehow she managed to make it tremble ever so slightly, so that a kind of subtle but unstoppable energy seemed to be flowing from her body into mine. "You see," Helena said, not taking her eyes from mine, "*this* is how I took Möbius's hand as I rose to leave. And while I was doing so, I asked if he could explain to a poor unscientific person like me what he meant...about the phenomenon thing."

"And his explanation was?"

She paused, trying to recall Möbius's precise words. "Something about...how an event, no matter how impossible it seems, can become probable if the cause can be traced with sufficient clarity. He said it's a theory he's been working on for a number of years. It's what he calls 'the philosophy of science'."

I gave Helena a skeptical look. "He told you this while you were holding his hand?"

"This, and more," she said, still holding *my* hand. "Truth is, I hadn't the foggiest idea what Möbius was talking about, so I asked him to put it in terms that I, a mere cellist, could try to comprehend. I was so humble! And Möbius loves that. Female humility seems to arouse some men, doesn't it?"

I withdrew my hand. "I wouldn't know," I said. "Can we please stick to the topic...I mean Möbius's so-called philosophy of science?"

"Perhaps Möbius's explanation will help—the one he

offered when I said I didn't quite comprehend. He said,"
again Helena paused to recollect, "he said, if people fear
a certain possibility long enough and intensely enough,
the possibility they fear will become a probability. In other
words, the event they're terrified of will probably occur. It
sounds like absolute nonsense to me, Hermann."

With a start, I rose from the divan and stepped
quickly to my desk. I took a fresh sheet of stationery
from the drawer, dipped my pen into the inkwell and
was poised to write. To Helena, I said, "Will you repeat—
slowly, please—the example Möbius gave."

Helena looked at me as though I was losing my
senses. "Hermann, you're *not* taking this stuff seriously!"

"Please," I said firmly, "tell me again slowly, in his
exact words."

She repeated what Möbius had told her, word for word,
giving me time to get it all down on paper in large easily
readable letters. I then propped up the piece of stationery
against a pile of books, read it and re-read it. I could not
take my eyes from it. I said the words aloud: "If people fear
a certain possibility long enough and intensely enough,
the possibility they fear will become a probability. The
event they're terrified of will probably occur."

"Tell me the truth, Hermann," Helena said, "is the
world about to come to an end? Should I be making my
peace with God?"

"On the contrary," I replied, my gaze still fixed on
what I'd just written. "Nothing is coming to an end. In
fact, the very opposite is happening!"

Chapter Twenty

M y encounter with Professor Wieck and Willy Hupfer, though brief, struck me as bizarre, indeed so bizarre that I felt compelled to relate the scene to Schumann while the details were still fresh in my memory. I hoped that, though the Maestro might find the apparent acquaintanceship of these two disturbing, he might shed some light on it that would reinforce my newfound suspicions. Next morning, I decided to pay Schumann a visit. I expected that he and his wife would have returned from their "escape" to Bad Grünwald, and it turned out that I was right. What I did *not* expect, however, was to find that the Maestro was already fully (even rather nattily) dressed for an outing and emerging from the Schumann residence, a stout walking stick firmly in hand.

"Good morning, Preiss," he called out as I alighted from my cab. "What a pleasant coincidence!" He seemed in unusually high spirits.

"Coincidence?"

"Yes. You're just in time to join me for a walk. A wonderful morning, eh?" With his walking stick he pointed to a cloudless sky. "Haven't seen sunshine like this for days. We must take advantage of it. Exercise, my friend: good for a man's body, mind and soul!"

I am a night person, and the prospect of physical exercise, even at mid-morning, was less than appealing. "Thank you, Maestro," I said, "but the only time I take a walk at this hour of the day is when duty absolute requires it."

"Then consider it your absolute duty to accompany me," he countered with a cheerfulness I had never before witnessed in him.

"Very well," I said, making no secret of my reluctance. "Once around the block then."

"Nonsense!" he said, laughing. "I'm off on my favourite route. It'll do you a world of good on a brilliant day like today, Preiss. In fact, it'll do us *both* a world of good." I began to protest, but he wouldn't hear of it. "Whither I go, there also goest thou!" he said with mock severity.

"It sounds as though you're off to St. Lambertus," I said, referring to the famous thirteenth century church not too distant. "You're not going to try to make a religious man out of me, are you?"

"No indeed, Preiss. The very opposite. We're heading for the real heart of Düsseldorf, my friend." I knew he meant Königsallee. Where else?

"I'm always up for a visit to Königsallee," I said, though such a visit wasn't remotely on my agenda at the moment.

"I enjoy going there too," Schumann said, as we headed west toward Königsallee, a distance of about three city blocks from Bilkerstrasse. "I call it 'The Poor Man's Champs Elysées'...about the only place we have in the whole damn country that reminds me of Paris."

I'd never been to Paris but had read enough to understand what he meant.

So much of Düsseldorf is marinated in the past. Many of its parish churches and cathedrals date back to the 1600s and even earlier. The Old Town takes up a square kilometre on the banks of the Rhine. Within its borders, one can hear history in every creak of its rusted hinges, every groan of its ancient floorboards, every clatter of a wooden wheel rim on its rough cobblestone lanes. I can look toward the Rhine from any street in the Old Town and have no difficulty imagining myself to be a fifteenth century farmer toting a burlap sack of onions over my hunched back to market, or a potter pulling a cart heavily laden with my latest earthenware for sale there, or a tattered follower of Martin Luther crying aloud from some makeshift street corner pulpit to passersby to turn their backs forever on Rome.

Königsallee, on the other hand, is the brightest, liveliest, most fashionable precinct in the whole of Düsseldorf. I fell in love with Königsallee the first time I walked its length years earlier as a penny-pinching recruit. Its luxurious offerings of clothes and jewellery and food were there to be looked at, and maybe touched, but nothing more at the time. To a young man from Zwicken, Königsallee was heaven on earth, and in the early days of my career in the constabulary, that one street had more to do with my burning ambition to succeed than all the homilies that rained down upon my youthful head from parents and teachers and clergymen, not to mention my superiors in the force.

"Shall I tell you something funny?" Schumann said as we began our walk, he setting a remarkably vigorous pace. "I'm not a particularly religious man, but I thank God regularly for creating Königsallee. Today I have a mission: for each of my children a small toy, nothing elaborate, just something to brighten their lives on these wintery days, the way they constantly brighten my life. Ah, but for Marie, the oldest, something special, a bracelet perhaps. Eight years old, Preiss, and already she's following in her mother's footsteps. You must excuse a father's pride, but the fact is my Marie is going to be another Clara. As for me, I'm in the market today for a box of good Dutch cigars, a bottle of Napoleon cognac, and one or two of those cravats that Spiegelman's imports from Milan, pure silk they are, much finer than the British. Oh, and a shawl for Clara, too, also from Italy."

Schumann seemed excited about the prospect of these

purchases, but I couldn't help wondering where he got the money to buy all these things. I said, "Maestro, you sound as though you've just won a lottery."

He chuckled. "No, Preiss, no lottery. But Clara's recent concertizing has been profitable. Besides, a letter came in the post this morning from my publishers. Seems they like my latest suite for piano. Well, hell Preiss, what's money *for?* Come to think of it, with so much winter still ahead of us, I might treat myself to a new hat today, one of those fur ones that the Russians are famous for. I saw a beauty in the shop window of Menkes the Hatter. Looked like sable."

Arriving at Königsallee, we carried on north and passed several outdoor cafés where coffee drinkers, bundled up in overcoats and looking almost desperate in their determination, were taking as much sun as they could this time of year.

Passing one of these cafés, my ebullient companion suddenly tugged at my sleeve, stopping me short. "Look there, Preiss, a fortune teller!"

"She's a palm-reader, Maestro," I said, making no attempt to conceal my contempt. From past experience, I knew how these people plied their trade. They travelled in packs—*wolf* packs is how I referred to them. Magicians, acrobats, assorted freaks, people who'd seldom if ever done an honest day's work. They were clever, these masters of the art of distraction, and could skin alive anyone who came within reach of their practiced fingers, be he a poor unsophisticated villager or well-heeled man-of-the-world. I had prosecuted more than a few of the rogues in my time, and word was out that pitching their tents in my territory was risky business.

This fortune teller, a hag of a woman probably in her late fifties, apparently hadn't heard of me or, having heard of me, simply didn't give a damn. Looking first to me, she said, "Read your palm, sir? You strike me as a man with a bright future. Only fifty pfennigs, sir."

I nodded in the direction of Schumann. "My friend here...*he's* your customer, not I."

Squinting, she looked Schumann up and down. "Well, now," she said, breaking into a smile of approval, "*there's* a distinguished-looking gentleman if I ever saw one. I can tell a senior public official a mile away. I'd bet my crystal ball—if I had one, I mean—that you're a retired general, sir. Do sit down."

Schumann shot me a wide grin. He seemed, with good reason, to be gaining immense enjoyment out of being mistaken for a military man. Taking a folding chair across the small table from the woman, he asked, "Which hand, madam?"

"Which hand do you normally favour?" she said.

"I work with both," Schumann said with a perfectly straight face.

"Of course, sir," the palm reader said. "It's only natural in a leader of men."

"You flatter me," Schumann said. I could tell he was struggling not to laugh.

"Not at all, sir. I assume you are a skilled swordsman. So let me examine the palm of your right hand, if you will."

Obediently, he offered his right hand to her, palm up. "Ah, yes," she said after a moment or two, "the hand of a man who has seen many a battle for king and country and won 'em all. The palm of a hero. Well, sir, I'm happy to tell you this—" She traced with her index finger a long crease in the palm of Schumann's hand, one that extended from thumb almost to wrist. "This line," she said, looking him soberly in the eye, "represents the reward that will soon come to you, sir. Before the year is out, you will receive a generous pension for meritorious service—"

Schumann interrupted her. "My God, a pension, you say! My prayers are answered!"

"Wait, sir, that is not all. You will inherit a château in the south of France—"

"Do you hear that!" Schumann shouted to me over his shoulder. "A château!"

"Oh, but there is more," the woman went on. "Your bachelorhood will come to a happy end—"

"And not a moment too soon!" Schumann said, going along with the palm reader with enthusiasm.

"Indeed, sir," she said, "for you will marry a young woman of the Spanish royal family no less."

Schumann was beside himself. "My cup runneth over!" he shouted. "Is there more, madam?"

"Yes, but it will cost you an extra fifty pfennigs, sir."

"To hell with the cost," Schumann said, brimming with good nature. "I've not heard tidings of such great joy since Napoleon was defeated at Waterloo."

"You were at Waterloo, sir?" the palm reader wanted to know. She seemed momentarily impressed, and I began to wonder who was fooling whom here.

"Yes," Schumann said. "I was a young subaltern seconded to the British Army. On General Wellington's personal staff, as a matter of fact. You've heard of Wellington, no doubt?"

"Oh, yes," the woman replied quickly. "Who hasn't? Well, in that case, I can tell you that, in addition to the honours I mentioned before, a square in the heart of Düsseldorf will soon be named after you. You said your name was—?"

"I didn't," Schumann said. "It's Schumannheink. Major General Maximilian von Schumannheink...at your service, madam."

"Of course," the woman said. "I should have known. How stupid of me. The name Maximilian von Schumannheink is on the lips of Germans from Bremen to Berlin and beyond. An honour to meet you, sir! That'll be one hundred pfennigs, sir."

"It's worth two," Schumann said.

The palm reader's eyes narrowed. She gave Schumann a suspicious look. "Two what?" she said.

"Two *hundred* pfennigs," Schumann said. "As a bonus, you understand."

Her look of suspicion changed instantly to one of relief. "That's very kind of you, General," she said.

Schumann reached inside his jacket to fetch his wallet. Smiling benignly at the palm reader, he said, "It's a pleasure, I assure you." Suddenly his face darkened. "What the devil!" he whispered hoarsely. "I'm sure I took my wallet with me when I left the house—" He looked over at me. "My money's gone! All of it!"

"Not really," I said, and took a couple of steps to my left, where a young man who'd been watching us was beginning to move away. Seizing the man by the collar, I pulled him sharply toward me. "We'll have your wallet and money in a second or two, Maestro," I said and roughly twisted the fellow's right arm up behind his back, forcing a scream of pain from him. "Cough it up!" I ordered the young pickpocket.

"You're breaking my arm!" he screamed again as I tightened my hold.

"I can break much more than your arm. Tell me where the wallet's hidden," I said, giving his arm an extra twist for good measure.

Barely able to speak, he blurted out, "Back pocket, pants, right side. *Damn!*"

Not letting go of his arm, I reached with my free hand into the back pocket of his pants and pulled out the wallet.

The palm reader sat frozen in her chair, glaring up at the young man. "Tell him to let go," he pleaded, looking over his shoulder at the woman. "He's killing me!"

"And so he should." Her voice was pitiless. "You clumsy fool! How many times have I told you not to hang around after—"

The resemblance was unmistakable. The blackish hair, the sunbeaten complexion, the eyes that looked like black olives. These two were mother and son.

I handed Schumann his wallet, expecting, if not a glow of gratitude, at least a sigh of relief. Neither I, nor the culprits, were prepared for what came next. His face almost purple with rage, he gripped with both hands the small table at which he and the palm reader had been seated. With one mighty effort he sent it flying, a deck of playing cards that had been kept there scattering in the air like leaves blown by a sudden windstorm. The woman sat in horror, watching the simple implements of her trade disappear, in all likelihood never to be recovered. Indeed, the flimsy table, landing close to a group of startled spectators, disintegrated into dozens of fragments.

But Schumann was not finished. Now he lunged at the woman, his outstretched hands reaching for her neck. I had no choice. Letting go my grip on the young man, I threw myself between Schumann and the woman.

"Out of my way, Preiss, damn you!" Schumann demanded, straining to get at her. The force of his onslaught and my attempt to interfere caused us both to topple heavily against her, and her chair tipped backward, leaving her flat on her back, her arms and legs flailing the air.

Somehow my own physical strength prevailed, and I managed to put an end to the chaos in a minute or two, by which time the palm reader's accomplice had disappeared into the crowd. But at least I had his mother back on her feet and firmly under arrest.

And here is the strange scene that followed: instead of venting her rage at me—which I as a policeman had every reason to expect—she aimed her screaming imprecations at Schumann. No French château and noble Spanish bride this time. Now she had him rotting in hell, slowly and painfully.

Shaking her grubby fist in Schumann's face, she yelled in a voice that could be heard from one end of

Germany to the other: *"May everything you fear become a reality in your life!"*

Hearing this, Schumann shrank back, a look of alarm on his face such as I'd never before seen on him. It was as though the woman were a leper or a carrier of smallpox whom he had touched and who had fatally infected him. White with fear, he was breathing with difficulty, so much so that he seemed about to collapse.

I let the woman go, roughly shoving her away. "Go, and never set foot anywhere in Düsseldorf again," I said, "or so help me God, I'll see you behind bars for the rest of your miserable life!"

The woman dragged herself off without another word, but she had already said more than enough, for Robert Schumann was now reduced to a trembling wreck. "What did she mean, Preiss?" he said.

"Dr. Schumann," I said, trying to sound dismissive, "if I took every criminal's curse seriously, I would never leave my bed in the morning."

"No, no," he said, "that was no ordinary curse. I remember every word she said, *'May everything you fear become a reality in your life.'* And she said this to *me*, not you. My God, look at me, Preiss. I can't stop shaking. What kind of man am I?"

*   *   *

Schumann's question haunted me long after I had escorted him back to No. 15 Bilkerstrasse, where I left him still badly shaken after his experience with the palm reader on Königsallee.

What kind of man was he? One moment in high spirits, fun-loving, going along with all the palm reader's absolute nonsense, enjoying it to the hilt. Next moment terrified by what I regarded as nothing more than a hag's evil eye.

But what struck me with sudden force was the similarity between the woman's curse, and Dr. Möbius's dictum as told to Helena. Weren't these two saying the same thing? *The ghosts you fear are the ghosts you invent; the consequences you dread are the ones you bring upon yourself.* More to the point, was Robert Schumann himself bringing to reality everything he feared? If this was so, then what was the point of my continuing to involve myself? Schumann simply may have been the inventor of his own tragedy. Tragic as that fact might be, his case would have to be written off just as a bad debt is written off, I would return to my normal duties, and the world would go on spinning on its mysterious axis.

But then two things happened.

Following my last conversation with Helena, I decided that a gift to show my gratitude for her devotion to duty was long overdue. Walter Thüringer's jewellery shop was located in an arcade in the fashionable Königsallee and, while I was hardly in a position to be counted a regular patron on an inspector's salary, I managed from time to time to purchase the odd ornament from Thüringer. The old jeweller was aware, of course, that discounts on merchandise sold to a public official or civil servant were capable of being construed as a form of bribery, but it was uncanny how, whenever I expressed interest in some bauble or other, it was at that very moment due to go on sale for less than the ticketed price. I never took the trouble to question these coincidences. Nor did I bother to question the origins of certain valuables on display that were supposedly purchased from estates of deceased aristocrats but which, I had little doubt, had been stolen from houses as far away as Paris, London, Vienna and even St. Petersburg.

As always, Thüringer greeted me as though I were a long-lost brother. "Ah, Inspector Preiss, how marvellous to see you! And looking as impeccably turned out as ever! I get older and older, and you, Preiss, get younger and younger." The shopkeeper shook his head ruefully. "In my next life, God willing, I shall be a policeman, I swear."

"Thüringer, save your flattery," I responded. "You know perfectly well I'm a man of limited means."

"Nonsense!" Thüringer said. "My entire stock is at your disposal."

"I'm not in the market for your entire stock," I said, "only a small gift."

"A small gift, you say? That sounds to me like there's a woman involved."

"A very special woman, yes."

Thüringer spread his arms wide. "Make yourself at home, Inspector. Look about, and I'll be back to you presently. I must finish with another customer, if you will please excuse me."

He bowed low, as though I were a tax collector delivering an unexpected refund, then hereturned to the only other customer in the shop, a man standing nearby, his back to me.

"It's a charming piece," I heard Thüringer tell the man. "Of all the lockets in my inventory, it is undoubtedly the finest. French craftsmanship, of course. And the price will include the engraving on the back of it."

"Speaking of price," the customer said, "is it the very best you can manage?" The speaker had lowered his voice, but I could still hear. "I really didn't anticipate having to spend this much."

In his best avuncular manner, Thüringer said, "My dear young man, the recipient of this locket will treasure it surely for the rest of her days. Such a gift has value beyond price."

A little reluctantly, the customer replied, "Very well, then, I suppose I must make the sacrifice."

It was at this point that the man turned partly, and I recognized him at once. "Herr Brahms?"

"Inspector—uh—"

"Preiss," I said. "Hermann Preiss."

"Yes, yes, of course," Brahms said. "We meet again."

"We meet again" was an expression I'd become all too accustomed to—usually spoken by someone who was anything but thrilled to see me. Nevertheless, I attempted to sound cheerful. "It seems," I said, "that you and I are on similar missions. I too am buying a gift for a woman, and if I know this old rascal Thüringer, I too will end up spending more than I'd intended."

Thüringer loved it whenever I teased him, and chuckled amiably; anyway, both he and I shared this truth: he really *was* an old rascal. Brahms made an effort to be amused. "Well, Inspector," he said, "I will leave here with a lighter wallet thanks to Herr Thüringer, and a lighter heart thanks to you. I bid you a good day, sir." Buttoning his coat, he said to Thüringer, "May I count on the engraving being done by this time tomorrow?"

His hand over his heart, the jeweller replied, "You have my word on it."

I waited for young Brahms to depart. Turning to Thüringer, I said, "I need a favour, my friend."

"Name it," the old man said.

"That locket you just sold...are you acquainted with the buyer?"

"Johannes Brahms? Yes. A musician of some note—no pun intended—from what little I know of him."

"The inscription you're to engrave on the back of the locket—"

"Yes, what about it?"

"I need to know what it says, Thüringer."

Thüringer took a step back, and his face took on a shocked expression. "But you must know, my dear fellow, that such things are confidential. To reveal to you what I'm to engrave would be like opening someone's private mail. I have my ethical standards about such things."

Quietly, I said, "Thüringer, listen to me. Priests have

ethical standards. *You* are not a priest. Do I make my point? Now then, Thüringer, what's to be engraved on the back of that locket?"

"You are placing me in a terrible dilemma," the jeweller protested.

"Then permit me to resolve your dilemma at once," I said. "In return for your cooperation, I will see to it that the next police inspection of your inventory of antique pieces is conducted by Inspector Hermann Preiss, rather than by someone with—uh—*keener* sight."

Without another word, Thüringer handed me a slip of paper that he'd just deposited in a drawer behind one of the display cases.

"Whose handwriting is this?" I asked.

"His, Brahms's."

I read aloud: "To dearest Clara, my life's blood." Below these words was a single initial—J.

I handed back the slip to Thüringer. "Thank you," I said. "You have my word that no one will hear of this. Now then, there's a set of pearl earrings in the window—"

I purchased the earrings (yes, by coincidence, they had just gone on sale at a considerable discount) and placed a small white card inside the gift box. It read: "To dear Helena, whose ears hear what mine cannot."

Then, the Beethoven manuscript. Leaving Thüringer's, I decided it was time to give *myself* a gift, albeit a modest one, nothing more, in fact, than a half-hour or so at my favourite coffeehouse, Schimmel's. A good strong cup of coffee, a slice of Black Forest cake, and a chance to browse through the latest arts journals from Berlin were precisely what I needed to free my mind from the Schumann affair.

The coffee turned out to be fresher and stronger than I could recall from my past visits. "That's because it's imported direct from Colombia," Schimmel explained to me with great pride. "The British," he went on, "get theirs from somewhere in Africa, which proves of course that they know absolutely nothing about coffee." The Black Forest cake, too, was perfect. I sat back, stretched my legs, and snapped open the first newspaper at hand, *Berliner Kunstzeitung.* Lazily, I scanned the headlines. Then my eyes dropped to the lower section of the front page, and my few minutes of rest and recreation came to an abrupt halt.

Beneath a photograph of a familiar musical figure, I read: FRANZ LIZST ACQUIRES RARE BEETHOVEN PIANO MANUSCRIPT.

Chapter Twenty-One

S o, Preiss, this is how you kept your promise, is it?" It
was the morning after Franz Liszt's acquisition of the
Beethoven manuscript was reported in the *Berliner
Kunstzeitung*, and Robert Schumann had just stormed
into my office and hurled his copy of the newspaper
across my desk.

"My promise, Maestro?" I said, knowing perfectly well
what he was referring to.

"You allowed that devil Adelmann to get away with it,
didn't you? Was it carelessness, or am I to believe that
you, too, have joined the ring of conspirators?"

Calmly, I said, "Let me explain, please. I had a
meeting with Georg Adelmann—"

"Ah, so you *do* recall the promise you made me, after
all—"

"Please, allow me to finish. I met with Adelmann and
yes, he has the Beethoven manuscript…or rather, *had* it."

"And you got him to admit he'd stolen it, then?"

I took a deep breath. "Not quite, I'm afraid."

"I thought you were the cleverest detective in this
part of Germany. Don't tell me you actually saw the
manuscript but failed to confiscate it from him!"

I took another deep breath. "Correct on both counts.
I saw it, and I did *not* confiscate it."

"But why? *Why?*"

Schumann had been standing all this time, leaning
somewhat menacingly over my desk, as though he were
ready to pounce at any moment. "I think, Maestro, you

had better be seated," I said.

"Don't treat me like a child or like one of your moronic criminals, Preiss. I don't need to sit."

I rose from my chair and spoke sharply now. "You will be seated, sir, or this meeting is over. *Sit!*"

I watched Schumann slowly lower himself into a chair on the other side of my desk. There was, suddenly, something child-like and pathetic about the way he did this, and for a second or two I felt remorse at having shouted him into submission. In a steady voice I began again. "I have to tell you, Dr. Schumann, that when the subject of the Beethoven manuscript came up, Adelmann, without the slightest reluctance, went to a cabinet in his study and produced it. This was not the conduct one would expect of a thief. Indeed, he had a ready explanation as to how he came to possess it. Do you wish me to go on, sir?"

I imagined that Schumann would demur. Contrary to my expectation, he gave me a contemptuous smile. "Go on, Preiss," he said without hesitation. "What did that overstuffed rodent tell you?"

"I warn you, sir...what follows is neither pleasant to say, nor will it be pleasant to hear." I hesitated to go on, hoping Schumann would volunteer the explanation and spare me the embarrassment. No such luck.

"I told you to go on," he said. "What more do you want, a fanfare?"

"I must be blunt, then," I said. "Adelmann insists that you gave him the manuscript in return for his pledge."

"Pledge? What pledge?"

"Not to disclose certain sexual activities you apparently engaged in...in your younger years."

Schumann let out a forced laugh. "Certain sexual activities, you say? Well, thank God I wasn't born a eunuch, if that's what Adelmann's alluding to. What red-blooded German doesn't sow a few wild oats with the fairer sex in his youth, eh? Yes, I did enjoy the odd fling or two with women. Maybe more, in fact."

"Adelmann was not speaking about affairs with *women.*"

Schumann's eyes narrowed. "What are you saying, Preiss?"

"Please understand, Maestro, it's not a matter of what *I* am saying."

"Yes, yes, now get on with it. Well?"

"Apparently, in the course of his research into your past, Adelmann came across—or *claims* to have come across—several of your male friends...he used the term 'friends'...it is Adelmann's description, not mine...with whom it is alleged you indulged in homosexual activities with some frequency—"

At this point, I anticipated his vehement denial. Instead, Schumann's face became an expressionless mask. I was certain it concealed the truth. Quietly, I said, "I warned you this would be upsetting."

"What is upsetting," Schumann said, "is the thought that the laws of the land are in the hands of a pack of narrow-minded constables, men who are little more than night watchmen. When it comes to subtleties in human behavior...to inner truths...you are as hopeless as the fish in the Rhine."

"I beg your pardon, sir," I said, "but I'm not trained to search for so-called inner truths. I deal in evidence which can be seen, touched and heard. Inner truths? There are none, except those that novelists and liars like to dream up. So, regarding Adelmann's findings, what have you to say? Yes, he's right, or no he's wrong?"

Schumann rose abruptly and snatched up the copy of the *Kunstzeitung* that lay on my desk. "I refuse to be intimidated. From this point onward, Florestan takes charge of my case."

Florestan? Where had I heard that name before? Then I remembered: Adelmann had referred to Florestan and Eusebius, the two companions Schumann had long ago invented and who inhabited his imagination and supposedly spoke to him in times of emotional distress. Florestan, the man of action, bold, impetuous, even reckless; Eusebius, soft-natured, introspective, brooding. "Maestro," I said, "this is not a time to wallow in fantasy. We must stick to reality. I must know, is Adelmann's version as to how he acquired the Beethoven manuscript true...or is it false?"

With a look of grim determination, Schumann donned his hat and turned to leave, the crumpled newspaper in his firm grip.

"You haven't answered my question, Dr. Schumann," I called after him as he reached my office door and began to open it.

Schumann turned to face me. "Florestan does not answer questions. Florestan is not on trial here. To hell with you, Preiss. Florestan will get on without you."

Chapter Twenty-Two

I am not accustomed to being interrupted when I'm rehearsing." Clara Schumann's voice, sharp-edged, reverberated against the ornate panelled walls of the empty concert hall, where she would be performing in a chamber music program jointly with Helena's string quartet within the coming week.

"I do apologize, Madam Schumann," I said, walking down the centre aisle and stopping at the apron of the stage. "Ordinarily, I would never presume to disturb you at a time like this, but what brings me here is a matter of extraordinary urgency. You see—"

"I *know* why you are here," Clara said, "but you will simply have to excuse me."

"But madam—"

"*Not now,* I say."

"Your husband is a very sick man, Madam Schumann."

"I told you the night you were summoned to our house that he needed a *doctor,* not some meddlesome policeman."

"I'm convinced he needs both a physician *and* a meddlesome policeman. His judgment is badly unbalanced by everything and everyone around him, which is why he announced in my office this morning that he...or rather *Florestan*...is going to pursue on his own the investigation I began."

"Well, there's your proof," Clara said. "What more do you need, for God's sake, Inspector—an official Certificate of Lunacy signed by a battery of medical specialists?"

"I beg of you; you have influence with your husband. He must not attempt to play amateur sleuth."

With a hint of irony in her voice, Clara said, "Come to think of it, perhaps what Georg Adelmann needs right now is a good dose of my husband's temper, especially since you apparently prefer to handle Adelmann with kid gloves."

"Madam Schumann, I wonder if you understand the nature of Maestro Schumann's problem with Adelmann."

"The man has made off with one of our priceless possessions. Remember, you yourself cautioned me that he's a thief. What more is there to understand? Really, Inspector, you *do* try one's patience!"

"But there is another side to the story," I said. "When I confronted Adelmann, he not only denied that the Beethoven manuscript was missing but made a point of *producing* it right before my very eyes and without a moment's hesitation. He insisted Dr. Schumann gave it to him."

"*Gave* it to him?"

"Yes. As a gift."

"Whatever for? Why would Robert do such a thing?"

"Adelmann had come across certain facts in his research concerning sexual experiments—"

"*Experiments?*"

"There doesn't seem to be any other way to characterize them, I'm sorry to say. They involved other…other *men*. In all likelihood, these would have come to light and become public knowledge once Adelmann's monograph was published. Adelmann revealed this to me, and I in turn revealed it to your husband this morning."

"I'm sure Robert must have denied it," Clara said, sounding indignant but confident. When I failed readily to agree, she frowned. "Surely Robert denied it?"

I shook my head.

At this point, the first crack in her composure appeared. She looked away and closed her eyes, as though struggling to absorb what she had just learned. At last, she said, "So you did not bother to challenge Adelmann's account? You simply swallowed his tale, knowing him as you do? Is that what you call interrogation?"

"I heard no firm and absolute denial from your husband, I remind you. Instead, he raved on about 'inner truths'. He accused me of being too crude to understand certain subtleties of human behaviour, then stormed out of my office vowing to take charge of his case, as he put it. *Now* do you begin to understand my alarm?"

"What I begin to understand," she said, eyeing me coldly, "is that you've succeeded only in inflaming my husband by your tactlessness. And now, having been responsible for driving poor Robert into the guise of Florestan, you want me to perform what might amount to a miracle…to restore my husband to the passive role of Eusebius, since obviously you are incapable of undoing what you've done."

I said, "Madam Schumann, this is neither the time nor the place to debate the merits of my conduct. You must go to Maestro Schumann as quickly as possible. You must do everything in your power to see to it that he does not commit some rash and foolish act that *all* of us will regret. There's no time to waste!"

Clara Schumann's response startled me. Turning away from me, she brought both hands powerfully down on the keyboard of the Bösendorfer, at which she'd remained seated, setting off an explosive discord that must have shortened the life of that instrument by years. "You speak of time," she shouted angrily, "but no one…*no one*…speaks of *my* time. It's as though I've been evicted from my own life, as though my only purpose is to serve my father, my children, my impresario, my audiences…and of course my husband. *I am sick to death of all this.*"

"Please, believe me, Madam Schumann," I said, "my

only wish is to be of help to you."

She straightened her back, then looked directly at me. In a quiet voice now, she said, "If you truly wish to help me, then please leave me. I need some time...time to be entirely alone."

*   *   *

Disheartened by my latest encounter with Clara Schumann, I decided that the best antidote would be to return to my office at the Constabulary and bury myself in some neglected paperwork. Saturday afternoons were traditionally quiet times in my department. Lulls before the storms is what my colleagues and I called Saturday afternoons, the reason being that in Düsseldorf—and I suspect pretty much everywhere else—most crimes of passion, especially fatal ones, were committed on Saturday nights, when seemingly harmless revellers, by some trick of metamorphosis known only to the Devil, turned into murderers. By late afternoon, a stack of files over which my shadow hadn't fallen for days on end had been reduced to one last file, which I was about to open when a young assistant burst into my office. "Have you heard the news, Inspector?" he said. "Georg Adelmann...you know, the journalist? A report has just come in. His landlady found him in his apartment an hour ago. Apparently murdered."

Chapter Twenty-Three

"Any idea who might have done this, Preiss?"
Commissioner Schilling was standing with his
gloved hands firmly clasped behind his back, keeping
his distance from the body of Georg Adelmann lest
violent death, which pervaded the scene, rub off on him.

"None, sir," I said over my shoulder. Bent over the
corpse, I pointed to the right temple. "Whoever it was must
have possessed brute strength. A single blow did the job, by
the looks of it." All that was visible was a thin trickle of blood
that had leaked from an odd puncture in the skin.

"Come to think of it," the Commissioner said, "the
list of suspects could spread from one end of the country
to the other. After all, a journalist of his sort...you know,
full of high and mighty opinions, and a gossip-monger
to boot...probably accumulates enemies the way rotten
meat attracts maggots."

With more than a little effort (the act of bending being
no easy feat given his global girth), the Commissioner now
joined me for a closer inspection of the deceased. He
shook his head, as though admiring a work of art. "Well
now, Preiss, if one must die a violent death, this is the way,
I suppose. Quick. Efficient. Final. An elegant murder is
what I'd call it. Yes, indeed, elegant."

I said, "The question is: is it an example of elegant
homicide, or homicidal elegance?"

The Commissioner frowned. "That's the trouble with
you, Preiss. Always splitting hairs. Perhaps you'd best get on
with your note-taking whilst I examine the place for clues."

I reached into my coat for my notebook and began to jot down some initial observations:

Victim fully clothed but no neckwear (probably relaxing, informal), lying on left side suggesting attempt to avoid blow to right temple. Minor blood loss, some discoloration around temple. Neatness of clothing suggests no struggle or resistance but sudden unexpected assault...

I glanced around Adelmann's sitting room, then continued:

Body in centre of room. No sign of forced entry, therefore assailant probably invited in. Familiar guest rather than intruder. Room generally in good order.

"Think it might have been a robbery, Preiss?" The Commissioner called to me from behind Adelmann's large, ornately carved desk. He was holding aloft a black leather wallet. "Found this lying here, open, on top of this mess of letters and working papers. See here—" He spread open the compartments. "Empty. Not so much as a pfennig in it. Looks as though it was a robbery. A man like Adelmann would surely have carried a reasonable amount of cash on him."

"On the other hand, Commissioner," I said, "there's a diamond ring on Adelmann's left small finger...I'd estimate one-and-a-half to two carats. Also a gold pocket watch dangling there on a chain. A serious thief would hardly have overlooked those items."

"Then how to explain the wallet?"

"Simple, sir. Whoever killed Adelmann was a rank amateur, despite the efficiency of the lethal blow to the victim's temple. The wallet tossed helter-skelter...its contents gone...an old trick, sir." I stood up and heaved a world-weary sigh. "Criminals can be so damned unimaginative," I said.

I stepped across the room to the glass-fronted cabinet that held Adelmann's silver and gold collections. "No indication anyone attempted to remove anything here, Commissioner. And these are certainly worth a fortune—"

As soon as I'd said this, I realized I had made a mistake.

Schilling shot me a quizzical look. "Sounds to me as though you've been here before," he said. "You seem to have some acquaintance with the place."

"I was here once, just once...recently in fact."

My response did not seem to sit well with my superior. I imagined him asking himself how I, his underling, managed to be in the company of Georg Adelmann when he—Düsseldorf's Commissioner of Police no less—had never so much as received a nod of recognition from the man all these years.

"Tell me, Preiss, how *well* did you know this fellow Adelmann? The word among your colleagues is that you have a reputation for hobnobbing with these types from time to time."

Be humble, Hermann, I told myself. "Hobnobbing is putting too fine a point on it, sir. I would never *dream* of inserting myself into the circles frequented by Georg Adelmann. Fact is, he merely consulted me about the safety and security of his valuable collection, what measures to take to protect them from the criminal elements that have drifted in from the slums of Hamburg and Berlin. He was deeply concerned, and rightly so. As you can see, sir, this place is a veritable treasure house."

Without bothering to survey the treasures, Schilling said: "Look here, I'm a man of the world, if I may say so, and I can understand that a chap like you would be eager to seize any opportunity to advance himself...you know, rubbing shoulders so to speak with the local intelligentsia, upgrading yourself socially and all that. And I grant you, that sort of thing is all right, so long as it reflects credit on the Police Department—"

"I'm grateful, sir, that you approve—"

"Let me finish. Take my advice." He lowered his voice to a confidential level. "It doesn't pay to overdo that kind of thing. Mustn't lose our objectivity, you know. Remember,

Preiss, that even high-born persons—the *haut monde,* as they say in France—are known to run afoul of the law, not often mind you, but vigilance must always be our first priority. I have a saying: too much whipped cream spoils the cake! This little motto of mine—simple though it be— has stood me in good stead."

For a moment I was back at the train station in my hometown, Zwicken, pretending to absorb my father's parting admonitions into the deepest recesses of my memory—then letting them evaporate there.

Fortunately, something caught the attention of the Commissioner, sparing me the pain of thanking him for his words of advice. "Ah, what have we here?"

Schilling had discovered Adelmann's appointment book on the fireplace mantel. "Well, now," he said, his face revealing more interest than before, "this may tell us a thing or two, eh!"

The Commissioner—rather cleverly for him—turned immediately to the page for that very day. His expression turned dark. "Nothing," he said. "Not a damned thing. Bad luck."

"Well, sir, it's not entirely bad luck. At least it helps us to narrow the possibilities in a way."

"And that's another problem you have, Preiss, if I may be frank," said Schilling. "You exhibit this constant refusal to face basic facts. There is nothing…not so much as a chicken scratch…here on today's page. Now how in heaven's name does that help us?"

"One: it confirms that whoever killed Adelmann was an unscheduled visitor. Let's assume a surprise guest. This is further substantiated by the position of the body. Two: obviously the killer was invited into the room…*well* in, not simply left at the entrance. Therefore, he was probably known to the victim, perhaps even a friend."

"You say 'he' referring to the killer. Perhaps this was some sort of bizarre lover's revenge…a woman's wrath…that sort of nonsense. These journalist types are notorious for becoming involved in domestic scandals."

"I marvel at your insights, Commissioner," I said, "but no woman would have had the strength to deliver a fatal blow to Adelmann's head without the benefit of a stout weapon. There's no evidence to indicate that a weapon…say, a club or fireplace iron or heavy piece of sculpture…inflicted a wound. No, sir, this was the work of a man."

"And a damned angry one at that," said Schilling, "one whose physical power matched his anger. So who the devil could he be?"

In my own mind the name "Robert Schumann" had formed almost from the moment I had entered Adelmann's quarters, but I could not bring myself to say it aloud. Besides, having persuaded the Commissioner to let me pursue Schumann's tormentors, how could I possibly justify my efforts if Schumann himself were now perceived as a cold-blooded murderer?

Desperate to focus Schilling's attention on other possible suspects—*anyone but Schumann, for God's sake*—I said, "Let's examine the pages for the previous days, say, for the past week or so."

Schilling laid the appointment book open and flipped the pages back about seven or eight days. "I must say, for a writer, this fellow Adelmann had terrible penmanship. I can hardly read what's written here. Unfortunately, I've left my spectacles back at my office."

The Commissioner handed over the appointment book to me. "You have one advantage over me, Preiss," he said grudgingly, "your eyes are younger. Here, perhaps you can make out the names—"

Most of the names, which I read aloud, meant nothing to the Commissioner or to me, which brought a chuckle from Schilling. "Probably the butcher, the baker and the candlestick maker, eh? Even a famous journalist has to deal with the humdrum of daily life, I suppose."

"No doubt, sir."

"Well, continue. Maybe we'll encounter some names that ring a bell."

"May I suggest, Commissioner, that we take the appointment book back to the Constabulary," I said.

"Why? Light's just as good here as there."

"True, but—"

"But what?"

"I have a more powerful magnifying glass in my office. It would certainly help...I mean, to make out some of the names and notes—"

"You mean to tell me your eyesight isn't keen enough, Preiss? I find it astonishing, to say the least...a man of your age."

"I plan to consult an eye specialist very soon," I said. "Meantime, shall we take the appointment book back to—?"

"Yes, yes," Schilling said impatiently. "If we must, we must."

I breathed a silent sigh of relief. This would give me time to digest the names that appeared in Adelmann's appointment book for the three days immediately preceding the day of his death...names that *were* familiar to me: Friedrich Wieck, Willi Hupfer, Paul Möbius.

But one name that was also familiar to me—a name I suspected I'd find for certain in the appointment book—in fact was *not* there at all...Johannes Brahms.

* * *

"Well, Preiss, now you've got yourself a *genuine* crime, eh?"

Commissioner Schilling, gold-rimmed spectacles firmly fixed in place by his bulbous nose, stood peering over my shoulder, gloating.

"Genuine crime, sir?"

"As opposed to that frivolous business you've been involved with...much too involved, as you well know. I'm referring to the nonsense about that Schumann fellow, of course. Well, enough of that. Those names in Adelmann's appointment book...the ones that appear for the last two or three days...they mean anything to you? Read 'em again for me."

"Friedrich Wieck—"

"Go on."

"Wilhelm Hupfer—"

"Yes yes, go on. I see more there."

"Paul Möbius—"

"Ah, there's a name I recognize. Some sort of 'mind specialist', I believe."

"You mean a psychiatrist, sir?"

"Is that what they're called these days?" Schilling chuckled. "In my day they were called quacks and charlatans. I attended a lecture Möbius gave at the Police Academy several years ago. Never heard such idiocy in my entire life. Utter drivel dressed up in medical jargon. What do you suppose Adelmann was doing, mixed up with a...what did you call him?"

"A psychiatrist, sir. I have no idea why Adelmann and Möbius would be seeing one another."

"What about...Wieck, is it? And Hupfer?"

I shrugged. "Their names mean nothing to me, either, Commissioner."

"Well, Adelmann was a damned important figure. Better drop whatever's on your schedule and get busy on this investigation. Remember, Preiss, whenever the facts don't reveal themselves clearly, I always trust my instincts. Never wrong. In time, I hope you develop sufficient confidence to trust yours. I suppose you have some idea where to begin here?"

"I do indeed, Commissioner."

I knew exactly where to begin, but *my* instincts told me to keep it to myself for the time being.

"Well, then, carry on. Time flies."

Chapter Twenty-Four

So, Inspector Preiss, we meet again. Is this an official visit?" Brahms asked, "or have you come to discuss piano tuning? Don't look surprised, Inspector. I have my sources of information. By the way, how did you locate my lodging?"

"*My* sources of information," I replied. "And yes, this is an official visit."

I took a quick look around the room. My face must have betrayed disappointment, which my reluctant host did not fail to notice. "I must apologize for my humble abode. The realm has not yet seen fit to shower me with its coinage."

"Speaking of living quarters, Herr Brahms, I understood that you occupied a guest room at Number 15 Bilkerstrasse, the Schumanns' residence. Was I misinformed?"

"You were not misinformed," Brahms said, "but your information is slightly outdated. I moved here several days ago."

"Really? May I ask why?"

"You may ask," Brahms said, eyeing me steadily with those incredibly blue eyes, "but what's the point of asking when you already know the answer?"

"Ah, yes, of course. Living under the same roof as Robert Schumann would be next to impossible, wouldn't it? I mean, the man's unpredictable moods, his tempers—"

"Don't play games with me, Inspector. You know perfectly well my move had nothing to do with Robert.

The truth is, I found it next to impossible to live under the same roof as Clara Schumann, and I think you know the reason...or reasons," he said. Brahms's tone was so quiet, so confident, that for a moment I felt off balance.

"Did you happen to visit Georg Adelmann the day he was murdered?" I asked, anxious to change the subject and regain my sense of control. "That's really why I'm here, Herr Brahms."

"If you must know, I did go see the old bastard, because earlier that day Robert threatened to kill him. I persuaded the Maestro to let me deal with Adelmann. I didn't want Robert to get into trouble."

"You actually heard Schumann threaten to kill Adelmann?"

"Not in so many words, but whenever the Maestro is in one of his 'Florestan' moods, there is no telling what he will do, how far he might go if left unchecked."

"Did he tell you why he was ready to kill Adelmann?"

Brahms paused. "Well, you're not going to be pleased with the answer to that question, Inspector. Robert was bitterly disappointed over your failure to confront Adelmann and retrieve the stolen Beethoven manuscript."

"That's as much as Schumann revealed to you, then? Nothing more?"

"What more was there to tell?"

"The Maestro gave as his only reason the fact that, in his eyes, I had fallen down on the job?" I said.

"Inspector, with all due respect, when the man who is supposedly the finest detective in Düsseldorf catches a thief red-handed, fails to apprehend him, then to make matters worse, fails to retrieve a priceless item of stolen property, wouldn't you expect a man like Robert Schumann to become almost insane with rage?"

"So, the plan was," I said, choosing my words carefully, "that you would approach Adelmann yourself, hoping perhaps to accomplish what I allegedly failed to accomplish."

"Precisely, Inspector."

"And I take it that you were met with the same responses from Adelmann that I received?"

Brahms hesitated. I sensed for the first time since my arrival that he was unsure of himself. Looking steadily at me—which convinced me he was lying—he said, "Yes, I imagine he said the same things to me as he said to you."

"About how he came into possession of the Beethoven manuscript?"

"Yes."

"He told you what, then?"

Again a hesitation. "Well, I don't recall precisely."

"You don't *recall?* It was only yesterday, Herr Brahms."

"I'm doing my best to help you, Inspector—"

"I'm sure you are. Please try to remember Adelmann's explanation."

"His explanation?"

"Yes."

"Well...let me see now. His explanation...it was so convoluted that I'm having some difficulty..."

"I have all the time in the world," I said reassuringly.

"Well," Brahms said, "as I told you, the story Adelmann related...about the manuscript...and how it came into Liszt's hands...it was all so very convoluted...full of unfinished sentences, innuendos of one kind or another, non sequiturs, if you know what I mean."

"Herr Brahms, let me lift the veil from your memory," I said. "You undertook to call on Adelmann—"

"Yes, of course."

"But the truth is that you never fulfilled that undertaking, did you?"

"I beg your pardon, sir?"

"I repeat: you never showed up at Adelmann's."

"Nonsense!"

"I'm quite certain I'm correct, Herr Brahms."

"And what makes you so sure?"

"You never had a conversation with Adelmann about returning Schumann's prized possession. If you'd had such a conversation, you'd have no trouble recalling the reason it came into Adelmann's possession...or at least his version of it."

"Which was?"

"No, Herr Brahms, not yet. First let me tell you why you chose *not* to approach Adelmann. I'll come directly to the point," I said. "You had not the slightest intention of intervening. In fact, you intended the very opposite to occur; that is, you hoped, and probably expected, that Schumann would indeed kill Adelmann. As a convicted murderer, Robert Schumann would be imprisoned, in all likelihood for the rest of his life. And this would leave you free to cement your relationship with Clara Schumann, free to be with her openly instead of furtively. In short, you wanted Schumann out of the way, once and for all."

Brahms's expression remained impassive. "You believe I simply stood aside and cleared the way for Robert to murder Adelmann? And my reason for doing so was because I want to step into his shoes...to become the master of the Schumann household? Is that what you think?"

"Yes...and no...and maybe."

"Yes, no, maybe!" Brahms exploded. "What kind of policeman are you! You make accusations one minute, then you pussyfoot the next."

"Let me ask you something, Herr Brahms," I said. "When you sit down at the keyboard to compose, do you always know at the outset where a musical notion will ultimately take you?"

"I am an *artist,* sir," Brahms said, sounding insulted, "not a simple mechanic."

"Nor am *I* a simple mechanic, Brahms. You did *not* carry through with your undertaking to confront Georg Adelmann on Schumann's behalf. Am I correct? Yes or no?"

Brahms roughly seized a chair and sat down. He took what must have been a full minute to study me. Plainly, I was not prepared to put up with evasions. "Well, yes or no?" I insisted.

"Yes."

"Yes, what?"

"Yes, you are correct...I mean about not going to see Adelmann. The reason is simple. You see, Inspector, I have one goal and one goal only in my life—"

"And that is?"

"To be a great composer. Music is my religion. Without music, there is no story to my life. I know this sounds egotistical, but the truth is, I want nothing...absolutely nothing...to stand in the way of my career."

"Well, at least we have the answer as to whether or not you kept your appointment with Georg Adelmann, and why in fact you didn't."

"Correction, sir," Brahms said. "You have only *half* the answer."

"I don't follow you—"

"Look, I *am* infatuated with Clara Schumann...who wouldn't be?...but I am *not* in love with her, I mean so in love that I am willing to give up the thing I value most at the moment...my freedom."

I shook my head. "I'm sorry, Herr Brahms, but I've seen how you look at her."

"And I've seen how *you* look at her, Herr Preiss."

I felt a sudden rush of blood to my cheeks. Brahms gave me a shrewd smile. "Ahah! So now it's out in the open. We're both caught in this woman's net. And how does your cellist friend...I believe her name is Helena Becker, yes?...how does she figure into your domestic life these days?"

"I have no domestic life, Herr Brahms," I said, "not that it's any of your business."

"No thoughts of a sweet little hausfrau setting a

steaming plate of dumplings before you after a hard day, then?"

Brahms seemed to enjoy making fun of me. I'm afraid I allowed my irritation to get the best of me. "You mistake me for some kind of railway station guard," I said. "Fact is, I happen to value my freedom as much as you value yours, Brahms. It's not in my nature to come home every night to a hausfrau, a plate of dumplings and a rocking chair."

"I assume you've had the decency to make your position clear to your young cellist, Inspector."

"As much decency and courage as you display in your relationship with Madam Schumann," I shot back. "You are how old?"

"Twenty-one."

"And she?"

"Thirty-five."

"So every time you and she share some forbidden moments, you make it clear to her that you are prepared to commit yourself fully and honourably?"

"Of course not. The idea is preposterous, Preiss."

"And yet you lead her on, while availing yourself of her fame, her connections, her hospitality, her passion. You're a rather cold-blooded fellow."

"I am from Hamburg," Brahms said. "We North Germans as a rule do not wear our hearts on our sleeves."

"Maybe so," I said, "but surely the odd North German must be capable of feeling pangs of guilt?"

"If there is reason for me to feel guilty," Brahms said, his voice calm and matter-of-fact, "I'll have plenty of time to deal with my conscience later in life. For the time being at least, my art comes first."

"I'm not sure I believe you," I said.

"If you don't believe me, there can be only one explanation."

"And that is?"

"You are so totally enthralled by Clara Schumann that you cannot imagine a man like me, one who is close to her, being less than totally enthralled. But the fact of the matter is that I would no more seek to get rid of Robert Schumann, give up my precious freedom and take up with his wife than *you* would, Inspector Preiss."

Brahms rose from his chair and stood over me with a curious smile. "Come to think of it, it turns out that you and I have much in common, certainly more than either of us may have thought before this little conversation of ours." Suddenly Brahms broke into a laugh. "And come to think of it, perhaps *you* murdered Georg Adelmann hoping it would look like the work of Robert Schumann—"

I jumped up. "This is not a joking matter, Brahms."

Brahms turned sober. "Of course it's not," he said. "I was merely pointing out that I am no more a suspect than you yourself are. You're right, Preiss; I never met with Adelmann, but I never deliberately paved the way for Schumann to murder the man, either." Eyeing me coolly, he said, "Is there anything else I can help you with, Inspector?"

I was tempted to get into the matter of the piano tuning but decided to leave that touchy subject for another time. I wanted Brahms to think he had succeeded in persuading me of his innocence in this whole affair.

And yet, as I left him, I found myself with my feet firmly planted in mid-air as far as this Brahms fellow was concerned. Handsome, brilliant, articulate, witty…he was all these things. But was he also a liar?

Chapter Twenty-Five

It took a half-dozen sharp raps on the front door before the Schumanns' housekeeper opened it and greeted me with an apology. "I'm sorry, Inspector," she said, having trouble looking me in the eye, "but you'll have to come back later. Madam Schumann is extremely busy at the moment."

"That makes two of us," I said, and brushed past the hapless woman. "Kindly tell Madam Schumann I must see her at once."

My voice must have carried, for a moment later Clara Schumann emerged from the parlour. "What now, Inspector?" she demanded, adding quickly, "I have a very full schedule today, as always." She shot a withering look at the housekeeper. "I thought this was made clear to you."

I said, "Madam Schumann, perhaps we might speak in private—"

She gave an impatient sigh. "If we must," she said, and motioned me to follow her. "We'll use Robert's study. He's dashed off somewhere, as he has a habit of doing these days, whenever he's faced with something he finds disagreeable. God knows it doesn't take much to set him off."

I said, "Forgive me, Madam Schumann, aren't you at all concerned about his erratic behaviour?"

"We already have an army of doctors to cope with Robert's problems. You have to admit that their training and experience exceeds your own in such matters."

"But your husband has no confidence in the doctors. Take for instance this fellow Möbius—"

"*Doctor* Möbius."

"Witch doctor is more apt. The man belongs in a jungle."

"You seem so sure of yourself," she said. "Perhaps you've been a patient of his?"

"I've consulted him, though not as a patient."

"Then you're hardly in a position—"

"On the contrary, I am very much in a position. In addition to my own encounter with Möbius, a close friend of mine has had reason to consult him...as a *patient*. The man's a quack, nothing more."

"A friend, you say?" Clara Schumann's tone turned contemptuous. "What kind of 'friend' would confide that he or she was compelled to seek treatment for mental illness? It's hardly fashionable to talk openly of such intimate matters. Believe me, I speak from experience. Do you have any idea how mortifying it is, Inspector, that Robert and I find ourselves baring our private lives before one doctor after another? And how doubly mortifying when we must do so before a policeman? Be honest, Inspector," she said, "and admit the plain truth. You have no business being involved in our troubles. My biggest regret is that I gave in to Robert and wrote the damned note summoning you that night. It was a moment of weakness on my part, for which I will never forgive myself."

"About your friend, Brahms—" I began to ask.

"What about my friend Brahms?"

The expression on her face tightened, and a fierceness in her eyes gave me the feeling that somehow *I* was on trial here. I said, "I have some questions I must ask...about him...about you."

"I will not lie to you, Inspector," she said quietly, "though I assume you anticipate lies in these situations.

It is true that I have some affection for Johannes, a great deal, in fact. What normal woman would not?"

"Enough affection that—to put it plainly—you have given yourself to him?"

"I repeat, Inspector: what normal woman would not?"

"But you are no *normal* woman, surely," I said.

"In some respects," she replied, "I am normal. In other respects...well, see for yourself: daughter of a tyrant, wife of a man who has become as wildly unpredictable as the weather, mother of six demanding children, performing artist, and these days more and more the sole source of income for our family. I carry not one but several albatrosses about my neck."

"The only thing I observe about your neck is a locket, which I recognize."

"Really? How so?"

"I happened to be at Thüringer's Jewellery Shoppe the day Brahms purchased it. There's an inscription on the back—'To dearest Clara, my life's blood'."

"I don't know what you're talking about," Clara Schumann said. "What inscription?"

"Come now, Madam Schumann, you indicated there would be no lies."

She promptly reached behind her neck, unclasped the locket, and handed it to me. "Look for yourself, Inspector."

There was no inscription.

Had my ears and eyes played some kind of trick on me? Or was Johannes Brahms, clever devil, the trickster here?

"You see, Inspector," she said, "once again your policeman's imagination has run away with itself." She extended her hand in an imperious manner. "The locket...please give it back."

I confess to feeling sheepish and more than a little confused as I handed back the locket and watched as Clara replaced it around her neck. "Now, sir, if we are quite finished—" she said.

"No, madam, we are *not* quite finished," I said. From an inner pocket of my coat I withdrew one of my finest Irish linen handkerchiefs and unfolded it carefully to reveal a tuning fork. "Do you recognize this?" I said, watching intently for her reaction.

Without bothering to examine it closely she said, "You're asking me if I recognize a *tuning fork?*" She gave a little laugh. "Seriously, there must be thousands of such tuning forks."

"Quite so," I agreed. "I doubt, however, that all of them have bloodstains on the prongs, as this one does."

Her expression betrayed little interest. "You must forgive me," she said, "if I fail to find the artifacts of crime as fascinating as you do."

"This is no mere 'artifact'," I said. "This happens to be a murder weapon. This innocent-looking instrument, applied with immense force to the skull of Georg Adelmann, took the man's life."

"Then that must have been the last musical note the poor fellow heard, mustn't it?" she said, pretending to be stricken.

"Madam Schumann," I said, "this is not a time for clever jests. I'm certain this tuning fork belongs to your husband. He is known to carry one much of the time. I'm told, for instance, that whenever he's conducting, he and the orchestra's oboeist battle constantly over tuning, and the Maestro insists his own tuning fork must settle the pitch."

"Go on."

"He is also renowned for his seemingly uncontrollable fits of rage."

"I take it, then, that you think you have sufficient grounds to arrest my husband and charge him with the murder of Georg Adelmann?"

Before I could reply, the housekeeper burst into the study. "Madam Schumann, come quickly!"

Suddenly the house was filled with the sounds of a

scuffle. With Clara close behind, I followed the housekeeper into the entrance hall, now the setting for a scene of complete chaos. The front door of the house had been flung open and there, in the centre of the hall, three burly men in fishermen's apparel were struggling to restrain a fourth man who, despite the odds against him, appeared on the verge of overwhelming them and breaking free. A raw wind from the street blew through the open door, scattering that morning's newspaper, a stack of unopened mail, and a thick sheaf of music paper. Puddles were forming under the feet of the four men, and my nose caught the rank odour of river water. That same smell was on their clothing. There were cries, shouts and garbled words that made no sense.

The loudest of these came from the fourth man who was, of course, Robert Schumann.

Ribbons of what looked like seaweed dangled from his matted scalp. His complexion, which in moments of contentment had been a reassuring pink, was now colourless, the skin wrinkled as though it had been marinated in brine. His clothing—he wore only a thin suit but no coat despite this cold, rainy season—was soaked. I had seen drifters in the slums of Düsseldorf who looked less dishevelled.

Both Clara and the housekeeper had rushed to fetch shawls and towels to cover and dry him. His arms flinging about wildly, Schumann rejected everything. The man was clearly beyond being comforted. He cursed everyone, Clara and the housekeeper included, but aimed most of his hostility at two of the three men, accusing them of meddling. "Why didn't you leave me be?" he demanded, shouting at them in a voice growing hoarse, as though his lungs were filled with water and silt.

Then, in a sudden change of mood which I had come to know as typical of the man, Schumann sank into total surrender. He became lifeless, his face a blank canvas devoid of any visible emotion. Clara and the housekeeper could now resume with some success their attempts to warm him, for he had begun to shake and shiver, yet somehow he did not seem to be at all aware of his condition. It was as though his mind and body were disconnected.

I turned to one of the fishermen, who had now released his grip on Schumann. Without waiting for my question, without knowing who I was, he said, "We saw him...the other two were in their boat...I was on shore...and we saw him...well, actually, I saw him first. You know the toll bridge near here? Well, he started to cross, got part way, he was running at that point...then he stopped for maybe a second or two...and then, I swear to God, he just threw himself into the water. The others, the ones in the boat, went after him. God knows how they managed to pull him out; he was giving them such a hard time. They didn't know who he was, but I work at the toll bridge, and I was the one who recognized him, because he often takes walks along the riverbank."

Subdued and incredibly calm now, Schumann allowed himself to be led upstairs, saying only that he needed to sleep, repeating it over and over, paying no attention to Clara, who held his hand and urged him to hush, assuring him that Dr. Heller would come soon.

I introduced myself to the fishermen, praised them for their efforts, and made a note of their names and addresses explaining that I would be calling upon them to furnish their accounts of the incident in writing for a police record.

The wind had grown cruel as I started back to the Constabulary; however, I denied myself the luxury of a cab, feeling instead an urgent need of a long solitary walk and time to stitch into some logical pattern the events of the past hour. Schumann, the intended victim, had himself become a murderer. Of this I was now certain beyond a split second of doubt. My duty, therefore, was clear; it was not to be misted over by counterfeit sentimentality and misplaced sympathies.

Within sight of my headquarters, I touched the inside of my coat to make certain that the fateful tuning fork was securely stored. And over and over again, I repeated, as though bracing myself, "My duty is clear."

Chapter Twenty-Six

The following day, I waited until mid-morning before presenting myself once again at the house on Bilkerstrasse, hoping that by the time I arrived, the bustling Schumann household would be sufficiently settled to allow me an uninterrupted interval with Madam Schumann. There were too many hanging threads now—especially after the events of the previous day—for me to put off my investigation even for twenty-four hours. The housekeeper, admitting me this time after only a single knock on the door, shook her head in a sign of utter hopelessness. "I do not know what they are going to do with him," she lamented, her eyes travelling up the staircase. "Quiet one minute, terrible the next, and it goes on and on like this." She shook her head again.

"Who are 'they'?" I said.

"The doctors. Four of them now."

"Hellman, and who else?"

"Dr. Möbius. Dr. Gruhle. They've been here before. Then there's a new doctor, Dr. Hasenclever——"

Ah yes, Richard Hasenclever. I knew of this fellow. Physician, would-be poet, would-be conductor, dilettante. A man who basked at every opportunity in the Schumanns' fame, he boasted that he had collaborated with Schumann on the composition of a choral ballade. He was also a prominent member of the Music Society of Düsseldorf. But when it came to the practice of medicine, the man had as much claim to expertise as my chimneysweep.

"You said there are four doctors up there," I said to the housekeeper.

"Yes. The fourth is also someone I haven't seen here before. A Dr. Böger."

I was familiar with this physician as well. His qualifications consisted solely of experience in military hospitals, where he purported to treat soldiers suffering from an affliction which had only recently come to be known as shell-shock (and which the Commissioner, who had once been a battlefront officer, preferred to call cowardice). I imagined that Dr. Böger's advice to Schumann would be along the lines of "You must pull yourself together," or something equally simplistic.

"I suppose you wish to see Madam Schumann?" the housekeeper said.

"It may be a bad time to tear her away," I said, expecting that, along with the four doctors upstairs in their bedroom, she was attempting to calm her husband and somehow stabilize him.

"I will let her know you are here," the housekeeper said. To my surprise, instead of climbing the stairs, the woman stepped across the hall and knocked gently on the door of Dr. Schumann's study. I heard Clara Schumann instruct her to usher me in.

I found her standing before a well-laid fire. A heavy shawl was draped about her shoulders, its dark strands defining the mood in the room. Her expression was cautious and hinted of resistance. This would not be an easy conversation.

"Madam Schumann," I said, "I'll try not to detain you too long. I'm sure you feel a need to be with Dr. Schumann."

"If I thought I could be of use, I would be there instead of here," she replied in a voice that conveyed almost palpable defeat.

"I'm sorry to bother you at a time like this," I said, "but the law requires that attempted suicides be reported and investigated where there are questionable circumstances, as there are here. Yesterday you mentioned fleetingly that you and your husband had had a disagreement over some issue, and that he chose to dash off rather than come to grips with it. But there must be more to this...certain details you left out. After all, domestic spats don't ordinarily drive a man to attempt to drown himself."

"Robert has been drowning himself for a long time," Clara said. "Drowning himself in rages that have no sense, not to me, not to anyone."

"We need to be specific here. What drove your husband to attempt suicide?"

"It is a private matter. It is none of your business, really."

"I take it you would prefer, then, to submit to questioning by a panel of magistrates," I said. "I *can* have you summoned before them. Believe me, their patience does not stretch nearly as far as mine. Please understand, madam, I am not insensitive to what you are suffering, but I have a duty to perform. You *could* make it easier for both of us."

She stood motionless, studying me as though attempting to satisfy herself that I truly meant what I said.

"Inspector Preiss," she said at last, "kindly be seated. You say you need details? Very well, then. I have something to tell you, and I warn you: I am going to tell it to you fully, unconditionally, and without shame."

She offered me a chair, then looked away for several moments as though composing herself. Finally she spoke, her voice steady, her expression unflinching. "The disagreement Robert and I had...it was more a quarrel, an almost violent quarrel at that...really a continuation of what took place between him and me on the night you were first summoned to this house..."

They had gone to bed later than usual, Clara Schumann said, both of them exhausted.

It had been a typical day for her: children to get off to school; the day's meals to plan and a shopping list to compile for the housekeeper's trip to the grocer's; four hours of rigorous practice (two before lunch, two after lunch, in preparation for a cycle of nine Beethoven sonatas to be performed over three nights in Vienna the following month). She'd had household bills to examine and pay, a letter to write to her father, dutifully wishing him a happy birthday and adding Robert's best wishes (a lie if ever there was one). Before the children's bedtime, there were little tales of their joys and woes to listen to, bed-time stories to tell, and last-minute promises to make that there were absolutely *no* ghosts lurking in the seldom-visited attic directly above their heads.

Her husband, too, had reason to plead exhaustion. That morning he'd begun in a state of high expectation a new suite of piano pieces to which he'd given the title *Papillons.* Clara could hear him happily humming one of the sprightly opening themes as he came into the kitchen for the midday meal. So excited was he then that he passed up a plate of food set for him, contenting himself with nothing more than a quick cup of coffee and a freshly baked bun before closeting himself again in his study.

But by mid-afternoon, Clara could hear groans and curses, the latter growing louder and more vehement, emanating from her husband's workplace. The piece was not going well, that much was clear to her. What she did not know at the time was that the "A" sound had begun to re-appear, flowing in, receding, flowing in again, receding again, incessant, like waves along a shoreline, distracting Schumann to the point where he could no longer focus on the melody at hand.

Perhaps a cup of tea would help, she thought, but when she tapped gently on the study door, a tray laden with tea and another bun in hand, there was no response. She opened the door to discover he'd gone.

He did not return until after the children were asleep. His clothes reeked of cigar smoke. His breath reeked of ale. He'd had nothing to eat for hours but refused the supper that had been kept warm for him. The day, which had begun full of the brightness of creation, was coming to an end full of shadows. As Clara put it, her husband did not so much undress as *abandon* his clothes on their bedroom floor, after which he collapsed into the bed. She heard him mumble something about his mind and body being sapped of their strength as never before, but this was nothing new to her ears. Whenever he smoked and drank too much, it was always the same complaint.

"And then," she continued, "after I had slipped beneath the bedcovers...by now I was *aching* for some rest...I hadn't bothered to say goodnight because I believed him to be fast asleep...suddenly he came to life and was all over me. When Robert is aroused, there is no resisting him, so despite my extreme fatigue—"

"Madam Schumann," I said, beginning to feel uncomfortable in the extreme, "there's no need to go on. I'm a policeman, not a priest, and this is not the sort of confession—"

"Oh no no, Inspector," she said, her voice loud and overriding mine, "you cannot back away now. It's too late. You said you needed details...specific details—"

"Really, I've heard more than enough—"

"But we've barely scratched the surface," she protested, "and I'm sure you will find the rest of what I have to tell you not only enlightening but entertaining. I mean, let's be frank: a little prurience is to a detective what honey is to a bee. Is that not so, Inspector?"

I shifted to the edge of my chair. "I don't find your sarcasm entertaining," I said, "and I prefer to leave the balance of this interview for another time. Now, if you will excuse me—"

"Wait!" She had moved forward, standing so close to

me now that I was unable to leave my chair. Then, in a more moderate tone, she said, "Please, there is something I want to show you...something you must see with your own eyes."

I sat back and watched her throw open the bottom drawer of her husband's desk and remove a thick book, its black leather cover bearing in gold letters "Day Book, 1854."

Handing me the book she said, "Here, look for yourself. Go on, open it."

"But it's Maestro Schumann's private diary—"

"Since when would that stop a policeman? I thought you have your precious duty to perform. Let me help you, Preiss."

She snatched the book from my hands, flipped through its pages, her fingers turning them furiously, and settled on the first page of the current month.

"Before you set your eyes on this, let me fill in the scene a bit more. Where was I? Ah yes...Robert is all over me, and the endeavour is proving to be entirely unsatisfactory for both of us. And I feel as though my life's blood is draining out of me, but he will not stop. I say to him, 'Robert, this is the seventh time this month and again—*nothing*—is happening.' He looks at me, frowning, and begins to protest. 'It is *not* the seventh, Clara,' he says. 'Oh, but it is,' I tell him. 'Don't pretend to be surprised,' I say to him when he gives me a look of disbelief.

"'How can you possibly be so sure?' he wants to know. And then, despite the partial fog he's in, it dawns on him: almost screaming, he says 'Clara, you've been snooping in my Day Book...my personal diary!' He jerks himself free of me, and next thing he's standing in his rumpled nightshirt at the foot of the bed. Still screaming, and stamping his foot like a child, he accuses me of violating his privacy. I point out that after ten years of marriage and as many pregnancies, his private thoughts are as much *my* property as *his*.

"I admit to him...for the first time, mind you, Inspector...that I now know what all those 'Fs' stand for in the margins of his Day Book. He plays dumb, says he doesn't know what on earth I'm referring to—"

"What *are* you referring to, Madam Schumann?" I asked, though I put the question half-heartedly. Truth is, I wanted at that moment nothing more than that she should call a halt to this narrative. But that was not be.

She thrust the Day Book back at me and pointed to the margin of the page that lay open before me.

"I have no stomach for this—"

"*Look!*" She jabbed at the margin with her index finger. "Don't turn away, Preiss. You see what looks like an F, although it could also pass for a sixteenth note."

I nodded.

"And what's written in tiny print beneath it?"

"Unfinished."

"Yes. Unfinished. I said 'Robert, what does it mean?' He said it was to remind himself to write an unfinished symphony. Franz Schubert, he said, had written an unfinished symphony, which achieved enormous popularity and he—Robert—proposed therefore to do the same. This was my husband's idea of a joke, you see."

She turned several more pages and pointed to a similar marginal F, under which "one minute" appeared in similar tiny print.

"Robert insisted it was a reminder that he should get around to composing a Minute Waltz similar to Chopin's, again because the public loved it, and it could be very lucrative. That, too, was Robert's idea of a joke."

Several pages further on, two more Fs showed up. Beneath one Schumann had penned "Disappointment" in such small script that my nose almost touched the margin as I struggled to decipher what he'd written there. Two more Fs were brought to my attention, one of which had a thick black frame around it, like a miniature death notice.

"Robert began then to offer excuses: it was the onslaught of winter, a season he hates. It was the imminent visit of my father, a person he despises. It was the prospect of another tour, an aspect of our lives he abhors because he finds travel too much to deal with. And then, without warning, he let out a frightening wail. It was this 'A' sound again, he cried. I told him I thought it was preposterous, that he was allowing this hallucination of his to get the better of him, that it was ruining not only his life but mine as well. And the moment I started to mention his doctors' advice, he flew into an uncontrollable rage.

"Once again, he insisted that he was the victim of a criminal conspiracy...that he was being driven mad. The only way I could placate him was to agree—much against my better judgment—to send for you, Inspector Preiss."

"And the next morning, what happened?"

"I suppose it was a mistake on my part, for when I took him to task for what I considered his ridiculous conduct the previous evening, once again he flew into a rage and...well, we know the rest of what happened, don't we."

Giving me that same unflinching look, she said, "Brahms alone is what sustains me. So now that I have finished saying what I have to say, now that I have furnished you with every excruciating detail, I suppose it is up to you to do whatever the law bids you to do, is it not?"

Chapter Twenty-Seven

I arrived back at my office at the Constabulary to find a report routinely filed by my staff at noon daily summarizing the crimes uncovered during the past twenty-four hours and the arrests made. I scrutinized the report, noting the usual tiresome offenses: petty thefts, drunken assaults, indecent exposures in public places. Nothing here that would excite a senior inspector. I was about to toss the report aside when, to my astonishment, one name leapt from the bottom line of the page: *Walter Thüringer*. Opposite Thüringer's name appeared the offense with which he was charged: "Receiving stolen goods, to wit, one pair of diamond earrings, the property of one Countess Maria de Cecco of the City of Rome, Italy." The arresting officer was Constable Fritz Hesse, a recent addition to my staff, who had not as yet been tested in anything serious, such as homicide or rape, but who possessed a bloodhound's sense of smell whenever someone's jewellery went missing. *Bad luck, Thüringer,* I thought. Then, in a sudden fit of compassion, I decided to pay him a visit. I pictured him cringing in horror in one of the tomb-like holding cells in the basement of the Constabulary, sharing his confinement with a half-dozen of Düsseldorf's most unappealing citizens.

Which is exactly how I found the poor devil.

"Preiss," he cried out, "thank God you're here!"

"I'm known as *Inspector* Preiss in these quarters, Thüringer," I said, not wanting his cellmates to think he and I were bosom friends, but feeling a bit mean-spirited at the same time. I motioned to a nearby guard to approach. "Release this man into my custody," I said, "for questioning in the interrogation room."

I waited for a moment or two while Thüringer composed himself in the small private room just down the corridor from the cells, then fixed him with the most disapproving look I was capable of.

"I know what you're thinking," he said, "but I swear by everything I hold sacred—"

"Oh please, Thüringer," I cut in, "save the 'everything I hold sacred' speech. You're going to need it later. I've read Constable Hesse's report. The diamond earrings he spotted in your shop perfectly fit the description of the ones stolen from the hotel suite occupied by that Countess and her husband, the couple from Rome. My God, man, have you no shame? Our fair city is desperate to maintain its reputation as a cultural mecca for tourists…the birthplace of Heinrich Heine, no less!…and here you and your myriad accomplices turn Düsseldorf into the kind of slum one would expect to find in…in—"

"In Rome?" Thüringer ventured, eager to assist me.

"This is not an occasion for humorous remarks, thank you very much."

"I was only trying to be helpful," he said. "I've always tried to be helpful, as you well know, Inspector," he added, giving me a wise smile.

"Meaning what?"

Thüringer looked over his shoulder. We were the only people in the room, and the door was firmly closed. Nothing short of cannon fire could have been heard through the thick stone walls. Still, the old man wanted to assure himself that there were no eavesdroppers. He leaned forward over the small wooden table that separated us, his bony white jeweller's fingers resting flat on the tabletop. "You know, Inspector, how you've come to count on me to inform you of anything suspicious that comes to my attention—"

"Excluding anything suspicious that you yourself are involved in, of course," I put in.

"Point taken," Thüringer said. Undaunted, he went on. "I have some information that might be valuable to you, very valuable indeed, my friend."

"Such as?"

"Well now, it depends." Again he gave me that wise smile.

"Depends on what, Thüringer? I have only so much patience, and absolutely none when it comes to playing games with people in your current position."

He sat back and crossed his arms across his chest, looking remarkably self-confident for a man who might well be facing a prison sentence (I was certain Hesse's report was infallible). "First, Inspector, we must make a—what shall I call it?—a bargain, yes, that's a good way to put it, a bargain. The earrings are returned to the woman from Rome, let us say they were waylaid through an innocent mistake or something of that sort, I apologize to the lady profusely and offer her some nice bauble for her trouble. The charge against me is withdrawn. And that's the end of the matter."

"And what else do you do for *your* part, Thüringer?"

The man paused, peering at me over his pince-nez, no doubt wondering with good reason whether or not he could trust me.

I repeated, "What else do you do for your part? Understand something: it's not often that I take the trouble to visit an accused felon as I'm doing now. Consider this a privilege I'm extending to you, but time is quickly running out." Again the man glanced needlessly over his shoulder, then leaned forward over the table as before. "Does the name Wilhelm Hupfer mean anything to you?"

I affected a blank expression. "Wilhelm Hupfer? What about him?"

"It has come to my attention—never mind how—that he's a piano tuner, of all things. How much do you think a piano tuner, even the most expert piano tuner, earns?"

"I couldn't begin to know."

"A man like Hupfer is lucky if his income is enough to supply him with three meals a day and a roof over his head. Piano tuners, even the best of them, are perhaps a step or two above shoemakers. How does a man like Wilhelm Hupfer suddenly manage to become one of my steadiest customers? I'd never heard of the man until a couple of months ago, not so much as a syllable of gossip or anything about him. And suddenly he's making weekly visits to my shop. One day he's purchasing a diamond stickpin. I ask myself, would a fellow like him even own a cravat? Next, it's gold cufflinks engraved with his initials. Then a French eighteen-carat gold pocket watch with Swiss movement. A few days, perhaps a week later, he's back. This time it's a ring, again eighteen carats, the setting for a magnificent sapphire. And that's not all, my dear Inspector. Unlike many of my customers, even the wealthy ones who often pay by giving me a note, Hupfer pays in cash! Yes, nice crisp genuine German banknotes!"

"Does it occur to you that Hupfer may be lucky at cards? Or perhaps a rich uncle has died and left him a fortune? Some Germans...you'd be surprised at the number...have recently made piles of money on the stock markets, not only here but abroad. One must always give a man the benefit of the doubt in such matters, Thüringer."

A half-smile appeared on the old jeweller's face. "I've known you too long, Preiss," he said, "and not once have I ever known you to give a suspect the benefit of the doubt."

"And who's to say this man Hupfer is a suspect?"

"Come, come, Inspector," Thüringer said, "I'm an old scoundrel, and you cannot fool an old scoundrel. The man *must* be a thief, an embezzler, maybe a blackmailer.

These nostrils of mine are never wrong. So, Preiss, do we have a deal? I cannot bear to stay another minute in that hell-hole down the hall. Get me out of here, and I will furnish you with enough solid evidence to back up all the suspicion I've just planted. Look at it this way: I'm just a little fish leading you straight to a possible shark."

We rose together, and Thüringer extended his right hand. "Deal?" he said.

Chapter Twenty-Eight

I proceeded without delay to fulfill my end of the pact I'd made with the devil, but it was not easy. To begin with, I had to persuade my zealous subordinate Constable Hesse that the charge against the old jeweller should be dropped. This I accomplished in two ways: first, I pointed out that since the robber himself (or herself, for that matter) had not yet been caught, there was no positive proof that Countess de Cecco's diamond earrings were stolen, nor could it be proved that Thüringer *knew* he was receiving stolen goods; therefore prosecution against Thüringer was not only premature but very likely to fail. Failure would most certainly reflect poorly on the police force in general, and on Hesse in particular, which would be a pity given his splendid record to date. Secondly, I informed Hesse that I was giving serious thought now to transferring him into the branch which dealt with more serious crimes—murders, rapes, kidnappings—which, I felt certain, would challenge his capabilities far more than the crimes he had been dealing with up to this point. Young Hesse virtually sailed out of my office, thrilled at the prospect of his coming promotion and vowing to retrieve the earrings promptly upon Thüringer's release from custody, following which he, Hesse, would personally see to it that they were returned to the Countess, together with whatever suitable "gift" the jeweller threw in to keep the Italian noblewoman happy.

That was not the only challenge I had to deal with. It was customary for copies of my staff's daily reports to me to be furnished as well to the Commissioner. Much of the time my immediate superior, being consumed these days with thoughts about his forthcoming retirement and pension, gave such documents no more than a cursory glance, hastily scrawled his initials to acknowledge he'd seen them, and back they came to my office for filing. But luck was not with me this day. Just as the name Walter Thüringer had leapt from the page when I first spotted it, so did it leap from the page when Schilling caught sight of it.

"Preiss, how the devil are we expected to uphold the reputation of our city, and indeed the entire nation, when innocent tourists are callously relieved of their precious possessions? And not ordinary tourists; no, by heaven, a count and countess, no less, according to the report." The Commissioner peered at me through his spectacles as though *I* were the culprit who had received the stolen earrings.

I said, "Permit me to point out that these tourists come from a part of the world where people are used to this sort of thing."

"I fully agree," said the Commissioner, "but damn it, man, two wrongs don't make a right. This fellow Thüringer, haven't I heard you recommend his jewellery shop? If memory serves, on more than one occasion you've mentioned him favourably. Don't tell me you're consorting with a man who habitually deals in stolen goods!"

"Sir, I would not say I've been *consorting* with Walter Thüringer," I replied, "but I have to explain that he and I have a rather unique relationship. The fact is, being in the line of business he's in, the man has a particularly keen sense of smell whenever there's even the slightest whiff of skullduggery in the air. He has been instrumental in my being able to apprehend a veritable army of thieves over the years."

"That's all well and good," the Commissioner huffed, "but if the man himself is a criminal, he must face justice, and that's all there is to it. I trust you'll see to it."

I paused, and the Commissioner frowned, sensing my hesitation. "Well, Preiss, that's all. You may go, unless there's something further."

I cleared my throat, then said quietly, "I've ordered Thüringer to be released, sir. In fact, my order has already been carried out."

"Are you mad, Preiss? Reverse your order, then, and see to it that this man is put back behind bars where he obviously belongs."

Retaining my composure, I said, "May I respectfully remind the Commissioner that, as senior inspector, I have complete discretion in such matters and am entitled, indeed authorized, to retain or release such persons from police custody if I deem it appropriate or expedient in the cause of justice...as I do, incidentally, in this instance."

"And may I remind *you*, that *I* am accountable to the mayor of this city who, I need hardly repeat, is anxious that Düsseldorf be regarded as one of the cultural capitals of Europe, and not a German version of Sodom and Gomorrah. I have already had hell to pay because our esteemed mayor has taken a personal interest in the murder of Georg Adelmann and cannot understand why the killer is still at large." Commissioner Schilling took a moment to regard me with a look steeped more in sorrow than in anger. "You know, Preiss," he said, sadly shaking his head, "I had high hopes for you. But you are fast becoming a thorn in my side. If you wish to redeem yourself, give me your assurance...no, better still, your *word*...that this business about that fellow Schumann is over and done with once and for all, and that I can expect your return forthwith to the *serious* business at hand."

Well, that wasn't difficult to give. After all, by my own definition, the "serious" business at hand came down to a single name.

*   *   *

Hupfer...*Hupfer...*

In the privacy of my room, I repeated aloud the name of Wilhelm Hupfer over and over again while turning the pages of my memory in an attempt to recall precisely the places and times I'd seen the man. I began to make notes:

Hupfer shows up at the house of Dr. Möbius, making his way in just as I am making my way out.

Hupfer shows up again at the Schumanns' while they are away for a few days of rest at Bad Grünwald and Professor Wieck just happens to be visiting Düsseldorf, and the two of them, Hupfer and Wieck, obviously cannot wait to be rid of me.

When I question Hupfer in his workshop about the possibility of untuning a piano, he is less than forthcoming, and I'm left with the distinct impression that he is lying.

Then there were these nagging questions:

Why does Hupfer spend two hours on the day of the Schumanns' musicale tuning the older of their grand pianos, but that evening only the newer of the two instruments, the Klems, is played?

Why does he later gossip to Liszt about what he overheard that day at the Schumann house (the bit of conversation between Clara and Brahms), and why does he mention to Liszt that Brahms apparently regulated the Klems himself using his own set of tools prior to the musicale?

My note-taking was interrupted by a soft knock on my door. "Inspector Preiss?" I recognized the voice of Henckel, the concierge. "A message for you, sir."

Henckel apologized (as he invariably did out of habit) for disturbing me, then handed me a sealed envelope bearing my name and address written in what can only be described as a ferocious scrawl. "Who delivered this?" I asked.

Henckel replied, "A gentleman. Same gentleman that visited you a few nights back. Came by carriage. Simply took off without a word. I *am* sorry, sir." Knowing that for some peculiar reason Henckel enjoyed feeling guilty (even when he had no reason to), I did the generous thing; I withheld forgiveness.

The note turned out to have been penned in the same wild handwriting.

"Preiss, I must see you. Please pardon my past rudeness and offenses. I desperately need your help!"

It was signed simply *"R.S."*

Chapter Twenty-Nine

Impeccably groomed and wearing a simple but fashionable frock, Clara Schumann offered me a civil "Good day" when I arrived at No. 15 Bilkerstrasse the next morning. At her side—not surprisingly—stood Johannes Brahms, who acknowledged me with a curt nod, as though I were on a mission to deliver bread from the local bakery.

"My husband awaits you in the study," Clara said.

I said, somewhat astonished, "You're aware, then, that he sent for me?"

"Of course," she replied. "Did you suppose I would interfere with his wishes at a time like this?"

"A time like this? I don't understand, Madam Schumann, what that means."

My tone must have been a bit too officious, for Brahms immediately stepped forward. "Clara...that is, Madam Schumann...is suffering greatly under the stress of the Maestro's illness. At least a *little* sensitivity on your part would be in order, don't you agree? In fact, Inspector, your valuable time might be better spent if you went directly to the study where Dr. Schumann awaits."

There was something in the air at that moment, something in the manner of Clara Schumann and young Brahms, that smacked of an arrangement on the brink of being carried out, something now unstoppable.

Without bothering to knock, I opened the study door and entered to find Schumann standing before a fire. He was fully clothed, and a thick woollen cape was

thrown over his shoulders. Close by stood a pair of brawny
male attendants, each wearing an overcoat, despite the
heat in the room. Schumann, his voice gravelly, said to the
two men, "Leave us, please."

One of the men spoke up. "Sir, we have strict orders
to—"

"To hell with your orders!" Schumann shouted. "I
said leave us, or so help me God—"

The men exchanged quick glances. The taller of the
two gave me a pleading look. "We have a carriage due
here momentarily, Inspector, and a long journey ahead
of us," he explained.

"Go!" Schumann said, almost screaming.

Judging by the way they shrugged, the two attendants
were accustomed to such outbursts. Without another
word, they retired from the room, Schumann eyeing
them suspiciously. "And close the door behind you," he
commanded. Satisfied that we could not be overheard,
he said, "They're like parasites. They cling to me day and
night. Imagine, Preiss: I, Robert Schumann, am granted
privacy only when I use my toilet, and even then I'm not
certain! Have you any idea what it's like to be spied on
around the clock? It's those bastard doctors. Even Clara
and Johannes have been forced to submit to the
collective will of these medical monsters."

"But Dr. Schumann, perhaps they're only seeking
to…I mean, given what occurred."

"Do not interrupt me, Preiss. Let me finish what I
have to say. *Someone* must listen to me. There's not much
time, don't you see? They're taking me away. Today. Any
moment now."

"Away? Where to?"

"They call it a hospital, in a town called Endenich,
somewhere near Bonn, run by another one of these
medicine men, a Dr. Richarz. Never heard of him. But I
can guarantee you, it's not a hospital; it's an asylum for

the insane. Please, Preiss, I beg you, stop them. Look at me: I am *not* insane. You know that, don't you? All I want now is to do my work, to be in my home. Don't let them do this to me. You, of all people, have the power to stop them. If they take me away, I know I will never see Düsseldorf again. I will live in a cage, and die in a cage. Help me, Preiss."

Tears had formed in Schumann's eyes. His lips quivered. His sallow cheeks became wet with his tears. He reached out to me with his right hand, silently urging me to take it, to be his saviour.

I stood staring at his hand as though it were somehow detached from the person to whom it belonged, and I could not for the life of me reach out and take it. And in that instant, what went through my mind was that, for whatever number of years I lived, I would neither forget my refusal, nor forgive myself. Instead of saying to Schumann what he so desperately wanted to hear, I said, "Are you aware, sir, that Georg Adelmann has been murdered?"

I was expecting a show of astonishment followed perhaps by a passionate declaration of innocence. After all, was this not how a typical suspect would react? I was not prepared, then, for Schumann's unhesitating response.

"Good riddance!" Schumann exulted. "Murdered, eh? Well, a fitting end for a blackmailer and a thief, I say. Some may mourn his death, but not I, not for a second."

"Adelmann was about to publish a biography of you, Maestro. Surely you have *some* regret?"

"Lies! That's what he was about to publish. Now he'll publish in hell!" Calming down, Schumann went on: "Anyway, Preiss, don't waste time over Georg Adelmann, because once a man's dead, he's dead, and that's all there is to it. I, on the other hand, am very much alive, and I am being killed steadily and mercilessly. And the pity is, I still have much to give. Believe me, music comes closest to the unknowable, and I, Robert Schumann, have seen the unknowable, heard it, even touched it in my way! So you see, don't you? I am *not* insane. Promise me you will put a stop to this exile. And this time you must keep your promise, not break it as you did before, I mean about retrieving my Beethoven manuscript."

What was the point of disputing Schumann's accusation? No excuse I could offer would convince him that I had not been derelict. "I will see what I can do, Maestro," I said.

The study door opened and Clara Schumann entered. "Robert dear," she said quietly, "the carriage is here."

Meekly, almost mechanically, a figure without strength, without hope, Robert Schumann, his hand in hers, allowed his wife to lead him to the open door of the house, where the two attendants waited. He said to Clara, "My pens and manuscript paper...you packed them?"

"Of course, Robert," she replied. "And your notebooks too, the ones with your most recent sketches."

"Clara, promise me you'll see to it that the oldest children keep up their music lessons, especially Marie, bless her. And make sure the jar on the writing desk is well-stocked with pfennigs. They must have their rewards, you know! By the way, Clara, when Marie has mastered those finger exercises Carl Czerny sent for the children, I want her to have a whole thaler to spend as she pleases."

Schumann turned to Brahms. "I mean to compose another symphony, Johannes," he said, smiling at his protégé. "It will be my fifth. I've already sketched the opening movement. It will be like Beethoven's fifth, only better, more melodious. One of these days, my dear Johannes, you must try your hand at composing a symphony."

Brahms stepped forward and gave Schumann a brisk embrace. "Perhaps I'll get around to it by the time I'm forty," he said.

"Forty! My God, Johannes, I'll be serenading Satan by then!" Schumann said, giving Brahms a fond poke on his arm. Then, turning his back on Clara and Brahms, with an attendant at each side, Schumann started out of the house.

Suddenly, he came to a halt and turned about. "I've forgotten something," he called to Clara.

"Forgotten what, Robert?"

"I must get it," he said, elbowing away the attendants and moving back into the house with resolute steps. I watched him enter the study, pull open the centre tray of his worktable, and remove an object which I could not recognize until he held it aloft for all to see with an air of triumph.

"My trusted tuning fork!" he said, smiling at it as though the thing was human.

Instantly, Clara Schumann's eyes and mine met, though not a word was said.

A minute later Schumann and his attendants were tucked into the carriage, ready for the six-hour journey to Bonn. Another minute, and they were out of sight.

Chapter Thirty

W hat *would* you do without me, Hermann?" Helena Becker was saying in that teasing manner of hers as she ushered me into the sitting room of her small but comfortable apartment. "Your message sounded as though you couldn't wait to see me." She took a moment to inspect me with a critical eye. "I note that as usual you come empty-handed. Flowers would have been nice." She'd forgotten about the gift of pearl earrings, but it would have been bad taste on my part to remind her.

"Helena, what *would* I do without you?" I said. "You have a way of making me feel humble, and God knows, a man needs a healthy dose of humility now and then."

Offering me a chair, Helena said, "Now that you've gotten that lie off your chest, what really brings you here?"

"This brings me here," I replied. I took a large white handkerchief from my coat and unfolded it to reveal a tuning fork, which I laid carefully on a table between us.

"A present for me?" Helena said.

"Hardly," I said.

"Just as well," Helena said. "It's rather badly stained, isn't it?"

"Those are bloodstains."

Helena bent to take a closer look. "How fascinating," she said without a trace of enthusiasm.

I said, "What you're looking at happens to be a murder weapon."

Helena's eyes glazed over. "Tea or coffee?"

"I've no time for either. What I need are your ears and your cello."

"You *do* sound desperate, Hermann."

"I'm under extraordinary pressure, Helena. The Commissioner, you understand."

She laughed. "That toothless old dinosaur?"

"That toothless old dinosaur would love nothing more than a good excuse to sack me. He says I'm a thorn in his side. Go fetch your cello, because we have an urgent experiment to perform, you and I."

I watched her remove the honey-coloured cello from its case, seat herself, and set the instrument between her legs, her bow at the ready.

"Now what?" she said.

"Let me hear your 'A'," I said.

Helena lifted her bow from the strings. "Please, Hermann," she protested, "not this Schumann thing again!"

She shrugged as if to say I, not Schumann, was the person going mad, then brought the bow across the thinnest of the four strings. "I think I'm a bit flat," she said, frowning, and began to twist the tuning peg for that string with her left hand while continuing to bow with her right, the resulting changes of pitch sounding like the wailing of an alley cat. At last she was satisfied that the 'A' was where it ought to be.

"Now listen carefully, please," I said. I took the tuning fork and struck it hard against the marble mantle of her fireplace. "Well?" I said.

Helena's frown returned. "Sounds sharp to me. Not by much, but just enough to be annoying. Are you sure it's a tuning fork and not the kind you eat with?"

"Listen again, just once more." I struck the fork even harder.

"You can strike it from now till doomsday," she said, "but that's not a true 'A'. Granted, it's off by just a touch, but sharp is sharp."

"How good is your memory?" I said. "Think back to the musicale at the Schumanns'. Would you say it's the same 'A'?"

"Let me tune my string to it," Helena said. "Strike it again."

Again Helena gave me the same response. "It's very much like the 'A' we tuned to at the Schumanns' that night, but what's it got to do with a murder?"

I tucked the tuning fork back into the handkerchief. "I'm sorry, my dear," I said, putting on the most officious airs I could manage, "I cannot possibly divulge the facts and circumstances of a case while it is under investigation. Anyway, I thought you found all this rather tedious."

"What has the tuning fork got to do with a murder? Stop torturing me, Hermann!"

"Very well," I said, "but not a word of this gets out until I say so. I found this tuning fork under Georg Adelmann's body. I had reason to believe it belonged to Schumann and that he used it as a kind of weapon to attack Adelmann in a fit of rage."

"But what would drive a man like Schumann to do such a terrible thing?"

"He learned that a monograph Adelmann was writing about his life and career contained references—rather specific references, in fact—to some early homosexual activities Schumann engaged in. To make matters worse, Schumann was convinced Adelmann stole the Beethoven manuscript from Schumann's home, possibly on the night of the musicale."

"You say, Hermann, that you *had* reason to believe Schumann was the assailant—"

"Yes, but now I believe Robert Schumann did *not* kill Adelmann."

"Then who did?"

I picked up the bloodstained tuning fork. "The owner of this," I replied.

"And that would be?"

"Wilhelm Hupfer."

Chapter Thirty-One

I couldn't confront Hupfer solely on the strength of the tuning fork revelation. That single item of evidence, for the moment at least, had to be regarded as purely circumstantial, and certainly not enough to induce a voluntary confession of guilt. I had to satisfy myself as to Hupfer's motive for slaying Georg Adelmann. I have to admit that I owed a debt of gratitude to—of all people—Walter Thüringer. It was he who had given me the key: Hupfer's craving for money. The man must have been receiving, one way or another, substantial sums of cash. But from whom? And why?

I took a fresh page from my notebook and wrote down the following list of names in alphabetical order:

Adelmann
Brahms
Liszt
Möbius
Schumann (Clara)
Wieck

I propped up the notebook against a pile of books atop my desk, sat back, and stared at the list. Had I omitted anyone? Any artist of Robert Schumann's stature was bound to have numerous rivals, enemies, critics; yet it seemed to me that only the persons whose names I had set down on paper would have had sufficient connection to be taken seriously. One by one, I began to consider the suspects.

Adelmann? Would he have bribed Hupfer to so undermine Schumann that the poor fellow would eventually be driven to attempt suicide? Adelmann was about to publish what would doubtless quickly become a highly-readable (not to mention profitable) biography of Schumann. Surely, it would behoove him to do everything to prolong, not curtail, the composer's life. I dipped my pen into its inkwell and ran a thick line through the first name on the list.

Brahms? No. Too young, and therefore too impecunious to be in a position to lavish large sums on Hupfer. Besides, perhaps he *was* being truthful with me about the limits of his feelings for Clara Schumann, after all. Brahms's name was therefore struck from the list.

Franz Liszt? A bitter enemy for artistic reasons, yes. But much too full of his own eminence to risk being caught up in shabby criminal activity. Though the great man was no stranger to the *civil* courts—breach-of-promise suits and claims for unpaid bills had turned him into a professional defendant—the thought that Liszt would engage in any conduct that would render him liable to a term in prison was simply too preposterous. His name, too, was ruled through.

Dr. Paul Möbius? I strongly suspected that someday, probably after his time and my own, the world of medicine would come to regard this physician as an unpardonable fraud. But that wasn't the point, was it? The point was that, at this moment in time, many of his colleagues took him seriously, and no one took him more seriously than he himself. Consumed with his so-called theory of mental illness and its relationship to creative endeavour, he would regard Robert Schumann as his experimental animal, his guinea pig, so to speak. His remark to Helena Becker came to mind, about how fears have a way of becoming realities. Obviously, the doctor was intrigued by this idea, especially as it pertained to Schumann. I concluded, therefore, that Dr. Möbius would benefit more by Schumann's life rather than his death, and his name, too, was deleted with the stroke of my pen.

Would Clara Schumann be the one supplying Hupfer with generous amounts of cash? Not likely. Every thaler this woman earned went of necessity toward feeding, clothing and housing her family. With her husband largely incapacitated, there would be no money to spare. True, whenever their eyes met, the spark between Clara and Brahms was as palpable now as when I first noticed them together, and though my questions and doubts about them had begun to run like veins through my reasoning, I could not imagine that she alone, or the two of them together, could produce the quantities of money Hupfer was spending at Thüringer's jewellery shop. And so Clara Schumann's name, like the others before hers, was struck off.

This left the name at the bottom of the list: Professor Friedrich Wieck. I pronounced that name several times, and found myself each time adding the cliché "Last but not least." Indeed, last but not least!

Another thought came to mind: Hupfer's appearance at No. 15 Bilkerstrasse while Wieck conveniently was present at the house and the Schumanns conveniently were away at Bad Grünwald…

Then something struck me—something that had not caught my attention at the time: Hupfer had shown up *without* his leather satchel that contained the tools of his trade. What, then, could have been the purpose of his attendance at the house? If he came unequipped, was this purely a social call? Or was Hupfer calling on Wieck to collect money?

Chapter Thirty-Two

I made it clear that my plan was to be followed to the letter, beginning with the delivery of a note by the Schumanns' faithful housekeeper to Willi Hupfer. This was to be done precisely at twelve o'clock noon, when Hupfer—a man of unswerving habits according to Clara Schumann—would have returned home from wherever he might be working and be sitting down to his big meal of the day.

"I have to tell you," the housekeeper reported on her return, "that he was very annoyed, Madam Schumann, very annoyed indeed. He said he was very busy, too busy, in fact. I pretended not to hear, but he definitely uttered an oath I would not dare to repeat."

"Yes, yes," Clara said, "but will he *come?*" The housekeeper threw up her shoulders as if to say "Who knows?"

One hour later, Clara had her answer. Out of breath, a scowl leaving no doubt of his annoyance, Wilhelm Hupfer was admitted to the parlour of the Schumann house. "Willi!" Clara said, springing from her piano bench, "thank God you've arrived!" Looking about him at the members of the Düsseldorf Quartet already assembled in the room, he seemed taken aback. "I did not expect to find all of you here," he said.

"You see how important you are," Clara said taking the man's coat, folding it, and laying it neatly over the back of a chair. "The five of us have been sitting here completely immobilized. You, and only you, Willi, have the power to rescue us."

"You flatter me, Madam," Hupfer said, slowly warming.
"I assure you, it's not idle flattery," Clara said. She
turned to the members of the quartet. "Whatever would
we do without our technical genius!" All four players
chimed in with extravagant praise.

Instead of responding with a mixture of gratitude
and pride, as one, knowing him, would have expected,
Hupfer indulged in an uncharacteristic show of
modesty, reminding his admirers that he had always
striven to do his best, but adding quickly, "Though, God
knows, occasionally I do fall short because of my habit of
demanding too much of myself."

Everyone in the room nodded in sympathy with him,
and Clara broke in with, "Ah, but God knows how hard
you try, so perhaps your rewards will come in the
afterlife."

To this bit of optimism, Hupfer's response was a
dismissive shrug. "Perhaps," he said, "but I am not
counting on it. And now, if you will excuse me, to work."

Resuming a businesslike manner, he put down his
leather satchel containing his tools next to the Klems
grand piano. "I did caution you and the Maestro about
this instrument, Madam Schumann," he said, sounding
like a schoolmaster chiding an errant pupil.

Relishing the fact that five very dependent souls
anxiously awaited his next move, Willi Hupfer sat himself
down at the keyboard of the Klems. As though he were a
virtuoso about to perform, he took a minute or two to adjust
the piano bench, fussing with the knobs until the height of
the upholstered seat was exactly to his satisfaction. He
shifted the bench, now back a little, now forward a little,
until the toes of his shoes were within comfortable reach of
the pedals. He rubbed his hands together vigorously to
warm up the fingers. At last, he raised his right arm, brought
his hand down, and played at moderate speed the C-major

scale on the upper two octaves of the Klems. This was followed by a similar demonstration over the lower two octaves. He paused at this point for dramatic effect. "Well, I suppose one gets what one pays for," he said, his lips pursed in contempt for the instrument. "At least the upper and lower ranges are tolerable."

"Try the middle range, Willi," Clara Schumann suggested.

"Of course," Hupfer said, "you realize that any deviation is not my fault. A Klems is *not* a Bösendorfer, you know."

"I understand," Clara said, full of deference. "Nobody is blaming you, Willi. Could we hear middle A now? My friends here—" She nodded in the direction of the four string players sitting by attentively. "My friends were not at all happy with the pitch."

"Oh?" Hupfer said. "And what is supposed to be the trouble with the pitch, may I ask?" There was a slight edge now in his voice.

The second violinist, Martin Stollenberg, spoke up. "Not *'supposed* to be the trouble'; there really *is* some trouble."

Hupfer, peering over his spectacles at the impertinent fiddler, said, "Do you purport, sir, to have perfect pitch?"

"Not at all," Stollenberg replied. "But I know when a note is sharp, and the middle A on this piano is definitely sharp." Stollenberg's three colleagues muttered their agreement in unison.

Clara interjected, her eyes on a mantel clock, "Willi, we must get on with this. We have a heavy program to rehearse for this coming Sunday. Would you kindly oblige us by sounding middle A and doing whatever is needed so we can proceed." She gave him a seductive smile.

"If you will pardon my frankness," Hupfer said, rising from the piano bench, "I really believe you are being unfair to yourselves. The older piano is a far superior instrument. Better tone. The pins, even in an earthquake, won't loosen and throw the strings off. Why don't I—"

"But Willi," Clara cut in, "I explained to you in my note

that the Klems is far better suited to a chamber arrangement, especially in a setting like this. Remember, we are not performing in an auditorium. *Please.*"

Plainly reluctant, Hupfer seated himself again at the Klems. The members of the quartet brought their bows up to their strings, and waited for him to sound middle A. Hupfer's right index finger came down on the key so softly that it barely created a sound. The string players made no move to tune their instruments. The leader, Rudy von Schirach, affecting a jocular air, called out to Hupfer, "Come, come, Maestro, the note needs to be played *fortissimo!* Again, if you will."

Hupfer shook his head. Quietly, he responded, "You are all making a grave mistake."

"The *A,* Willi," Clara said, her voice firm, "and louder this time."

"This is deeply offensive to my sense of profess-ionalism," Hupfer said, looking her straight in the eye. Returning to the keyboard, he pressed his index finger down heavily on middle A.

"You see," Stollenberg said, "I was right. It's absolutely sharp."

Clara moved close to the Klems, hovering over the piano tuner, then boldly set her own finger down hard on the middle A key. "Oh dear, this will never do. Get out your tuning fork and do what must be done." She stooped, picked up Hupfer's satchel, and handed it to him. "The fork, Willi—"

Slowly, Hupfer unfastened the belt that encircled the leather satchel. The bag fell open, each half revealing tools neatly arranged, each tool in a specially fitted holder. The piano technician's face darkened. "That's very odd," he muttered. "For some reason it's not here."

"The tuning fork?" Clara Schumann said.

"Yes. I must have left it in my shop." Hupfer shook his head, as though angry with himself. "I cannot believe—"

For a moment he fell into an awkward silence, then abruptly got to his feet. "I do apologize," he said, addressing everyone, "but if you will bear with me, I will dash back to my workshop and—"

"There's no need to go to the trouble, Hupfer—"

I had slipped suddenly into the parlour from the adjoining study and called out to him. Sliding doors separating the two rooms had been left open sufficiently that I had been able to spy on his actions since the moment of his arrival. "Here…here is your tuning fork," I said, holding it up so that it was in plain sight.

Hupfer pretended to be disgusted with himself. "Ach! How careless of me! I must have dropped it somewhere in my rush to get here." He turned to Clara Schumann. "Whatever would we do without detectives!"

"Thank you, Herr Hupfer, for the compliment," I said. "By the way, would you like to know where I found it?" I watched Hupfer's face for any sign of unease, but to my surprise I saw none.

"What does it matter where it was found? The important thing is, it was found."

He started toward me and reached for the fork, but I swiftly drew back my hand, placing the instrument beyond his grasp. I gave him a quizzical smile. "Aren't you the least bit curious, I mean about how I came upon your tuning fork?" I said.

"Please, Inspector, we have no time for games."

"We? You mean *you* have no time for games. Very well, Herr Hupfer, I too have no time for games."

"Good," Hupfer said. "The tuning fork, please."

"But first let me tell you where I found it—"

"I said it does not matter!"

"In the apartment of Georg Adelmann, Hupfer, that is where I found it. Perhaps you have an explanation for your presence in his apartment, bearing in mind that among the myriad treasures with which Adelmann managed to surround himself, the one thing he never got around to was a *piano.* "

"I don't know what you're talking about," Hupfer said. "Come to think of it, I can't even be certain if what you're holding in your hand *is* my tuning fork. All tuning forks look alike."

"There's one distinguishing feature. Allow me—" I struck the tuning fork firmly against the edge of Helena's wooden music stand.

"That's *it!*" Rudy von Schirach exclaimed, "that's the A we tuned to at the musicale."

"You're sure, von Schirach?" I said, not taking my eyes off Hupfer.

"Sure?" von Schirach said. "I'd wager my Guarneri del Jesu on it!"

Chapter Thirty-Three

We were in the interrogation room deep in the bowels of the Constabulary, just the two of us, Wilhelm Hupfer and I, he perched uncomfortably on the edge of an unforgiving wooden bench, facing me, the same bench on which some forty-eight hours earlier Walter Thüringer (now at least in one sense my key witness) had bought his freedom by informing me of Hupfer's lavish acquisitions. Ever since my first exposure to this room as a fledgling detective, I have regarded it as a windowless, dank entranceway to Hell, a checkpoint where one's criminal credentials are finally certified before one makes that final passage into the eternal fires. Indeed, in the flickering gaslight that provides the only illumination, even visiting saints take on the look of sinners.

Not that Wilhelm Hupfer was a visiting saint. Far from it.

"The tuning fork, Hupfer...you tampered with it, didn't you? Fixed it so that it would be just sharp enough that someone like Schumann would go out of his mind hearing it, remembering it, isn't that the truth?" Putting this question to Hupfer, I made a point of holding the fork almost touching his nose. "Look here, Hupfer. See, one prong has been shaved ever so slightly. One can barely notice it. In fact, you actually have to run a finger along each prong to discover that one is different from the other." Rudy von Schirach had demonstrated this for my benefit, and now I was inviting Hupfer to test the instrument. "Here, see for yourself—"

"No no no! Von Schirach is wrong!"

"You knew, didn't you, Hupfer, that Schumann suffered from auditory hallucinations, because you have been in contact with the doctor who was treating him, Dr. Möbius? And you knew that these hallucinations would be aggravated if you mis-tuned his pianos, isn't that correct?"

"I know nothing about such mental nonsense," Hupfer said. "Besides, I've never heard of Dr. Paul Möbius."

"Oh, so you know his first name is Paul?"

"Did I say Paul?"

"Not only did you say Paul, but let me remind you that one morning recently, as I was leaving the doctor's residence, you were making your way into that same house. Why?"

"I have absolutely no recollection of that," Hupfer said. But all the classic signs of lying were now showing up: the biting of the lips, the shifting of the eyes, the veins beginning to stand out at the man's temples.

I said, "Tell me, why did you kill Georg Adelmann?"

"I did not murder Adelmann!" he cried out. "You must believe me!"

"And why should I believe you, Hupfer? You've already lied to me twice: once about the condition of the tuning fork, and a second time about your acquaintanceship with Dr. Möbius. So why should I believe you?"

"Because I will now tell you something, and you will know I am speaking the truth."

"Go on," I said. "I'm waiting."

"I am *not* a murderer, Inspector. I had absolutely no reason to kill Adelmann. I don't even recall meeting the man, although our paths might have crossed...maybe at Schumanns', maybe elsewhere, who knows. But yes, there *was* a plan to destroy Schumann, and I confess I was part of it, though I did not originate it, I swear to God."

"Then who did?"

"Wieck…Madam Schumann's father…it was all his idea. Wieck and Dr. Möbius, those two had become close, close enough that Wieck knew all of Möbius's theories concerning hallucinations, especially Maestro Schumann's. And I became involved because Wieck figured out that Schumann, being as sensitive to pitch as he was, would be driven out of his mind by a combination of his own mental problems and my ability to manipulate the tuning of his pianos. Which explains why Schumann complained constantly that the A sound kept running through his head."

I wanted to know how Wieck would have possessed the technical knowledge required to concoct his scheme.

"Anybody who has been around pianos as long as Wieck learns a few basic principles about sound. For example: a normal human has a hearing range which extends all the way from one vibration per second to twenty-thousand. When a piano is perfectly tuned, A vibrates four hundred and forty-times per second. But then there are what we call 'partials'. If you press the key for A above middle C on an instrument that is properly tuned, yes, you hear the fundamental A-440, but that is not all. You should also hear a series of partials that are multiples of four hundred forty…such as eight hundred eighty, thirteen hundred twenty, seventeen hundred sixty, twenty-two hundred, and so on right up to a fifteenth or even twentieth partial."

"In other words," I said, "if I depress a single key, the result is an entire *chord* of partials?"

"Precisely."

"So it stands to reason, Hupfer, that if one distorts the tuning by sharpening A, the resulting partials entering sensitive ears like Schumann's can become not simply irritating but downright maddening if carried on over a sufficient period of time. Am I correct?"

Hupfer dropped his head. I thought I heard him whisper, "Yes."

"Why would a man with your skill, your reputation, become an accomplice...*why?*"

"As I said to you at my shop, the performer gets the adulation and the money. But all a man like me earns is a reputation. Wieck paid me much more generously than Schumann ever would or could."

"But the Schumanns *trusted* you, Hupfer," I said. "You were 'Willi' to them, you were like family. You knew— how could you of all people *not* know?—how fine a line Schumann walked when it came to his emotions and his tempers."

Hupfer looked me straight in the eye. "Think of me what you will, Preiss," he said, "but I have told you the truth about my part in Wieck's plot. And I am telling you the truth about Adelmann's death. The tuning fork is mine. But I swear before God *I did not kill him.*"

Chapter Thirty-Four

S o, Preiss, let me see if I understand what you've been up to—"

Over the years, I had learned that whenever Commissioner Schilling commenced a review of my activities with these words, the threat of crucifixion hung in the air. Fingering my report, a one-page document containing as little specific information as I could hope to get away with, he cleared his throat noisily several times (I hated to imagine what he was coughing up) while I stood awaiting his summation.

"It seems, firstly, that you saw fit, acting as usual solely on your own initiative, to give this jeweller Thüringer his freedom in exchange for some tidbit of information no doubt of questionable value considering its source."

"Well, sir, that's not quite—" I started to explain.

"Kindly do not interrupt," the Commissioner barked. "Walter Thüringer…a thief and habitual receiver of stolen goods…that is a fact, is it not?"

"Well, Commissioner—"

"Yes or no?"

"Yes."

"Secondly, having gone to the trouble of acting upon the tip from the jeweller and arresting this piano-tuner…what's his name?"

"Hupfer, sir. Wilhelm Hupfer."

"Right. Hupfer. Apparently a devious lowlife who confesses—*confesses, mind you*—that he's been the technical mastermind behind a plot aimed at driving that fellow Schumann insane...am I correct thus far, Preiss?"

"You are indeed, sir."

"Yes, and what do you do about him, eh? You release *him* as well and send him back to society! And why? On what grounds? On the excuse that the victim of this evil plot is ensconced in an asylum somewhere and in no position to testify against the perpetrators? Since when is that a reason not to proceed with prosecution?"

"If I might explain, sir—"

"Again you interrupt! I will *not* be interrupted, Preiss, is that clear?"

"Absolutely, sir."

"Now then, I want you to examine this so-called report—" Schilling thrust the page across his desk "—and be so good as to tell me what it says about the one *important* case on your assignment list. I'm referring of course to the murder of Georg Adelmann. I would have expected," Schilling said, "that by this time you would have produced a suspect, a murder weapon, a clear motive, perhaps even a witness or two, certainly enough that we could assure the public that Düsseldorf is not Hamburg, that we do not tolerate crime and molly-coddle our criminals. But what does your report say of all this, eh?"

"Nothing, sir."

"In other words, Inspector," Schilling said, reaching across his desk and seizing the sheet of paper, "this sorry account...two men arrested, the same two released...*this* is all you've managed to accomplish, while whoever killed Georg Adelmann in cold blood is presumably dining at this very hour on roast goose with a good bottle of Moselle at Emmerich's. And what's worse, probably laughing up his sleeve!"

"Not quite, sir," I said.

A deep scowl darkened the reddish blotches on the Commissioner's face.

"Not quite? What the devil does that mean, Preiss?"

"I'm certain the person who killed Georg Adelmann is *not* dining at Emmerich's. Nor is he laughing up his sleeve. On the contrary, he is probably suffering greater tortures than any convict you or I have ever sent to prison."

"You're talking in riddles," the Commissioner said, his anger rising another notch. "You know, Preiss, I've always suspected that at heart you're a romantic, but all these cultural pretensions of yours don't fool me, not for a minute. It's plain to me that you haven't the slightest notion who Adelmann's murderer is, and so you attempt to mask your failure with some fictional nonsense. Tortures indeed!"

Schilling made a scoffing sound through his nose as he once again thrust my report back at me. "Tell me something, Preiss," he said, "can you think of one good reason why I should not, here and now, on the spot, dismiss you from the force?"

I stood pondering the question for a few moments.

"Well?"

I took another moment or two, then said "Baron von Hoffman."

Schilling eyed me suspiciously, but nervously now too. "What about the Baron?"

"I simply point out, sir, that he has on several occasions recently made certain overtures to me—"

"Overtures? What sort of overtures?"

"As you will no doubt appreciate," I said, "the Baron and Baroness are concerned in these increasingly crime-ridden times about their personal safety as well as the security of their manor here, their country estate, and their valuable contents. And since the Baron's time is very much taken up with his public duties—you will recall that, among other functions, he is chairman of the committee which determines retirement benefits for senior civil servants such as yourself—he has too little time to attend to certain personal needs of an urgent nature. He has therefore suggested that, with your concurrence of course, it would be most beneficial...I mean beneficial for him and the Baroness...if I were delegated to look into arrangements concerning their safety and security, especially when they find it necessary to travel abroad. I assume this would not unduly inconvenience you, sir?"

I put this last statement in the form of a question, knowing full well what the old man's response would be.

"The Baron wants this, eh? Well now—" Again much throat-clearing. "We'll have to give this some very serious thought, will we not? One certainly cannot overlook the wishes of one of our most important citizens, can one? Imagine the shame that would befall our fair city should the Baron and Baroness come to grief! Very well, Preiss, I will expect a detailed plan by the end of this week regarding the von Hoffmans. In the meantime, give me something—*any*thing—that I can present to the mayor regarding this damned Adelmann affair."

There followed a strange moment of silence, and I had the feeling that Commissioner Schilling wanted to say more but was holding back. Cautiously, I said, "Does the Commissioner have any further instructions? Otherwise, I take it that I may return to my office and resume my duties."

The Commissioner rose and came around to my side of his desk. In a quiet confidential tone, he said, "It occurs to me, Preiss, that a day or two ago you had quite a confrontation with an itinerant group of gypsies."

"That is correct, sir. So I did. And a not-too-pleasant band they were."

"Ah, yes," Schilling said, nodding agreeably. "Trouble-makers, every single one of 'em, eh?"

"Why do you mention this?" I asked.

Lowering his voice still more, Schilling said, "It would be very convenient...for *all* of us, you understand...if we could report to the mayor that Adelmann was likely done in by one or more of these here-today-gone-tomorrow gypsy types. You know how these journalist types like to mess about. Never saw one that didn't have a bohemian streak in him. You understand, Preiss, I'm sure."

"Perfectly, sir."

"Well then, enough time wasted, eh? Back to work!"

*   *   *

For the record, Baron von Hoffman had not in fact approached me with a proposal to protect him and his wife and their precious possessions. But he was instantly enthusiastic when I approached *him* with the idea (which, in fact, I made a point of doing not more than an hour after my latest encounter with the Commissioner).

"I do admire a man like you, Preiss," the Baron said, beaming and clapping a friendly hand on my shoulder. "Imagination, that's what gives a man a place in the sun, eh?"

I was keenly aware that the Baron had *inherited* his place in the sun, but why split hairs? "Thank you, Your Excellency," I said. "I look forward to being of service to you for many years to come."

"Indeed you will!" said the Baron. "One of these days we'll be considering a successor to Commissioner Schilling. Face it, the man deserves a good long rest, don't you agree?"

Hoping I sounded generous, I said, "The Commissioner deserves more than that, sir."

His hand still pressing my shoulder, the Baron said, "You're a good man, Preiss. You must dine one evening soon with the Baroness and me. Oh, and be sure to bring along that charming friend of yours, the cellist—"

"Fräulein Becker—"

"Yes, by all means. Fine musician, that young woman. And not hard to look at, eh? Made quite an impression on me that evening at the Schumanns. By the way, I hear

Schumann had to be carted off to some hospital near Bonn. Endenich or some such place. From all accounts, it sounds like the poor fellow has gone mad. Pity about these creative people, isn't it? All sorts of wild rumours floating about, too. Mostly about his wife and this young musician Brahms." The Baron regarded me with a cagey smile. "You happen to know anything about all this, Preiss?"

"Very little," I said. "Domestic matters of that sort are really no concern of my department."

"Of course," the Baron said, nodding in an understanding way. "Just a bit of idle curiosity on my part. Anyway, composers come and go, don't they. We lose one, we gain another. I'm old enough, Preiss, to remember when Beethoven died. Everyone moaned and groaned about the musical world coming to an end. But it didn't come to an end, did it? Which reminds me: anything new about the murder of Georg Adelmann? You know, the last time I saw the poor fellow was at the Schumanns' musicale. I happened to wander into the Maestro's study, and there was Adelmann, all alone, standing transfixed before a cabinet, gazing at an original Beethoven manuscript. I left the room, but Adelmann couldn't seem to tear himself away from it. Odd how one thought leads to another, eh?"

"You have no idea, sir, how odd," I said and left it at that.

Chapter Thirty-Five

E scorting me to the massive oak doors at the front entrance of his mansion, where his valet stood holding my coat, Baron von Hoffman abruptly brought me to a halt. "I hope you'll not take offense, Preiss," he said, "but I cannot help observing that you look exhausted. I insist you take one of my carriages back to the Constabulary." I began to protest that his offer was much too generous. "Nonsense! Not another word!"

The carriage turned out to be one of those fine English-built four-wheel coaches with oversize shackles and luxuriously padded seats that cushioned the passenger against the winter-ravaged cobbles. I sat back, silently congratulating myself on my good fortune. I had managed to learn—albeit by accident—that at one point during the evening of the Schumanns' musicale, Georg Adelmann had been observed by the Baron in Robert Schumann's study standing alone; he would have been entirely free to steal the precious Beethoven manuscript which so obviously entranced him. There was now not the slightest doubt in my mind: Adelmann had lied to me about the manuscript having come into his possession as a gift—a bribe, really—from Schumann.

But the Baron was right. I *was* exhausted, and it did not take long for the steady clip-clopping of the horses and the gentle swaying from side to side of the driver perched up front to mesmerize me. My eyelids were growing heavy and beginning to close. I was aware that I was falling asleep there, in the comfort of that splendid vehicle, when suddenly—as though the coachman's whip had flicked across my face—my eyes snapped open, I sat up, and heard myself sharply call out, "Stop! Please stop!"

Obeying instantly, the driver turned about in his seat, a worried look on his weather-beaten face. "I beg your pardon, sir," he said, "I did not mean to drive so fast. Please excuse—"

"No, no," I said, "that's not it at all. I need to walk."

"But, sir, the Constabulary is at least three kilometres—"

Paying no heed to the fellow, I abruptly dismounted. "Kindly convey my thanks to the Baron."

"But, sir," the driver said, rolling his eyes skyward, "any moment now those clouds are going to open up and—"

I dug into my coat pocket and found several coins, which I pressed into the driver's palm. "Rain does not dare to fall on police inspectors, but I thank you for your concern."

I watched him turn about, shaking his head as though I were mad to make him abandon me under a threatening sky. I began to walk, at first with a slow, measured pace; then, gradually, the pace accelerated until, a half-kilometre from the Constabulary, I had launched into a full march. So absorbed was I in my thoughts that I hadn't noticed that my hat and coat were soaked and the insides of my shoes wet from sheets of water being flung across my path by winds off the Rhine.

Reaching the Constabulary, I ignored the perfunctory greetings from the guards posted at the entrance and bounded up the four flights of stairs to my office in record time. To an orderly stationed in the corridor outside my office I called out that I was not to be disturbed for the next hour under any circumstances.

"Does that include the Commissioner?" the startled orderly inquired.

"It includes God!" I shouted back, slamming my office door behind me. Then, on second thought, and to make certain I was left alone, I locked my door, something I rarely if ever did.

I removed my soaked hat and coat and tossed them carelessly over the nearest chair. Who cared that, once dry, they would look slept in? I could feel my stockinged feet swimming inside my shoes but this, too, did not matter.

I sat myself down at my desk and found a large sheet of stationery, which I laid flat before me. I reached for a pen, dipped the nib deeply into the well for an ample supply of ink, and printed out in large block letters:

ROBERT SCHUMANN MURDERED GEORG ADELMANN

I sat back staring at what I had just written, the pen still in my hand. I pondered the words, holding the paper now at arm's length, feeling for a moment as though I were a child who had just learned to write and was staring in wonderment at my first-ever sentence.

I placed the paper flat in front of me again, replenished the ink on the nib, and ran a heavy line through the sentence. Underneath it, I then printed, again in large block letters:

ROBERT SCHUMANN KILLED GEORG ADELMANN

It was all beginning to make sense to me now.

I recalled that Schumann had agreed with Liszt about the piano having been mis-tuned. To prove it to himself, Schumann somehow must have got his hands on Hupfer's tuning fork, probably lifting it from the unsuspecting technician's tool bag. Satisfied that the fork had been deliberately tampered with, Schumann must have fallen into one of his rages, the fires within him ignited beyond extinguishing when he next discovered that his Beethoven treasure was missing. Clara would have stoked the fires further by pointing to Adelmann as the culprit, based on the information I had passed on to her about the journalist's penchant for stealing. The sequence of events led to one conclusion and one conclusion only.

Another dip of my pen into the inkpot. Another fresh sentence:

FLORESTAN KILLED GEORG ADELMANN!

Florestan: Robert Schumann's inner man of action. Or so Schumann would have me believe if, at this moment, he were standing in my presence grimly facing a criminal charge. But Schumann was *not* here, was he? No, he was cooped up in a secure private room in an asylum in Endenich. Or was he? Cooped up, that is? Perhaps it was more to the point now to think of him as being conveniently tucked away. Oh yes, he had protested mightily against being taken away the other morning, begging me to intervene, no doubt knowing full well that I could not or would not interrupt the process of his removal. I recalled the sudden acquiescence as he was escorted by his two attendants to the carriage, the way he made such a point of rushing back into the house to retrieve his own tuning fork, making sure this did not escape my notice. As he rode off that morning, was Florestan contentedly smiling to himself?

Slowly, deliberately, I folded the sheet of stationery in half, then in quarters. I began tearing the paper into strips, so many strips that when I was finished I had created a small pile of thin paper noodles, not unlike the thin noodles that lingered in what passed for soup in my threadbare childhood. I threw the pile into an envelope which I stored in the inner pocket of my suit jacket, next to Hupfer's tuning fork.

On a fresh sheet of paper, in my most meticulous penmanship, I wrote the following report to the Commissioner:

March 12, 1854

Sir:

I beg to report that, to date, the identity of the person responsible for the slaying of Georg Adelmann has not been ascertained. Unfortunately no suspect has come to light nor

has a murder weapon surfaced. Nor have I located any
witness or witnesses despite a thorough canvass of the
immediate neighbourhood. In the absence of scientific means
of detecting how crimes of this nature are committed, I can
only pledge to you that I shall continue with all due
diligence and despatch my investigations in the hope that
the perpetrator is apprehended and brought before the bar of
justice for due conviction and punishment.
   Respectfully,
   Preiss, H., Senior Inspector

Despite the discomfort, I donned my hat and coat, still damp right through to their linings, and left my office, brushing past the orderly, curtly informing him that I would be gone for the remainder of the day, and instructing him to deliver my report.

A fog had begun drifting across the city from the river, coiling itself around the ancient buildings that lined my route to the same bridge from which Robert Schumann, or Florestan, or Eusebius...make your choice...had leapt into the chilly waters of the Rhine. Once at the bridge, I determined with satisfaction that not a soul was in sight. It was as if the inclement weather had been made to my order.

From the inner pocket of my jacket I took the envelope and Hupfer's tuning fork, the latter still carefully wrapped in a handkerchief. I paused for one more glance from one end of the bridge to the other to assure myself that I was alone. I leaned over the cold, wet masonry of the railing, holding the envelope and tuning fork (now unwrapped) in a firm grip. I opened the palm of my hand and released the contents. I watched the metal fork touch the black rain-pocked surface of the river without so much as a ripple and immediately disappear. The envelope also touched the water unceremoniously, but it was captured by a wave and swiftly carried away, reminding me of paper boats I made as a child. Before long, it too was out of sight.

Chapter Thirty-Six

I left the bridge at a brisk pace, each clack of my heels against the paving stones like the sharp steady beat of a metronome, the tempo reflecting a sense of urgent unfinished business. I flagged down the first cab that came in view and called out my destination. The driver, noticing my bedraggled appearance, gave me a skeptical look, as though I couldn't possibly reside in the fashionable neighbourhood to which I had directed him.

"You *live* there, sir?" he asked.

Insolent bastard. "Of course I live there," I replied.

Properly silenced, the driver returned to his business. I settled back in the cab, grateful at last to be out of the unrelenting downpour, and began pondering the acts I had just committed back at the bridge. That I had willfully broken the law by doing away with incriminating evidence was of course beyond question, and yet in the expected tide of self-condemnation, I felt not the shallowest ripple of remorse. Instead, what consumed me more than anything else at the moment was the irony of my situation. I was drifting without restraint from the safe narrow confines of inspection into the dark uncharted spaces of introspection, searching for reasons that would justify not only what I had done…but what I was about to do.

Inner truths. I smiled ruefully to myself, recalling how resolutely I had dismissed, even scorned, the idea as nothing but romantic foolishness, the stuff of poets, not policemen. Motive, opportunity, means…that was all that mattered. Or so I told myself until my path was crossed and re-crossed by this man Schumann, alias Florestan. I wanted nothing more now than somehow to right the wrongs done him. To accomplish this, one further item remained on my agenda: I must get rid of Adelmann's papers, his draft monograph on the life of Robert Schumann exposing details the Maestro was so desperate to suppress.

A block short of Adelmann's address, I ordered the driver to stop, paid the fare and waited on the sidewalk until the cab rounded the next corner and was out of sight. I had earlier appropriated a key to Adelmann's apartment from his landlady, citing "official police business," and was able to let myself in without being noticed. Fortunately, there was sufficient light, despite the gloom outdoors, to permit a thorough search. I began, of course, in his study, ransacking his desk, an unruly depository of just about every shred of paper the man had ever touched, or so it seemed. But there was not so much as a tittle about Schumann. I then went from room to room, sparing nothing. I probed every stick of furniture, and poked behind curtains, under carpets, even upturning the bedding upon which the man had slept. Not a single nook or cranny escaped my scrutiny.

The papers were nowhere to be found.

I found it hard to imagine that out of some rare spirit of charity or compassion, Georg Adelmann would have voluntarily destroyed his work in response to Schumann's bidding. Besides, as a renowned journalist, Adelmann no doubt took pride in his research and had scruples about expurgating what he regarded as essential facts, even if they were potentially ruinous to someone's reputation. Nor did I overlook the probability that a literary exposé of Robert Schumann's private sex life would have found a wide audience and stuffed Adelmann's pockets with cash…those pockets which were not already stuffed with stolen valuables, that is.

But there was another possibility. What if Adelmann's monograph had fallen into the wrong hands, perhaps those of some professional gossipmonger, and was destined to be widely circulated in the press? Apart from the legitimate newspapers and periodicals in the country, a growing number of scandal sheets had sprung up like poison mushrooms in major cities like Berlin and Hamburg and Frankfurt, places where prurience knew few limits, not only among the masses but among the newly wealthy as well. I could not bear the thought that two personalities like Robert and Clara Schumann, geniuses who once upon a time had lit up the pluperfect realm of music, overnight would become objects of public ridicule and shame. I felt an overwhelming compulsion now to warn Clara about what I feared lay in store for her husband and her. Letting myself out of Adelmann's rooms, and making certain to lock the door behind me, I made straight for No. 15 Bilkerstrasse.

Chapter Thirty-Seven

"Madam Schumann is practicing," the Schumanns' housekeeper said, "but I will let her know you are here, Inspector."

"Never mind. I know where to find her, thank you." I went directly to the drawing-room, parted the heavy oak doors, and boldly entered to find Clara seated at the older of the two grand pianos. She did not bother to look up, nor did she stop playing, though she had to know I was there (I am, after all, not a small man, nor was the Schumann drawing-room all that spacious). She was bent over the keyboard, her head almost touching the keys, in what I had come to know as her customary posture at the piano. Player and instrument, it seemed, were as one. Her fingers did not strike the keys; rather they squeezed them. Under the touch of her hands—which for the first time struck me as surprisingly large for so compact a woman—the piano responded in a way that I did not think a piano was capable of responding: it sang, as though it possessed a human voice.

Suddenly, she halted in the midst of a phrase. I quickly apologized for the intrusion and for my dreadful appearance. She gave me a critical look, indicating that I had failed to pass inspection. I began to stammer a second apology only to be interrupted with a firm *"Please..."* followed by a flickering smile. "No need to make excuses, Inspector," she said. "It appears that Düsseldorf has been chosen as the site of the second Great Flood—" she paused, and her smile warmed a bit, "though I must say, you *do* look as though you were on Noah's ark and fell overboard."

"May I ask what you were playing?" I said. "It doesn't sound familiar to me."

"It is my own composition, something I've been working on for several months...a set of variations on a theme of Robert's that I'm especially fond of."

"Pardon my ignorance, Madam Schumann," I said, "but I was not aware that musical composition was among your many talents."

She smiled ruefully. "Then you must have been listening to my husband, Inspector. Robert went out of his way to discourage my attempts at composition, though from time to time he would allow that something I'd written was, as he put it, rather *charming*. Have you any idea, Inspector, what it feels like to be told something you've worked on is 'charming'?"

"I cannot possibly imagine," I said. "Certainly in *my* line of work, a word like 'charming' has never cropped up nor, I expect, will it ever."

Rising from the piano, she beckoned me to join her at the fireplace, where the two of us sat facing one another, she looking unexpectedly serene, I on the other hand feeling a deep sense of unease.

"I wasn't born yesterday, Inspector," she said. "You didn't come here merely to listen to the bleating of a frustrated female."

"I hardly know where to begin," I said.

"Well, I suppose one ought to begin at the beginning. You've satisfied yourself that our friend Hupfer is guilty of the murder of Georg Adelmann?"

"I'm afraid not," I said. "You see, 'our friend' Willi Hupfer did not murder Georg Adelmann, as it turns out." As I said this I watched for Clara's reaction. I thought I noticed her eyes narrow slightly. "The fact is, madam...the fact is that I am now quite positive that

Adelmann was killed by someone wanting it to look as though it was the work of Willi Hupfer."

"Well now, Inspector," Madam Schumann said, "you surprise me. I thought the whole point of that demonstration you so cleverly staged...I'm referring to the business with the tuning fork...was to prove beyond doubt that Hupfer was Adelmann's slayer. You even arrested the man right there, before our very eyes! Now you're telling me the entire exercise was in vain?"

"Not entirely. One mystery *has* been resolved as a result of that arrest. Willi Hupfer confessed to being partly responsible for a series of deliberate mis-tunings over a period of some months which exacerbated the hallucinations your husband suffered. So there's now no doubt whatsoever about the legitimacy of your husband's complaints."

"Is that your way of making me feel smitten with guilt because I doubted Robert's complaints were real rather than imagined? If so, then you've succeeded, Inspector."

"I'm only stating established facts," I replied. "Your feelings? Well, I suppose those are entirely up to you, aren't they?"

"You say Willi admits to being *partly* responsible. Only partly?"

"There was a collaborator, madam, a man whom I'd describe as the mastermind behind the plot. This 'mastermind' was well aware of the frightening damage these heightened auditory hallucinations could inflict. In Hupfer he found the perfect man to carry out the technical part of the plot. And he saw to it that Hupfer, who made no secret of his bitterness over the scant rewards of his trade, was handsomely paid for his efforts."

"And are you at liberty to disclose who this collaborator is?"

"Unfortunately, there is no tactful way to tell you this. He is none other than Professor Friedrich Wieck...your father."

I had expected this announcement to elicit from Clara Schumann some highly emotional response. And who would have blamed her at this point if, like a prima donna in some melodramatic opera, she had heart-wrenchingly sworn bloody revenge against the evildoers? Instead, after a full minute or so of silence, with incredible calmness, she said, "So you are completely satisfied that Hupfer has told you the truth about my father's role in all this?"

"When one has been in my profession long enough, one develops what people in your profession call perfect pitch. Hupfer was telling the truth."

She paused again, then in that same unruffled manner, said, "So you will now travel to Endenich and arrest Robert."

I found it strange that she put this in the form of a statement rather than a question. There was even a hint of resignation in her tone, as though the facts had emerged plainly in black and white: Who else but Robert Schumann would have had the reason, the opportunity, and the strength to murder Adelmann?

I was not at all prepared for her next remark. "That would be a grave mistake on your part, Inspector," she said, her gaze intently fixed on me, "a very grave mistake."

"How so?"

"Robert did not kill Georg Adelmann."

"You know this for certain?"

"Yes."

"You mean you have some *opinion* in the matter?"

"Not an opinion, Inspector. Call it knowledge."

"Knowledge? Your own, or someone else's?"

"First-hand knowledge, Inspector. *I* killed Georg Adelmann."

"I beg your pardon?"

"It was *I* who killed Adelmann."

I said, "It is very noble of you, Madam Schumann, to

want to protect your husband's honour, but the powerful blow that took Adelmann's life could not possibly have been administered by someone of your physical stature."

She took this as an insult. "Look at these hands!" She extended her hands, the long fingers splayed. "Do you have any notion at all how strong a pianist's hands are? How strong our arms and wrists must be? Even our shoulder and back muscles? I choose to avoid pounding the keys the way Franz Liszt pounds them, but I assure you my hands and fingers are every bit as steely as any male's, pianist or otherwise. A single blow is all it took for me to dispatch Adelmann."

"There were marks on his temple suggesting that whoever struck him—"

"Not 'whoever', Inspector. It was *I* who struck him—"

"—used a tuning fork or an instrument very much resembling—"

"Again I have to interrupt you, sir. The tuning fork you found is the instrument I used."

"Hupfer's tuning fork?"

"Yes. Why do you find this so hard to accept?"

"How did you manage to acquire Hupfer's tuning fork? Don't ask me to believe that it suddenly materialized out of nowhere, madam. Tales of coincidence do *not* sit well with police inspectors."

Clara Schumann gave me a faint smile. "Inspector Preiss, I would never insult your intelligence by offering you some fantasy about how it came into my possession."

"The truth had better be simple. I have no time for anything else."

"The truth is always simple, isn't it, Inspector? Think back, if you will. You recall, I mentioned that Willi Hupfer is a creature of rigorous habit. One might say his life is set in stone. You've seen how meticulous he is, everything in its place, a place for everything, as they say.

And proud too. You've seen ample evidence of his pride. But pride leads to smugness, and smugness leads to carelessness, doesn't it?" I had the uncomfortable feeling that Clara Schumann's point wasn't confined to Wilhelm Hupfer, that she was aiming her barb at me as well.

"To answer your question fully about Willi's tuning fork, I have to take you back to the night of the musicale here in our house. The last thing Franz Liszt said as he was leaving was that the piano I'd played on was out of tune."

"Yes, and you and your friend Brahms protested— rather vehemently, I must say—and continued to protest even after Maestro Schumann appeared on the scene and acknowledged that Liszt was right. Frankly, it was my impression that you and Brahms were chiefly concerned with allaying any suspicions about yourselves, and to hell with Dr. Schumann."

"You're *half* right, Inspector," Clara Schumann said. "My denial was not aimed at allaying suspicions about *me*; rather, I was anxious to shield Johannes from suspicion. After all, when you consider Robert's temperament, it would not have taken much for him to conclude that Johannes was a participant in the conspiracy. And I say this despite Robert's deep affection for Johannes. So, yes, my protests were, as you put it, vehement. And with good reason."

"But the *tuning fork*, Madam Schumann—"

"Bear with me. I mentioned that pride, smugness and carelessness inevitably follow one another. And here—" She reached for a sheet of stationery that lay on the lid of the Klems. "Here is proof." She handed me the sheet. At the top, the printed letterhead read, "Wilhelm Hupfer, Master Piano Service Technician."

"You will notice," she said, "the date, which is the Saturday of the musicale. It is an itemized list of work done by Willi Hupfer that afternoon. This was one of Willi's many habits. After every visit, he would leave behind a detailed record of each item of service he'd performed, no matter how routine. It was his way of impressing us with his thoroughness. It was also his subtle way of attempting to make us feel guilty because he considered himself underpaid. His penmanship, like his workmanship, is impeccable, so you should have no trouble reading it."

I began silently to read.

"No, Inspector," she urged, "please read it aloud."

I read: *Klems exhibits premature wear and tear due to secondary quality parts and construction!*

Cleaned keybed, polished pins, checked all hammers and tapes.

Tightened all action screws.

Polished action brackets.

Checked damper lever springs.

Regulated and eased keys wherever necessary.

Re-strung A above Middle C (original strings too slack to pull up).

I looked up. "I'm no technician, but one question immediately jumps out of this report: isn't it curious that, for a piano that is supposedly cheaply constructed, among all eighty-eight keys and over two hundred strings the only strings, that required replacing were those for A above middle C?"

"That is not the only peculiar thing," she replied. "Suppose one must order a new set of strings. The closest manufacturer of strings suitable for our Klems piano is in Berlin. It can take up to two weeks before such an order is delivered. So one must produce strings from scratch in an emergency. It is a highly skilled and time-consuming process. I've watched Hupfer make them. First, he takes a length of thin but very strong steel wire, hammers both ends flat and forms them into loops, then hooks the wire onto a spinning contraption, something like a woodcraftsman's lathe. Then he wraps a length of copper wire around the steel core and spins the two, feeding the copper one very deftly between his thumb and forefinger so that it spirals down the steel wire to form a covering. As you can appreciate, Inspector, piano wires don't grow on trees."

"Which means Hupfer wouldn't have been capable of producing the new A strings on the spur of the moment," I said.

"Exactly."

"Which also means he must have planned to replace the A strings in advance...*well* in advance. Whether or not it needed restringing was beside the point. But I'm not sure if it was carelessness or just plain stupidity that made him refer to it in the list."

"It was both," Clara said, "but it was also greed. In his anxiety to make certain he collected every possible pfennig for his labour and material, he made the mistake of listing the A-string replacements. As soon as I read the list, I realized in a flash that something foul was going on."

I asked, "When did you first see the list?"

"After everyone had departed, the night of the musicale, Robert flew into one of his worst tantrums. Naturally, he was outraged by Liszt's patronizing response to our music. He was angry with me because he felt that I hadn't adequately supervised the tuning of the Klems or at least tested it after Hupfer was finished. He professed again and again that the A sound was constantly ringing in his ears. I'm ashamed to admit that I finally resorted to giving him a tumbler of schnapps large enough to put a regiment to sleep. It worked. Then I came back down to Robert's study, found Hupfer's list and request for payment. As soon as I saw the last item...well, you can imagine the rest."

"May we return, then, to the matter of Hupfer's tuning fork?" I said.

"Ah yes, the tuning fork. I *did* warn you, Inspector, that we would have to go back in time."

She moved to the Klems and stood at the keyboard. "Let me show you something," she said. Raising her right hand head high, she suddenly plunged it downward, striking A above middle C with her index finger with such force that the resulting sound pierced the air like a scream, causing me to wince. It was the kind of attack that would have shaken no less a fortress than a full-size Bösendorfer. "Now watch again, please," she said. Again her right hand ascended, this time slightly above her head, then descended even more forcefully, the index finger drilling into the same ivory key like a meteor biting into rock. But instead of the note sounding, there was a loud snap.

"My God, what was that?" I cried.

Her smile was almost triumphant. *"That,"* Clara said, "is the sound of a piano string breaking loose from its tuning pin."

"Very impressive," I said, somewhat amused. "How often do you do this kind of thing?"

She shook her head. "I leave such antics to Franz Liszt," she replied. "Every time Liszt causes a piano string to pop, a million female hearts pop. Women love masculine displays of that sort. But let me get to the point of all this, Inspector. I fear I'm taking up too much of your time."

"Yes, please. The point—"

"When a string is new, it tends to stretch. If the piano hasn't had the benefit of several thorough re-tunings so that the new string can settle in, an extra-hard strike can cause it to snap. As you've just witnessed, even a seasoned string may react the same way. Sunday morning, after I'd perused Hupfer's statement of account and become suspicious, I needed an excuse to summon him."

"On Sunday? Wouldn't that be unusual?"

"Yes, of course. But I made it sound like a matter of life and death. Also, I made a point of mentioning that his latest bill would be paid at the same time, together with any additional charges, just to sweeten his Sabbath."

"And your excuse for sending for him?"

"I did just what you saw me do, Inspector. I delivered a blow to his newly-installed A string that could be heard from one end of Düsseldorf to the other."

"And the string snapped?"

"Like a dry twig. Well, it turned out that Willi was able to re-attach the string, which I suppose is a tribute to his skill, because a factory-made string might not have survived the experience. Then, out comes Willi's tuning fork, because the string must be re-tuned, following which he deposits the fork in his tool satchel. I insist that he stay for a slice of warm strudel, his favourite. While he's distracted in the dining room, I suddenly remember something I've left behind in the parlour. His satchel lies open next to the Klems. I locate the tuning fork, pocket it, and close the satchel. After Hupfer's departure, I test the tuning fork and the new string. Need I say more, Inspector?"

"You left the tuning fork concealed under Adelmann's body hoping that it would be traced to Hupfer. In other words, you acted with all the forethought and craftiness of a hardened criminal...or so you would have me believe."

"You needn't sound so skeptical, Inspector," Clara said. "You happen to be perfectly correct."

"And your reason for going to Adelmann's apartment in the first place?"

"Why, I should think my reason was obvious. I wanted him to delete from his monograph that filth about Robert. At first, I asked him very politely to do so. That was met by a refusal, some lame excuse about not wanting to compromise his precious integrity as a journalist. I tried reasoning with him. When reasoning failed, I tried pleading. Pleading too failed. I humbled myself and resorted to begging. He laughed in my face, then made some lewd remark about my relationship with Johannes Brahms and accused me of being hypocritical, attempting to shield Robert's reputation with one hand while cheating on him with the other. Finally, I *demanded* that he not publish the offensive parts of the monograph. Again he laughed in my face. That was Georg Adelmann's last laugh."

I sat back in my chair staring at the woman, shaking my head from side to side, at a loss for words. Finally, I said, "I did not come here expecting to listen to what I can only call an incredible confession."

"Then why *did* you come?"

"To warn you."

"Warn me? About what?"

"About the fact that Adelmann's monograph is missing and may well have gotten into the wrong hands. You may have to prepare yourself for—"

"For a scandal?"

I said, "You seem strangely resigned about all this, almost indifferent. Have I not made myself clear? I mean, if these events become public knowledge—"

Without replying, Clara rose from her chair, took several steps across the drawing-room and stopped before a massive mahogany armoire that occupied the better part of one wall and stood at least a half-metre taller than she. From a pocket of her frock she removed a large brass key, which she used to unlock the armoire, its two heavy doors falling open like the doors of a tabernacle, revealing shelves crammed with what appeared to be music manuscripts, notebooks, thick orchestral scores and some ancient-looking textbooks. Pointing to the uppermost shelf whose contents were barely visible, she called to me, "I need your assistance, Inspector."

At her request I reached up and brought down a package wrapped in a carefully folded linen cloth and securely tied with a black silk ribbon.

"*Voilà!*" she quietly said, presenting me with the package. "You see, Inspector Preiss, I told you the truth. It was I who went to Adelmann's rooms, I who killed him, I who found and removed the monograph you now see before you. I trust you no longer find my account incredible."

"Despite what you say," I protested, "it *could* have been your husband. After all, he was capable of doing exactly what you insist *you* did."

"Physically capable, yes. But mentally? Never! Robert floated from Eusebius to Florestan to Eusebius to Florestan, on and on in that fashion, the way the tides in the Rhine ebb and flow endlessly. He was like Hamlet; full of determination one minute, completely irresolute the next. It was amazing that he managed to accomplish as much as he did. So, I suppose there is nothing more to say, is there?"

"I'm not certain I agree with you," I said.

"Now, now, we mustn't be stubborn about this. You have all the evidence you need—the tuning fork, Adelmann's manuscript, my own confession. If you will pardon the pun, there is no need to soft-pedal whatever it is your duty requires you to do now. I'm not Beethoven; the poor man couldn't bring himself to end a piece of music in fewer than twenty bars. I know a finale when I see it. I am ready to face justice. I've made suitable arrangements for the care of our children. As for poor Robert, it's best that he remain distanced from the real world, at least for the time being."

Once again, I found myself speechless. She had handed over the papers in what was intended to be a gesture of surrender, and I had taken them from her mechanically, my mind still frozen in disbelief. Even my body seemed incapable of reacting to this turn of events, my shoes feeling as though the soles had been nailed to the floor. Was she telling me the truth? Or was she a devilishly clever liar? And then again, given what I myself had done at the bridge, did it really matter?

"Well, Inspector?" she said, again with that remarkable calmness.

Slowly, I found my tongue. "There is one problem,

Madam Schumann…from my standpoint, that is: The tuning fork? Well, it is no longer in my possession. It lies at the bottom of the Rhine—"

Clara Schumann's eyes grew suddenly large. Her mouth was agape.

"I put it there," I said.

"You did *what?*"

"I disposed of the tuning fork."

"You mean…by *accident?*"

"On the contrary. I deliberately threw it into the river."

"I—I don't understand, Inspector." Her expression now was one of disbelief. "Surely what you did flies in the face of what you are duty-bound to do, I mean, to solve mysteries."

"Perhaps," I said, "but then again, some mysteries are not meant to be solved. At least, that is what I'm beginning to believe."

I moved away from the armoire and returned to the fireplace on the other side of the drawing-room. "That's a fine blaze," I said, "and very heartwarming on a day like this."

She remained near the armoire watching me.

Almost in a whisper, I said, "Dust to dust, ashes to ashes." Then I knelt down and laid Adelmann's papers carefully atop the burning logs, staying in that kneeling position until I was certain that the flames had licked their way well into the bundle, the sheets browning and curling and disintegrating and rising up into the chimney in bright orange flecks.

I stood up, pulled my coat securely around me (by now the warmth of the fire had made it dry and comfortable) and said, "And now, goodbye, Madam Schumann. I hope we may meet again one day…under clearer circumstances."

She came toward me and offered her hand which, without daring to look up at her, I kissed. I left her standing there, in the middle of the drawing-room, and let myself out. It would be—I felt certain—the last time I would ever find myself in that house.

*   *   *

That evening, again warmed before a blazing fire—this time in the peace and quiet of Helena Becker's sitting room—I indulged in a confession of my own. I related in precise detail each and every sin I had committed on this cold, wet, miserable day in Düsseldorf.

Without being coaxed or cajoled, I admitted that I had renounced—at least for the present—whatever credible claim I might have to the moral high ground that was supposed to be a police officer's habitat. "Some day, Helena," I said, my mood wistful, "when I'm long into my dotage and have nothing to lose, I see myself parked in some working-class tavern and, over a glass or two of beer, raising the eyebrows of fresh-faced young colleagues with tales of my misdeeds. But do you think they will understand?"

"Not for a moment," Helena said. "Nor would *you* have understood until the Schumanns turned your life upside down. Life is really about *dis*order, isn't it?"

"Perhaps I ought to become a monk, then. Or at least retire to a monastery as Franz Liszt proposes to do, and spend an orderly year in search of my soul."

"Hermann, you are expert at many kinds of investigation," Helena said (I had the feeling she was trying with difficulty not to laugh at me), "but men will land on the moon before you discover the whereabouts of your soul."

That said, my confessor, in her own way, offered me absolution, gracefully given, and gratefully received.

Once again my father—or to put it more accurately, the man whom I was brought up to regard as my father—proved to be wrong. There *was* such a thing as a good surprise.

Chapter Thirty-Eight

The English have a saying: *Leave well enough alone.* Ironically, it's a piece of advice the English notoriously fail to heed, judging by their penchant nowadays for marching, or sailing, into far-off places, ignoring the local populations there, planting their Union Jacks in foreign soil, and proclaiming ownership of that soil. Frankly, it's a characteristic of the English that I've always admired, that ability to preach one thing but do the very opposite. Which accounts for what I did one day, but let me explain: After my final encounter with Clara Schumann, the day I dropped the tuning fork into the Rhine then, as an encore, tossed Adelmann's monograph into the fire, I told myself that my involvement with the Schumanns, while not neatly settled by any means, should be considered at an end. I wanted nothing more to do with them, or with their circle for that matter.

Leave well enough alone.

The Commissioner's irritation with me faded, and I found myself restored in his sight now that I had begun to throw myself into my regular line of police work with greater devotion. Several memoranda of praise actually landed on my desk from my superior, although I've no doubt he penned these encomiums bearing firmly in mind my connection to Baron von Hoffman)

Helena Becker swore I had changed for the better, despite breaching my sworn duty as an officer of the law, and her tenderness towards me now carried with it a tinge of respect, something I confess I hadn't always earned in the past in my dealings with her.

As for my relationships with my fellow officers, I became less stand-offish. After spending so much time exposed to the pretensions, jealousies, and unabashed backstabbing that prevails in Düsseldorf's cultural world, I suddenly found the simplicity of Düsseldorf's taverns refreshing. There is more honesty in beer than in wine.

Leave well enough alone. And that is what I did; I left well enough alone.

Then, some fifteen months after Maestro Schumann's arrival at the hospital at Endenich, I awoke one morning before dawn after an inexplicably restless night and, as though sleepwalking, dressed, left my rooms, hailed a cab, and found myself at the train station purchasing a ticket for passage on the recently installed rail line to Bonn. Several hours later, still in a trance-like state, I took a cab from the centre of Bonn to the outskirts, Endenich, instructing the driver to take me to Number 182 Sebastianstrasse. I had not been in Bonn for a number of years, and under ordinary circumstances, I would have taken in the sights like a typical tourist as the horses clopped along, but I recall little or nothing about that carriage ride until the driver pulled into the stone-paved entranceway, swung round in his perch and, giving me a sad-eyed look, asked, "Do you need some assistance, sir? I can call for help if—"

Only then did I snap fully awake, or so it seemed. "No, no, *I* am not a patient," I quickly assured him, though I'm afraid my protestation was not convincing, since he continued to look at me with nothing less than pity. "I'm here to *visit* a patient, but thank you anyway."

If the hospital I was about to enter was a place for the storage of the insane, one would never have known it from the look of the place. Apart from a discreet bronze plaque which announced that it was a hospital (in fact the only private mental hospital in the Rhineland), everything about the building and the acres of ground upon which it sat suggested that here was an estate anyone of noble birth or recently acquired wealth would be proud to inhabit, an estate where great parties could be given and where, on a fair June afternoon such as this, on lawns upholstered with patches of meticulously arranged flowerbeds, guests could meander as though they hadn't a care in the world, except to locate the next glass of Champagne or a canapé.

This was the hospital of Dr. Franz Richarz, the domain of perhaps the only psychiatrist in Germany, indeed in Europe, who at the moment regarded mental illness as exactly that—an illness—rather than some form of moral failure or punishable evil.

The main building was a two-storey structure Dr. Richarz had remodelled to house no more than fourteen psychiatric patients. I presented my credentials to the doctor at his office on the ground floor. "I apologize," I said to him, "for not communicating with you in advance about my plan to visit Dr. Schumann, but the pressures of my occupation are such that I never know from one day to the next…"

Dr. Richarz's eyes struck me as the kind that were capable of looking not only directly at me but *through* me, and whether or not he believed my flimsy excuse, he graciously accepted it. "I *am* aware of your interest in Dr. Schumann's troubles," he acknowledged with a forgiving nod, "and, if you will pardon me for saying so, the only surprise is that you didn't come to see him sooner."

His tone, though gentle, seemed to call for an apology for this, too. "Police inspectors are not prized, I'm afraid, for their hospital visitations," I said. "Usually when we show up at someone's bedside, we serve only as a grim reminder of some crime that's been committed."

The doctor gave me a warm smile. "No fear of that here, Inspector Preiss. Dr. Schumann is not bedridden... at least not much of the time, only occasionally...and I'm certain he'll be glad of the company. Let me escort you to his room."

Mounting the broad stairway that led to the second storey, I asked if Schumann received many visitors. "Not many," Dr. Richarz replied, "but the few who come are obviously close to him and of great importance to him, which is gratifying not only to the patient but to me as his doctor. It is so vital that he remain connected to the world outside, you see. Much of the treatment I render is based precisely on personal contacts being maintained as often as possible between the patient and his family and friends and professional colleagues." At this point, Dr. Richarz halted suddenly and looked intently into my face. "Please understand, Inspector...Robert Schumann is not a freak."

"But I never thought of him as a freak."

"Others did. Others still do. I'm sorry if I offended you, Inspector Preiss." We continued up the stairs. "Fortunately, his friend Brahms and his favourite violinist Josef Joachim visit fairly frequently. Paul Mendelssohn, the brother of the late Felix, sends letters, and I happen to know that he has assisted Madam Schumann financially because of her worries about money. A woman by the name of Bettina von Arnim paid him a visit not long ago; I gather, however, that, unlike the others, she was not favourably impressed with our facilities, nor with me apparently. Word got back to me that she found everything here, to quote her, 'dreary'." At the top of the stairs, the doctor paused again, and sighed. "I like to think that I've made *some* progress discerning the human mind, but *women?*"

We both laughed, but the truth was, as we approached the door to Schumann's room, I had an increasingly uneasy feeling about what I would find there.

Whatever fears I had vanished the moment the door

opened. Schumann's bedroom, it turned out, was flooded with sunlight that poured through a generous pair of windows. Facing south and east, they offered a fine landscape, with mountains along the Rhine forming a backdrop. Opened wide, they permitted a gentle breeze to enter the room. The furnishings—a small writing table, a chest of drawers, several chairs, a bed with a handy night table—though modest, were almost pristine. Altogether these quarters were a far cry from the accommodations I had seen from time to time in my visits to asylums supported by the state, institutions whose long, dark corridors reeked of overcooked food and unemptied chamber pots and teemed with grotesque men and women milling aimlessly about, some muttering, others screaming, the air filled with hopelessness.

As I stepped into Schumann's room, I found him standing at one of the windows taking in the view, his back to me. Dr. Richarz called out "Maestro, you have a visitor." Then, in a whisper, he said to me, "I'll leave you two alone; I'm sure you have much to talk about. Do take your time, Inspector." I thanked him, watched him make his exit, quietly closing the door behind him, then called out, "Good afternoon, Maestro."

Schumann remained standing at the window, his back still to me. "Why do I know that voice?" he called back. Then, very slowly, he turned to face me. Several times he blinked, then shut his eyes tightly, then re-opened them, like a blind man suddenly regaining his sight. His mouth twisted into a suspicious smile. "I believe I have been blinded by the sun. Or maybe you're an apparition. Is it really you, Preiss?"

"It is I, Maestro. Inspector Hermann Preiss...at your service, sir."

Schumann let out a cynical laugh. "At *my* service, you say? You mean you're finally getting around to arresting me, then."

"Good God, no!" I said. "I give you my word—"

"Your *word?* If memory serves, your *word* has a tendency to evaporate much the way a spy's ink becomes invisible. Your word, if I recall correctly, does not always stand up when exposed to air and light."

"Please believe me, Dr. Schumann," I said, "this is strictly a social call."

"A social call? Inspector Hermann Preiss, one of Düsseldorf's finest, travels all the way to Endenich to make a social call, eh? Well now, I suppose we should pull over a couple of comfortable chairs, sit ourselves down, and have a nice chat about the good old days... not that there were many. Tell me, Preiss, how is everyone back in Düsseldorf?"

"You mentioned chairs, Maestro Schumann. I could use one right about now. It's already been a rather long day, you understand."

"Oh, I *do* beg your pardon, Inspector." Schumann reached for a chair, offered it to me, then took one for himself. His apology, and his movements—all haste and flourish—struck me as false. "There now, that's better," he said. "You were about to bring me up-to-date on people and events back home. Let's start out at the lowest level, in the underground tunnels and sewers."

"You're referring to?"

"Wieck and Hupfer, of course."

"Let me begin with Hupfer," I said. "You may recall, Maestro, that a family by the name of Steinweg—a father and two or three sons—became well-known builders of excellent pianos in the vicinity of Hamburg. Well, the family moved not long ago to the United States of America, to New York City in fact, and established a piano factory there. Apparently, the Americans are becoming increasingly civilized, not to mention wealthy, and are fond of adorning their parlours with none but the finest instruments. The Steinwegs changed their name to Steinway, presumably to blend in better with New York high society."

Schumann's face broke into a wise smile. "Surely, Inspector, you're not going to tell me Hupfer's working for them in America."

"He's not only working for them, Maestro, he's their chief technician."

"Their chief technician! Tell me more, Preiss. What of my dear father-in-law? What's *that* creature up to these days?"

"Professor Wieck? Not much. Apparently, he's badly crippled. Arthritis, you know. No longer able to teach, I hear. It may please you a bit to know that Madam Schumann has made it clear her father is no longer welcome in the Schumann household."

"It pleases me more than a bit, Inspector," Schumann said. As though speaking to himself, he said in a quiet voice, "And God fulfills Himself in many ways."

"I beg your pardon?"

"Just a quotation...from some poem I came across. About Liszt...did I not hear...yes, Johannes informed me...he'd gone off to some monastery...trying to discover God, was it?"

"He supposedly found God," I reported, "during the better part of a year spent with some holy order. I've forgotten exactly where."

"Let me guess," Schumann said, "it must have been at the Church of the Reluctant Virgin. Be honest, Preiss; you don't imagine for a moment Liszt has really changed."

"Oh but he *has,* Maestro," I said. "He gave a recital recently in Düsseldorf. Played mostly his own com-positions. His music is now more solemn, more meditative. And he walks on stage looking like some kind of high priest from the Middle Ages. Dresses in black from neck to toe, hair white now, and longer than before, combed absolutely straight, like a waterfall down his neck and shoulders. Altogether a very spiritual effect."

Schumann was unconvinced. "Nothing makes a woman

swoon like the sight of a man who looks as though he's bearing within him all the pain in the world. Clever devil."

There followed a long silence, while Schumann looked away from me and sat, hands tightly clasped, gazing out his windows at the distant mountains. There was a kind of vacant contentment in his expression, as though the foothills glowing green in the sun were forever out of bounds for him, and yet it was probably just as well. At least within the four walls of his room there were demons he was familiar with. Out there, who knew what fresh and terrible demons waited for him? Whatever he was thinking at the moment, I thought it best not to interrupt him, but to wait for him to resume conversation.

At last he broke the silence. "Clara does not come to visit me," he said. His eyes were still fixed on the scenery well beyond the windows. His voice had taken on a hollow sound. "She writes...writes often...and her letters are tender...but she does not come to visit. Johannes has come a number of times, Joachim too, and occasionally they come together. They play for me—there's a fairly decent piano in the sitting room just down the hall—and sometimes I play for them. I played several pieces and songs I've written these past months, and they were very complimentary, Preiss. Johannes says they're some of my best work. But Clara? I can only imagine how painful all this must be for my poor, dear Clara. So she stays away."

I offered no comment. What was there to say?

"My children are fatherless, Preiss...fatherless. God knows, I think of them often, and wish I could see them. But they are young; they cannot understand, can they?"

I wanted to say that being fatherless was not necessarily a bad thing; after all, during my own childhood, I recalled, the prospect of becoming fatherless held great appeal. I mumbled something banal about children being remarkably resilient, then instantly regretted it. Turning sharply to me, Schumann said, "How would you know,

Preiss? You strike me as a man who has managed to insulate himself from anything that is remotely domestic. Your friend, that attractive cellist—"

"Helena Becker—"

"Yes, Fräulein Becker. Am I correct in guessing that you and she are still friends and nothing more?"

"I suppose you could put it that way, Maestro."

Schumann chuckled. "I'm not surprised to hear this. Not surprised at all."

"How so?" I asked.

"Because I noticed how smitten you were with Clara. The night you were summoned to our house...and Clara appeared at the top of the stairway, and you caught sight of her." Schumann chuckled again. "Oh, don't look so embarrassed, man. You may be a police inspector, but you're still flesh and blood. And I may be incarcerated here, but there's enough sanity in me still to understand my wife's appeal. In fact, I have to tell you, it pleased me that you were so obviously taken with her."

There was no use attempting to lie my way out of this conversation. "I didn't think it was that obvious, Maestro."

"You see, Preiss, artists can be as discerning as detectives. As a matter of fact, it would not be beyond the realm of possibility that *you* killed Georg Adelmann, wanting to make it appear like *my* work in order to get rid of me and have Clara for your own."

"That is utterly preposterous!"

"Calm yourself," Schumann said with a slight smile. "Of course, it's preposterous. I was only jesting. Besides, the truth is...*I* killed Adelmann."

I smiled back at Schumann. "Now you are *really* being preposterous, Maestro," I said. "I have already exhausted this subject with Madam Schumann. I saw with my own eyes the Adelmann papers."

"Which, according to my dear wife, you committed to a fiery end—"

"Absolutely."

"You read the papers first, of course?"

"There was no need to. The title page was all I needed to see to be convinced."

Schumann rose from his chair and went to the small desk. From the centre tray, he withdrew a thick sheaf of papers tied with a ribbon, not unlike the papers and ribbon produced by Madam Schumann on the occasion of my last visit to No. 15 Bilkerstrasse. Without a word, Schumann returned to his seat and handed over the bundle to me.

"What is this?" I asked.

"Well, see for yourself, Preiss," he said, his eyes fixed on mine, as though he could scarcely await my reaction. "Go ahead, untie it."

The ribbon slipped off easily, and I glanced at the title page. Quietly I read aloud: "Robert Schumann: A Life In Music." My eyes went down the page. Again, quietly, I read aloud: "By Georg Adelmann."

This time I turned the handwritten pages, not just a few at the top but those well down into the manuscript. I looked up at Schumann. "How did you get this? I thought there was only one copy."

"There was...*is*...only one copy. This is it."

"But how?"

There was no need to finish my question.

"That's right, Inspector Preiss. It was I who killed Adelmann and retrieved the monograph. Don't look for signs of remorse on my part. I have none. Besides, there is no necessity for me to demonstrate remorse in the hope of obtaining mercy. After all, Preiss, you cannot bring a madman to justice, can you?"

"One of you...I mean Madam Schumann or you... one of you has to be lying," I said.

"The Chinese have an excellent proverb," Schumann said. "'Life is a search for truth, and there is no truth.'

And now, sir, on that positive note, let me order coffee for us. The cook here makes excellent cream-filled buns. They will fortify you for your return journey to Düsseldorf."

Schumann and I spent the next hour mostly in silence. I was grateful for the coffee and cream buns, having had little to eat that day. Schumann, on the other hand, seemed indifferent to these refreshments and barely touched his. Instead he sat staring out one of the windows in his room, and I watched as the sun, beginning its late-afternoon descent, carved shadows into the soft features of his face. Finally, not just his face, but all of him was in darkness.

He did not stir when I announced that it was time for my departure nor did he make any response when I said goodbye. I could not be certain if he was even aware that I was leaving.

I was able to catch an early evening train to Düsseldorf and arrived back at my rooms well after midnight. Too exhausted to sleep, I poured myself a brandy and sat reliving the events of the long day just concluded. Someday, I told myself, historians, musicologists, surgeons, psychiatrists, novelists—some of them clever, others fools—would attempt to understand what made Robert Schumann the way he was. As for me, I probably should have left well alone. For the truth was that I had travelled to Endenich privately hoping I could hack a clearing, no matter how small, in the thicket that was his mind. The truth was that the man remained as much a mystery now as he did that night when he stood before me unkempt in his robe and slippers and insisted that he was being driven insane.

My last thought, before the brandy dulled my senses and I fell into a deep sleep, was that he was a mystery not meant to be solved.

Afterword

Robert Schumann died at 4 P.M., July 29, 1856, some two and a half years after he was admitted to the hospital at Endenich and following a steady decline in his mental and physical health. His death was hastened by self-starvation, a process no one was capable of reversing. Clara, who had returned to her career as a piano virtuoso, could not bring herself to visit her husband until just a few days before his death, relying on Johannes Brahms to visit Schumann periodically. Though Clara Schumann and Brahms continued to be close and supportive of one another's careers, she remained a widow until her death in Frankfurt am Main, May 20, 1896. Johannes Brahms died the following year, on March 3, in Vienna, a confirmed bachelor. While their devotion to each other was life-long, Clara Schumann's grief over the untimely and tragic death of her husband was genuine. From head to toe, she wore only black in every public appearance until the end of her days.

Photo courtesy Ian Pool and Christina Kufner

Morley Torgov was born in Sault Ste. Marie, Ontario. Torgov's first book, *A Good Place to Come From*, was published in 1974 and won the Leacock Medal for Humour. His second novel, *The Outside Chance of Maximilian Glick* (1982), also received the Leacock Medal.

In 1988, a feature film of the novel was produced and exhibited at the Festival of Festivals. It won top Canadian entry and was nominated for five Genie awards. The CBC also produced a twenty-six episode television series based on the novel.

This success was followed in 1990 by *St. Farb's Day*, which won the City of Toronto Book Award and the Jewish Book Award for fiction. *The War to End All Wars*, a novel, was published in 1998.

In 2005, he received the Order of Mariposa, a lifetime recognition from the Leacock Society.

Morley Torgov lives with his wife in Toronto, Ontario. *Murder in A-Major* is the beginning of a new mystery fiction series with RendezVous Crime.

Acknowledgments:

For their friendship, advice, and encouragement, my thanks to Beverley Slopen, Joanne DeLio, Henry Campbell, Malcolm Lester, Sally Zerker, and to my editors Sylvia McConnell and Allister Thompson.

NOTE TO THE READER

Because some of the principal characters in this novel actually existed, readers interested in tracking where historical fact and fiction cross each other's boundaries throughout the story may consult the following sources visited in my research into the people and their times:

Schumann: The Inner Voices Of A Musical Genius
        Peter Ostwald, M.D., 1985
The Lives And Times Of The Great Composers
        Michael Steen, 2003
Stories Of The Great Operas
        Ernest Newman, 1930
Great Symphonies
        Sigmund Spaeth, 1936
Franz Liszt: Volume 2, The Weimar Years 1848-1861
        Alan Walker, 1989
Piano: The Making Of A Steinway Concert Grand
        James Barron, 2006
The Steinway Saga: An American Dynasty
        D.W. Fostle, 1995
Perfect Pitch: A Life Story
        Nicholas Slonimsky, 1988
The Great Pianists
        Harold C. Schonberg, 1987
The Lives Of The Piano: Essays
        James R. Gaines, Editor, 1981